Waking Samuel

Waking Samuel

a novel

DANIEL COYLE

BLOOMSBURY

Published by Bloomsbury Publishing, New York and London
Distributed to the trade by Holtzbrinck Publishers

All papers used by Bloomsbury Publishing are natural,
recyclable products made from wood grown in sustainable,
well-managed forests. The manufacturing processes
conform to the environmental regulations of the
country of origin.

The Library of Congress has cataloged the hardcover edition as follows:

Coyle, Daniel.
Waking Samuel / by Daniel Coyle.—1st U.S. ed.
p. cm.
ISBN 1-58234-281-4 (hardcover)
1. Women—Washington (State)—Fiction. 2. Gunshot wounds—Patients—Fiction.
3. Washington (State)—Ficiton. 4. Nurse and patient—Fiction. 5. Children—Death—Fiction.
6. Islands—Fiction. 7. Alaska—Fiction. I. Title.

PS3603.O95W34 2003
813'.6—dc22
2003016238

First published in hardcover by Bloomsbury Publishing in 2003
This paperback edition published in 2004

Paperback ISBN 1-58234-442-6

1 3 5 7 9 10 8 6 4 2

Typeset by Hewer Text Ltd, Edinburgh
Printed in the United States of America
by Quebecor World Fairfield

To my brother, Maurice

1

Three-seventeen A.M.

In the upstairs bedroom of a white-curtained house near Seattle, Sara Black opened her eyes. Moving carefully, like a spy in enemy territory, she raised her head over her husband's shoulder and checked the clock glowing on the bedside table.

I should not go to him, was her first thought. *I should stay.*

Sara leaned back. Three-seventeen. That meant three hours and forty-three minutes until the alarm went off. Five hours and forty-three minutes until her shift started at the hospital. Seven hundred and fifteen days since the accident. Eighty-seven days until what would have been their son's sixth birthday. Sara closed her eyes, finding comfort in the stalwartness of each number. That was the reassuring thing about numbers: the unquestioning way they advanced and retreated, always remaining balanced. Numbers were honest. They gave her a foothold where she could locate herself.

Sara looked around, trying to see things as they were. The dark skylight. The pale white room, the blue patchwork quilt, the tidy house on Raven Lane where they'd lived for seven years now. She concentrated on sounds: a distant dog barking; the digestive gurgle of a street grate. Sara shifted slightly, and as she did she felt a pain shoot up her leg, a ghostly spark she welcomed because it carried her back to her purpose. *I won't go*, she told herself sternly. *I will stay here.* But even this reminder had the opposite of its intended effect. Instead of firming her resolve, it only made her see his face.

Stop, she told herself sternly, and for a second it worked.

To distract herself, Sara looked around the room, the garret-like space where she and Tom had spent half of their married life. When they had first moved here, she had thought of this place as an engine room, full of gleam and motion. But now the room felt more like a museum: placid, expectant, everything arranged just so.

Here was the blue wallpaper sprouting its golden field of flowers, the flowers of the condolence bouquets her neighbors, most of whom she barely knew, had sent for the funeral. There'd been so many flowers that they had blanketed every available table on their first floor, so many that the hungry birds and insects had mistaken their living room for a meadow, slipping through the open windows to feed among the end tables and the breakfront. For days afterward their upper floors were home to a number of small, batlike birds that darted from dark corners with such regularity that Sara had nearly begun to regard them as pets.

Here, propped on the windowsill, stood a clutter of family photographs, a seemingly offhand set of images that Sara knew was anything but, since all close-ups had been care-fully excised and replaced with photos that showed the family in a hazy middle distance, images that communicated, as the grief counselor had recommended, the *idea* of family without flesh-and-blood specifics. Or here, the vaguely dental shine of its combination lock visible through the open closet door, stood the red leather suitcase that had belonged to Sara's mother, a tattered and slightly rancid relic that Tom was constantly threatening to throw out and that for reasons she could not divine, Sara would not permit him to touch.

Sara tapped her fingers soundlessly on the quilt, craned her neck to recheck the clock. Three-twenty-one. Three hours and thirty-nine minutes until she and Tom would be rising, clicking on the coffeemaker, until they'd be sitting down to their scrambled eggs. Three fifty-four until they would watch their next-door neighbor Mrs. Wooding emerge regally from her door to pluck her newspaper from the sidewalk as if it were a particularly distasteful weed. Four thirty-nine until the workday began, the moment when Sara would be transformed into her official daytime self. But for now she lay here, watching the numbers, summoning her energies for the fight that lay ahead.

It was a fight. Sara would never admit that it was a fight (that was the most essential part of it, not admitting), but a fight was what it was. Specifically, it was a fight against a handful of concerned neighbors, tireless folk who drew their strength from the exhilarating conviction that they were helping her. There were not many – a half dozen, perhaps – but they seemed to occupy most of MountainLake Hills, padding smilingly down every grocery aisle, sidling casually along every sidewalk, fixing her with concerned eyes. Concern, that was the magical word, the one they liked to use. They were concerned about Sara, concerned at the way she was handling this. Concerned, they whispered, because Sara hadn't "come to grips with things," because she had "closed herself off." So those neighbors made it their duty to watch her. If Sara glanced at them, they would tilt their heads understandingly and smile their inscrutable dolphin smiles. If Sara walked away, they would follow, keeping a discreet distance. If Sara stayed home, they slipped through the phone wires, calling on the flimsiest pretense to pepper her with casual-sounding questions. So how are you feeling these

days? (*Have you started therapy? At least taking medication?*)
So I hear you've started back to work at the hospital. (*That, at last, is something. Maybe* they'll *be able to talk some sense into you.*) I want you to know that I'm there for you. (*Whenever you finally decide to rejoin the world, let me know.*)

"You can't hold it inside forever, hon," the psychiatrist had murmured, and Sara had nodded in violent agreement – she couldn't hold it in. But neither could she let it out. And how do you fight off someone who interprets your every move as a cry for help? *Such a terrible tragedy, who wouldn't have trouble coping?* they whispered. *We need to be there for her.*

Sara would have never said it, but in her heart she knew her existence had come to resemble that of a prisoner of war. She palmed her Zolofts and fed them to the dog. She logged an unhealthy number of hours driving the fateful section of highway with a ball-peen hammer in her purse, hoping for the opportunity to perform a make-good rescue (and spending some time considering forcing someone's car off the road so she could rescue them). At her doctor's insistence, she had attended meetings of Life Beyond Grief, When the Bough Breaks, and Listening to Your Heart, during the latter of which she had apparently fallen noisily and happily asleep. After that episode, she had sworn off therapy and replaced it with Aviation Weather, an hour-long loop of satellite maps and pressure contours that she found soothing beyond belief. She became obsessed with purging imperfections from her skin, marking her face with game trails of fingernail dents. She made midnight visits to the hospital to visit a patient whose name she didn't know.

Three twenty-five. Sara looked up, hoping to see a sign of dawn, but the skylight might as well have been painted black. During her recovery, Sara had developed the habit of asking

4

the skylight questions. It worked like this: She would whisper an inquiry, then wait for a reply. Signs from the air – a distant plane, a bird, a spinning leaf – meant yes, while those from the ground signified no. But tonight Sara did not ask any questions, because she had made up her mind that she would stay here, in bed.

She stared up, and the skylight seemed to react, its areas of deeper blackness pooling amoebically. *I don't even know his name,* Sara told the skylight firmly. *It makes no sense.* Seeming to hear her, the skylight morphed again. Sara knew it was an imperfection in the glass, a trick of light and angle. Still, she felt obliged to respond. *No,* she repeated silently. *Don't even try.*

I am arguing with a slab of glass, she thought, and smiled.

Sara leaned back and looked across the bed at Tom. He lay facing away from her, his square-shouldered, faintly whistling bulk reminding her of a cast-iron stove. He was listening, she knew. Tom never admitted it, but Sara knew he was awake, standing at the ready. Not because he thought anything would go wrong, but because this was the kind of role to which he was well suited, the rumpled yet vigilant watchman, jangling his keys, strolling the quieted rooms. *Now we're listening to each other listening,* she thought. She heard his measured breathing, felt his inner steadiness, the tick of his motor. Even in feigned sleep, Tom was good at emanating the sense that no matter what happens, everything will be okay. This bedrock certainty – the precise quality she'd fallen in love with – now made him seem as remote as the moon.

Lately Tom had begun acting strangely. The change appeared first in his voice, in a new brightness of tone that leapt on the first syllable of words – *Hell*-o. *Good* morning. Always a late sleeper, he'd started waking early, bounding out of bed to make breakfast, brimming with energy and ideas. Say, what did she think about redecorating the living room? Having the new neighbors over for barbecue on Saturday? Joining a bowling league? She did not know what to say. She only knew what not to say.

It has been forty-five nights since we made love.

You are becoming exactly like the rest of them.

I have found someone. I do not know his name. But he is lost, and I can help him, and that is all that matters.

Now Sara looked at Tom's body, studying its outline. It was muscular but not conventionally attractive – too hunched in the shoulders, a touch meaty in the butt, with a barrel-shaped chest whose contours were more automotive than sexual. Still, there had been a time when Sara could not keep her hands off him, when they had stolen away to kitchens, in bathrooms, on the stairway, when there was no time to make it to bed. Sara remembered the times while they'd been renovating this house when they'd come up to this very room and lain on the painter's tarps. When they were done, they'd lingered, looking at the unfinished ceiling and telling each other stories about what would happen in these very rooms. It had become a friendly contest between them, and they would take turns to see who could construct the most entertaining yarn – backyard epics of last-inning Little League home runs and calamity-filled canoe trips, excerpts from a family album whose pages had yet to be filled. Lying there next to Tom's warmth, safe within the ribs of the house, Sara had loved those stories. She could feel them, the words linking into sentences, the sentences ascending like breath-blown threads, reaching toward their shared future.

She looked. Tom's shoulder shone in the cold light, the same bone and muscle and skin, the powdery drift of freckles, the pale blossom of his vaccine scar. Automatically, she reached toward it, then stopped her hand in midair. If she touched him, what could they talk about? What stories were there to tell now? What words, whispered in the dark, could make any difference?

Three twenty-seven.

Silently, without warning, a blunt streak of white skidded diagonally across the skylight – a shooting star? A seagull? A windblown grocery bag? Sara chose the bird and pictured it gliding over the toylike grid of houses, headed east. She eased her leg to the side of the bed, letting gravity draw it downward, as if she were slipping from a boat railing into a dark current.

Sara drove quickly through the darkness, her face tipped into the dashboard lights. She was forty-one, with reddish curly hair and a runner's build. She was an attractive woman, with dark intelligent eyes set against a pale Irish complexion, but there was something slightly disproportionate about the geometry of her features, as though they had been knocked loose by some tremendous force and were in the process of migrating into a new arrangement. Sara had lived in the neighborhood for seven years, but it wasn't until the accident that her face had become a symbol of something, something whose very presence caused people to speak in whispers that Sara sometimes heard and sometimes didn't hear but always knew were spoken: *That's her. She's the one.*

Sara drove through the neighborhood, finding comfort in the familiar rhythm of the turns. Left, left, right, left, left. As she rounded the final corner, her eyes were drawn to a sunflower yellow Colonial, to a light in a second-floor dormer. She looked closer and saw the backlit profile of an upper torso – a petite woman seated at a desk, her hair tied in a collegiate ponytail, her head lowered in what looked like writerly contemplation. Brenda, Sara realized. Brenda Oliver, their neighborhood's official tragic celebrity.

Sara slowed the truck and examined the shadow more closely, noting its clerical tranquillity. She pictured Brenda's soulful blue eyes, her unfairly curvaceous body, her cheerful swoop of hair that was the exact same color as her house. Knowing Brenda, Sara assumed she was using this wakeful time for something ostentatiously productive, like working on her cancer fund-raiser or assembling one of her memory books about her late daughter. Or perhaps Brenda had guessed that Sara might drive past and was merely pretending to be engaged in work so that Sara would see her shadow and be inspired in the same way that medieval peasants were inspired by a stained-glass madonna. *That would be just like Brenda,* Sara thought darkly. No scheme was too elaborate, especially if it held the possibility of teaching a healing lesson, and God knew, no one was more in need of a healing lesson than Sara Black. Sara strongly suspected Brenda had been the one behind the flood of flowers at the funeral, as well as those mysterious sunflowers she'd been receiving each month on the anniversary of the accident. *Be happy today,* the unsigned notes read. *Somebody loves you!* It had been nice, the first few times, to find the flowers. But now, so many bouquets later, it seemed as if the giver had forgotten their original purpose and sent them out of childlike persistence – which was Brenda all over.

Sara hit the accelerator and the house shrank satisfyingly in the rearview mirror. She lowered the window to let the night air move through her hair. There was something reassuringly clandestine about driving, a solidity that returned her by degrees to her purpose. She was a nurse. She was driving to the hospital where she worked to check on a patient. That was all.

Sara's free hand traveled unconsciously to her knee, to the three titanium rods whose tips could be felt protruding faintly beneath her skin. She touched them in the usual order – thumb, middle, pinkie; one, three, five, a major chord. Sara moved the pins slightly but precisely, as one might wiggle a loose tooth, feeling the cat's cradle of metal within her bones. At her monthly visit the physical therapist had warned against doing this, had said it could create space for an infection, but Sara could not help herself. Before these pins there had been larger pins, along with an erector-set device to hold them in place that the doctors referred to as her "external fixation." She'd loved the plush sheen of the titanium, the way they vibrated like tuning forks when she tapped one with her wedding ring. *External fixation. Yes*, thought Sara. *That's it exactly.*

Sara pulled into the depths of the parking garage and walked to the elevator in her newly acquired old-lady shuffle. She rode to the fifth floor. The automatic door scraped open and she was subsumed by the underwater noises and the bright sour smells of King County Hospital. The facility, Seattle's largest, had been constructed in the fifties and had undergone a near constant renovation and expansion since. The resulting structure, swathed in scaffolding and plastic sheeting, linked by a crazy-quilt network of sky bridges and glass tunnels, seemed less like a hospital than a monstrous hamster cage. Sara limped smoothly through the blue expanse of the reception area, past lenslike panels of green glass, the tentacles of Christmas tinsel.

Four months earlier, Sara had returned to work – part-time, flexible hours, working not her old job in pediatrics, but a less demanding position as a fill-in. The other nurses tried their

9

best to make her first day an occasion, setting out cookies and pink lemonade beneath a computer paper banner. There had been toasts and hugs, informal speeches, and a presentation of a crutch festooned with red ribbon and a bicycle horn. Sara gave in; she had teared up on cue, she had laughed at all the right moments. As the gathering ended, she'd even made a stab at gallows humor – *better not let me behind the wheel* – that drew a discomfited explosion of laughter. She'd been an utterly believable heroine, so everyone – including Sara, for a few sweet, ephemeral moments – had believed her to be one.

Turning a corner, Sara heard the muted chirp of a tennis shoe and looked up to see a skinny blond-haired nurse fixing her with a toothy smile. Sara met her eyes, nodded pleasantly and kept walking, and saw the nurse's head swivel slowly. They had been watching her since the accident, all the nurses. Like the antennae of some vast subterranean organism, they monitored her moods, tracked her comings and goings, and registered small variations in her appearance (which, it was agreed, had slid). Their official purpose was to provide sympathy and support, yet behind the smiles and nods Sara caught the unmistakable whiff of pursuit. In the months since the cookie party, it had been noticed that Sara kept strange hours, coming and going in the middle of the night, spending an unusual number of shifts behind the red steel door of the TBI ward. It had been noticed that the good cheer she'd displayed during her welcome-back party had been replaced by a cryptic and unwholesome sneakiness. They watched her constantly, these sharp-eyed nurses, and as they did, Sara realized that they were not truly interested in her; they were interested in figuring her out, in unraveling her as if she were one of those dog-eared paperbacks in the waiting room. Sara limped briskly to the main nurses' station and signed in, keeping her head down. No one talked to her, and as she turned the corner she felt a cool wave of relief. She focused on her steps, counting. A few more seconds, she told herself, and she would be with him. She permitted herself to picture him for a second – not his body, just his face.

She was a few steps away when she heard a loud voice calling her name. Sara pivoted, bracing herself on her good right leg as if for a windstorm, and saw the light blocked out by a gigantic parrot-colored bulk.

"Hey there," a rust-plated voice behind her called. "If it isn't the early shift."

Sara blinked, slowly registering the apparition in front of her. Her friend Josephine was dressed as a Christmas elf: green tunic, candy-cane tights, red shoes. A tricorner hat listed alarmingly from her burnished curls like a tethered kite. She spread her arms and turned her massive body to the side like a chorus girl.

"You like?"

Sara glanced down the hall, half hoping Josephine would take the hint. But her friend paid no mind.

"Well, you better like it," she said, hiking up her red-and-white hosiery with an indelicate, elbowy gesture that reminded Sara of a football coach. "Administration told us to dress up on Christmas, for corporate morale. So I decided to give the dickholes more than they bargained for. Besides, lover boy can wait."

"It looks . . . good," Sara said kindly.

"It looks like shit," Josephine said.

Josephine was a six-foot-three-quarter-inch Belorussian woman. Her most notable feature was her hair, which was curled, doll-like, and dyed to a shade not far from that of an orange peel. But her hair, like the elf costume, was merely camouflage, a symbolic touch akin to hanging a fruit basket on the muzzle of a Sherman tank. Josephine belonged to a variety of recent immigrants all too aware of the perilous line that separated them from their former condition and who dealt with that perilousness by becoming a nation unto themselves. The Republic of Josephine was a pugnaciously independent rogue state, specializing in blood feuds and covert guerrilla actions. Before Sara's accident, Josephine had been one of the nurses whom Sara silently feared: she was too big, too profane, too aggressively American, a woman who did not work at the hospital as much as she invaded it, much to the chagrin of the dickholes – she pronounced the word with long Slavic vowels. But Josephine had served as Sara's night nurse for the first weeks after the accident. Heaven only knew what she had seen in Sara during those morphine-tinted days, but for some obscure, possibly perverse reason, Josephine had decided that the two of them would form an alliance against the rest of the nurses and doctors – against the rest of the world, for that matter. She had made it official one night just a week after the accident. "There," she'd said, kissing the astonished Sara sternly on the mouth. "Now we are friends."

So they were. Friendship with Josephine possessed a social utility that Sara was not unaware of, fending off other nurses' overtures by fulfilling the unspoken requirement that she have at least one close ally. And Sara liked Josephine; she truly did. But of what exactly their alliance consisted, Sara had a difficult time figuring out. Josephine's interests centered mostly on soap operas (*General Hospital* was, she announced, the reason she became a nurse – though the Russian subtitles were apparently more explicit than the spoken English version). Her personal life wasn't much different: there was her torrid affair with the skinny Scottish resident ("He knows how to use

12

it," she informed Sara), her porn-actress best friend in Tacoma, and her white piranha named Yeltsin that she constantly promised to serve on cabbage. Sara had also heard of the poverty of Josephine's youth in an agro-industrial outpost in the Urals, the infant brother who died of diphtheria, the miserly teetotaler uncle who died and miraculously left them enough rubles to come to America. Sara had come to think of Josephine as a kind of exact complement to herself: a noisy, vibrant exterior that contained sex, appetites, whole worlds. Sara, on the other hand, was a nondescript vessel emptied of all stories save one.

Now Josephine's big hand wrapped around Sara's. Sara fought the urge to pull away and then gave in. She felt its smoothness, its irresistible maternal force, and she understood. Josephine was her medication. Sara let herself relax.

"You don't look so hot," Josephine said, her eyes oscillating slowly as if scanning some invisible TelePrompTer.

Sara felt a rush of blood to her face. "Maybe I should've dressed up."

Josephine smiled and pulled Sara into her perfumey bulk. Then she pushed her back at arm's length, squinting at her.

"You have time for a little visit?"

Josephine looked around, the bells on her costume tinkling icily. She extracted an airline-size bottle of whiskey from her pocket and flashed it in her palm like a magician.

"Okay if he waits?" Josephine tipped her head toward the red door. Though they never talked about it, Josephine's instincts on this count were frustratingly accurate.

"Him?" Sara said quickly—too quickly, she immediately thought. "Sure. I'll get him after."

Josephine knitted her arm through Sara's and they walked a

few dozen yards down the hall to an abandoned waiting room safely out of sight of the nurses' station. They both knew what was going to happen. During Sara's recuperation, for reasons that were still mysterious to her, Sara had developed the occasional late-night habit of telling Josephine the story of her accident – not confessing, Sara pointed out to herself, just relating the facts in a cool, unemotional voice, like a police report. It had become their ritual: the covert drink and the telling of the story. Josephine liked to joke that she should bill Sara's insurance company for the whiskey, and her joke was true enough, because Sara had told no one else the story. But telling Josephine was permissible, according to the calculus of Sara's rebellion, for three reasons: 1) because her neighbors would never find out, 2) because they drank whiskey, and 3) because Josephine did not care about Sara's feelings. Josephine didn't listen to the story so much as midwife its delivery, her giant body leaned forward in the tiny waiting room chair, her face arranged in a professorial frown, giving Sara a bare minimum of attention (a monitoring glance, an authoritative pat on the wrist) so that she might devote ferocious attention to the story itself, so that she could receive it and care for it with stern devotion. So now, as they arranged themselves in the plastic chairs (a touch impatiently, Sara noted with gratitude) and Josephine poured the whiskey into tiny paper cups, Sara began to tell it again. She told it slightly differently every time, but the story was always the same.

The boy was in his car seat, talking. He was always talking, this boy, in love with the chattery music of his voice. *Hel-lo, ha-lo, ha-lo-la-looo.* He had just turned three and had given them some worries early on because he hadn't talked. Now those concerns seemed an ancient joke because he couldn't be stopped. With his oversize toddler's head and foreign-sounding modulation, he resembled nothing so much as a miniature sports commentator: *Now we're driving, there's a doggie, there's a yellow bus, now Mommy's waving, there's the blue water over there.* On this particular day, they were returning from a bout of last-minute Christmas shopping, and to assuage the guilt of leaving him in the outlet mall's day care facility, Sara had taken the long way home, along the shore. The vague idea was to find a spot for a mother-son picnic, but by the time they reached the Sound the light had begun to wane and a dense, bright fog had descended. Hieroglyphs of ice began to form in the corners of the windshield. Sara rinsed them away, and the boy prattled on: *Hell-o, good-bye-ee, halo, good-bye-oo.* She drove slowly, well below the speed limit, holding the wheel in both hands, trying to peer through the fog. She wished for a bigger car, she wished for Tom. She put in a tape for the boy, one of those sing-alongs. But the tape wouldn't play. She frowned, hit some buttons, and said something to the boy, something pleasant and motherly like "Just a minute, honey," and the music began to play and she looked up and saw the oncoming curve. The car began to skid. Sara panicked briefly, then saw the guardrail loom out of the fog and felt a wave of relief, knowing that would stop them. She felt brief, pre-emptive regret at denting the car – Tom would be displeased; he'd probably spend days fixing it himself. *Good-boo, good-bee, good-boy . . .*

The car flipped over the guardrail and fell down the embankment in a methodical tumble. Small items levitated as the car pivoted around them: a gum wrapper, an eyebrow pencil, a cup. Sara pressed her feet against the floorboards as if that would stop them, and when the car smashed headfirst into a boulder, she distinctly felt her leg bones stress and break. The car took one last fall and tipped with surprising gentleness on its back into the water.

They hung there, mother and son, upside down and ridiculous. The windows became aquaria, surreal and blue. Sara was surprised to hear her voice, motherly and calming, telling the boy everything would be all right. As she spoke, Sara watched water begin to flow in tidy cascades from the louvered air vents, pool on the ceiling around the dome light. The water rose slowly, touching her hair, her forehead, her eyebrows. She told him it would be all right again, and she looked back and she could see his eyes, fixed urgently on her – *Get us out of here!* – and then he began to scream, a high, bright, shining sound that seemed at once to come from him and from the rising water, and then the water smothered her.

Sara had seen the body. She wasn't supposed to see it, but she did. That first night after Tom fell asleep, she persuaded Josephine to wheel her down to the cold room and hold her up by the arms until she could prop herself on the slab. At first she felt a surge of hope – it was a mistake, some smaller, skinnier kid! – but then she looked closer. The salt water had dried his hair and pressed it to the side, as if he were leaning into a strong wind. He had a small cut on the corner of his chin, and she asked the orderly for a bandage, but it wouldn't stick, the edges kept curling like wings. She smoothed his hair. She touched his delicate ankles, her fingers brushing the crenulated sock marks as if they were messages written in braille. She whispered his name, half expecting him to sit up. Didn't that happen? Weren't children specially wired to survive drowning, didn't they lower their heart rates so that they masqueraded as dead, only to come back to life undamaged, perfect?

"Okay, enough," Josephine interjected. "You're done."

Sara and Josephine held hands in the fluorescent-lit silence, both pretending not to notice Sara's trembling. Josephine finished the story for her. She told Sara, as she always did, that no one could have gotten the kid out. The roof was caved in, the doors smashed. When the troopers pulled the car from the water, they had to use steel cutters and torches to get him. No one could have done more. No one.

Sara listened and tried to make Josephine believe that she believed her. This was their ritual, too. After a few moments she stood and patted her hands on her legs and said she'd better be getting on, or her patients would be wondering where she was. Josephine smiled at this and tucked the cups and bottle in her pocket and produced a bottle of mouthwash. When they were finished, Sara stepped out into the hall and began to walk back to the ward.

There were other things that she had never told Josephine or anyone. Such as the fact that she occasionally heard the boy's piping voice doing a play-by-play on her life: *Now Mommy's walking, now she goes boom, now she's wiping her eyes.* Or her recurring dream that the boy is alive and living in the remains of the smashed car. In the dream, she swims down to find that he has made a home out of the car's interior, fashioning toys, using the seat as a makeshift trampoline. (It is understood that he has inherited his father's handiness.) Sara looks in through the spiderwebbed crack of the windshield to see him chattering happily to himself, standing on the driver's seat, spinning the wheel. She taps on the glass with her knuckle. He is thrilled to see her and jumps up and down. He shows her all his toys and his new tricks he has taught himself – now he can do a somersault, now he can zip his own coat. Then he asks when he can come home, and all she can say is that it will be soon, very soon. He gets angry at this, he stamps his small foot and rages, and the car shakes, and he shouts her name, and he says, "Sometimes you're glad I'm gone," and his words make her tremble because she fears they are true. That's how the dream always ends, with the boy standing in his radiant underwater palace and speaking those words over and over in his high, clear voice. *Mommy's gone, Mommy's gone, Mommy's gone.*

2

Sara kept moving, flicking a nod toward the nurses' station while keeping her eyes focused on the red door at the end of the hall. As she approached, she slowed, breathing in the lemon-scented bleach the housekeepers used, feeling herself unclench. TBI: traumatic brain injury. The nurses liked to joke that the letters stood for "The Baby-sitter is In," and they were essentially right. Like newborns, TBI patients required only the most basic care; they needed to be fed, changed, rolled, and monitored, never-ending tasks that were happily consigned to nurse trainees and the magic of remote electronics. Sara checked the chart outside the door: the trainees had been here two hours ago and were not due to check for another two. Perfect.

Sara entered a stark room constructed of painted concrete blocks and lit by four fluorescent lights. Three beds stood arranged in an uneven semicircle around a small metal desk, their occupants propped up in the studied formality of a chamber orchestra. Two old women and a gaunt man with a shaven head. Sara's eyes passed over the man and went directly to the women.

"Good morning, good morning," she said to the two women softly. "How are my best girls today?"

They stared. One woman was white and one black, but Sara

thought of them as twins because they had suffered identical subcerebellar strokes that obliterated their ability to move or speak. Their hands were clenched into nutlike fists, their faces locked into elfin grimaces that may have once been smiles but now served, like inkblots, to animate any emotion the onlooker might wish to see. Their sole method of communication consisted of animalistic grunts and birdlike coos, which they now produced in soft chorus.

"Really?" Sara said. "I think so, too."

Sara went to work on the twins, checking IV tubes and oximeters. She checked the heart rate monitors, repinned stray hairs, wiped away frozen rivers of spittle and mucus, engaged in the demeaning acrobatics of the sponge bath, the linen change. Finally, she rolled the twins on their sides, adjusting them to some imagined level of comfort, placing their limbs in a natural position, arms on their blanketed laps as if they were at a quilting bee. She leaned down to kiss each one on the cheek. "Merry Christmas," she said. Then she swiveled their beds to the window – to let them enjoy the view, she told herself. She turned.

The tall man lay before her, his head tipped prayerfully to the ceiling, his slender body covered by an unwrinkled blanket. His face was angular, fringed by a faint halo of boyish stubble around his chin. His eyes were slightly hooded, intelligent looking with deep blue irises and tightly curled lashes – saint's eyes, Sara thought. She looked at the strong curve of his jaw, his wide, crooked mouth. She examined the architecture of his nose, the bowstrings of his neck. She looked with curiosity at his trach, that plastic-rimmed aperture at the base of his throat that dilated slightly with each breath, sending that whistling sound into the cool air. Though Sara had looked at his face many times in the past three weeks, she still had trouble fixing it in her memory. She decided, as she did each time she saw him, that it was in fact a thoughtful face, a trustworthy face. Not the face of someone who could put a pistol against the roof of his mouth and pull the trigger.

Sara checked his temperature – 101.7. She wet a cloth and pressed it to his forehead. She checked pulse, blood pressure, and respiration – normal, normal, normal. His expression showed no signs of pain or distress, only an intense and expectant concentration, as if he were listening to a piece of music.

Sara briskly united his soaked gown and worked it over his shoulders, exposing his dishlike breastbone, his tightly corded neck, and there, in its tender hollow, the tiny parodic mouth of his tracheostomy. She suctioned out the trach without looking into it (something about the trach unnerved her – its cavernlike darkness, the ropy wetness) and listened as the wand drew up a strand of mucus into the reservoir. She wet his mouth with a sponge, placed drops in his eyes. She carefully peeled off the four electrode patches from his chest, leaving marks like the kiss of a malevolent octopus. She slid aside the rest of the gown and coolly regarded the whole of his body: the gently protruding hipbones, the withered legs, the taut architecture of his feet. His body was unmarred except for a mole beneath his left nipple and a brandlike scar on his right leg. Sara liked to touch the scar; it was fat and pink, with a creamy, whorled surface that looked as if something were boiling beneath. According to his chart, he weighed 107 pounds.

The fever had made his skin oily, so she sprinkled baby powder on his chest in widening circles. With some effort she rolled him so she could reach his back, his shoulders, the pearl bumps of his spine, the doglike pads of his feet. She leaned close and covertly inhaled the scent of his skin, a sharp, clean aroma, like the ocean. At times, his body responded to her

21

touch by flexing unexpectedly – involuntary basal reflexes, common to brain-damaged patients, that Sara had experienced before.

Sara had been coming here for three weeks now, ever since her name was mistakenly listed in the schedule of unlucky nurse trainees who performed the yeoman's work. She had gone along on something of a lark – and why not? Whatever drooling horrors TBI might hold, it couldn't be worse than the stares and whisperings of the nurses. Besides, she'd been curious about the tall man. She'd remembered the day he had arrived, read the newspaper articles, spent a lunchtime idly gossiping about him with her physical therapist.

The tall man had been found eighteen months ago by a seventh-grade class on a field trip to a western corner of the Olympic Peninsula called Cape Flattery. He was lying face-up in a red wooden skiff, wearing jeans and a blue windbreaker, an antique .32-caliber pistol in his left hand. The braver children were poking him with sticks, thinking him dead, when his eye opened. When no one came forward to identify him, a moderate sensation ensued. One rumor had it that he was the despairing survivor of a Panamanian shipwreck that had occurred a month before. Another held him to be a Seattle drug kingpin who'd been killed by the DEA and set up to look like a suicide. Others said he was a hijacker, a CIA agent, a mental patient. The pistol had misfired, owing to its age and wet condition, and the bullet had tumbled weakly into his frontal lobe. Doctors estimated him to be between sixteen and twenty-two years old. Aside from the scar on his leg, there were no identifying marks.

As she liked to do, Sara flipped through his chart, examining the bricky checklists of physical exams, the seismographic jutterings of the EEG, the pointilist grays and blacks of MRI scans, the spare nuggets of information: He had broken his left arm as a child. His teeth had no cavities. Sara sometimes tried to read patterns into his chart, testing them against his various rumored identities. She kept a vague notion that he might be foreign – something in the curve of that jawline, the catlike cant of the eyes. A wealthy young sailor who fell from a yacht, perhaps.

His chart detailed the various infections he'd suffered early on: pneumonia, tetanus, and bacterial meningitis, along with recurrent seizures and periodic vocalizations, the latter of which ceased at the three-month mark. The remainder of his chart was filled with recordings of his battles with brain infection, clotting, and bleeding, an account that resembled nothing so much as an epic poem, complete with Hellenic names: heparin to thin the blood, cephalosporin and vanco-mycin to stop the recurrent infections caused by the presence of sinus tissue in his brain, dopamine to keep the blood flowing through the increasingly fragile tissues. Several times the doctors had used the clipped cadences of imminent death. *Multi-infarcts, widely distributed. Infection pervasive.* But the tall man had proven a failure at dying and had maintained himself in a state of suspended disrepair, watched over by trainees, visited once a day by a doctor or resident whose most difficult task was to hide his or her boredom.

After a few moments of massage, the tall man's twitching seemed to ease and with them Sara's concerns about his temperature. *It's nothing,* she told herself. *A cold, at most.* After laying out a blue absorbent pad, she rolled him on his back and wrapped more pads loosely around his legs. She wet a cloth and wiped down his skin again, allowing herself to slip by degrees into the warm pleasures of her routine. She worked in silence, folding and tucking more pads beneath his legs, his hips, and his elbows. *Cushion all points of contact*, that was the rule to prevent bedsores and infection. Sara adjusted the pads meticulously, feeling a pleasurable twinge of recognition as the tall man's body assumed its usual position on the bed. She blushed as she cleaned and sterilized his catheter – a foolish embarrassment, but one she had not been able to shake. Then she uncapped the narrow plastic wand of his stomach tube, attached the IV bag with 400 cc of Nutri-Gel, that brown, creamy liquid that smelled like baby formula, and watched it flow into his stomach with satisfying steadiness. She brushed his teeth, moving the toothbrush bristles in slow circles over his molars and incisors, over his tongue, around the ragged crater in his palate. She washed the tall man's feet, combed his hair, clipped his fingernails, plucked a stray eyelash from those eyes, in each step feeling a rhythmic gentleness that made normal conversation seem clumsy and ridiculous by comparison.

She checked him over, fixed a stray hair. Satisfied, Sara stood on a chair and stretched a surgical glove over the smoke detector. She positioned her chair safely to the side of his fixed gaze and turned the television to Aviation Weather – in case anyone walked in, she would appear to be watching the screen. She sat down and lit a cigarette – *Now Mommy's smoking.* Sara aimed a stream of smoke at the ceiling, watched it mingle with the spinning clouds.

"Lover boy," she said, imitating Josephine's accent, and she smiled.

At first the seizures followed a pattern, arriving like clock chimes every six hours. They began with fine, birdlike tremors in his fingertips, then spread in amplifying waves up his arms and into his chest, and soon the tall man's body was rocking

24

spasmodically back and forth, clenching and unclenching with soundless precision. The steel bed frame rattled like a machine gun. Sara tried strapping him down, but the restraints seemed cruel. Instead, she wrapped him in a blanket and held his body with her arms, his blond head burying and unburying itself in the crumpled landscape of her uniform. She felt his blind animal urgency nestling into her and tried to remind herself that it was a reflex. There was even a name for it: rhythmic myoclonus. But still she closed the scrim around his bed.

The doctors ordered blood drawn, shone lights into his good eye, took an MRI scan, massaged their chins. The tests for meningitis came up negative, so they switched to the next string of possibilities – virus, bacteria, epilepsy. They talked about taking a PET. *Keep a close eye on him,* they said grimly. So she had. Sara timed her visits around the tall man's seizures, using the intervals to take care of the twins. The trainees, who showed up each four hours to take vitals, were puppyishly amused by her constant presence.

Late the third night, Sara decided to wash the white twin's hair. She tipped the woman's head back into the small plastic sink and rinsed. The patient's eyes fluttered, as if in pain or pleasure, as the water pearled around her. Sara sat her up, dried the hair with a towel, and began combing. The woman had thick, luxuriant hair. The comb moved easily through the hair, furrowing it like water.

Sara experienced a memory of a night she spent near Cape Flattery when she was nine years old. It is September, and the sky is improbably clear and blue. In her memory she is sitting in the shadows of Flattery's low cliffs around a flickering campfire with a dozen blond-headed Mormon girls who all look like sisters because most of them, in fact, are related. They are roasting hot dogs on sticks and singing a religious song.

Sara, who does not have any sisters or brothers, does not know the words to the song because she's not Mormon. Sara's mother talked to the Mormons and arranged to have Sara join this trip. Sara's mother, Vera, is skilled at that sort of talk. She comes from a faraway and exotic place called Philadelphia. She calls Sara "my marvelous darling" and "my princess, my wonder, my one and only." Her mother's voice is difficult to describe — low, musical, sandpapery from cigarettes — but it is a movie star voice, definitely. Sara isn't exactly sure what a movie star is, but she is positive her mother must be one. What else could account for her beauty, her magical irresistibility? The last two summers, she had used that voice to land Sara on buses with the county's Baptists and Catholics, Presbyterians and Congregationalists, 4-H and 4-A Clubs, the garden club, and the chess club. Her mother travels, too, driving her sky blue Lincoln Continental with matching leather seats to Los Angeles and Seattle and Sacramento and other exotic cities, to adult places where kids can't go. Dad would go, except that he can't because he's always working on the ranch. That's why she has the red suitcase — movie star's luggage if there ever was — so she can have enough room to carry back presents for both of them: postcards, miniature plastic statues, new kinds of candy bars, talismans from a world Sara can only imagine. Vera's world: a place of secret jazz hideaways, hushed hotels, palm trees that arch like heavenly gates.

After the last doleful campfire song dies out, the group leader checks his pocketwatch and stands up, clearing his throat importantly. The head Mormon is a moonfaced man who has a habit of rising on his tiptoes whenever he talks to God, which he does quite often. Raising himself next to the fire, the head man announces to God that it's bedtime, and Sara watches as all the Mormon children obediently tuck their blond

26

heads into their neat row of tents. The head man tells God that the children are now picturing His face watching over them. Sara slips into her sleeping bag and lies there for a while picturing her mother and her sky blue Lincoln with the red suitcase, on her trip in California. Sara concentrates, and the picture comes into focus: Vera is standing beneath a palm tree on the starlit balcony of some expensive and ancient hotel in Los Angeles, casually sipping a glass of champagne. Sara closes her eyes and sees with miraculous clarity: her golden-piled hair, her secret smile, the velvet whisper of her blue Chanel dress. The swaying boom of the ocean. Somewhere in the distance an orchestra begins to play.

During the night, young Sara wakes. Perhaps there's a noise, or perhaps her sleeping bag is too hot. But something compels her to slip from her tent and walk away from the smoldering fire, down the beach. She knows this is forbidden – the head man had solemnly reminded God about that rule – but Sara does not care. She wades in, feeling the thrill of her disobedience, her paisley nightdress rising around her legs like a parachute. The bottom slopes imperceptibly, drawing her down into the cold. The small waves roll around her and she walks farther, and when she looks back all she can see is the dimpled outline of the tents against the sky. She walks farther and the stars come down over her so it seems they are not above her but all around her, electric in the water. She hears the faint sound of a voice, someone calling her name – the head man? her mother? But the voices are too faint to matter. She is a hundred feet out now, and the waves are stronger, lifting her off her feet and setting her gently in a new place, as if she is flying.

Sara was pulled from her memory by a high sound that seemed connected to the combing. A rhythmic sound, a musical screech.

27

She stopped combing. The noise continued.

"Hello?" she said, feeling foolish.

The tall man emitted three glottal, explosive sounds – *kaaa, kaaa, kaaa* – from the trach or the mouth, it was difficult for Sara to tell.

Automatically, Sara walked over and placed her hand across his lips, applying a light pressure that helped patients control numb facial muscles. His lips were cool to the touch, and she sensed a shimmer of continuous motion beneath them. His tongue flicked out, its live wetness surprising against her fingers. She pulled her hand away, conscious of the cooling stripe.

Sara paged Josephine. Twenty minutes later, he began again. Not the same sounds as before – these were longer, keening groans that seemed to come from his nose, amplified by his ruined sinuses. Sara felt her heart move inside her rib cage. She snuck a glance at Josephine, who seemed wholly unimpressed. She rose up sternly, a teacher addressing a tardy pupil.

"Lover boy!" Josephine exclaimed in mock indignance. "Nothing for so long, and now you sing?"

"Should we call someone?"

Josephine aimed a purple talon at his throat. "Laryngeal spasm," she said. "Not unusual."

"Is there anything we can do?"

Josephine arched her eyebrows theatrically. "Well, we could call Neuro. They would examine him, stick him full of needles, shock him, do PET scans. They can put him in the psych ward and do their tests and probes and anything they like, and then they can send him back to us when they're done."

The tall man groaned again. Sara heard the lifting effort in his voice, an animal plaintiveness. She closed her eyes and listened to the sound as it reached upward toward . . . toward what? She listened, and as she did she imagined him for the first time as part of a family. A mother, a father, perhaps a wife and family. A house somewhere, an empty bedroom. A family of strangers whose pain was familiar.

"Let's just keep an eye on it for now," she said quietly.

"Right-o," Josephine said.

"Maybe there are more low-impact things we could do. Simple things."

Josephine shrugged. "Do them."

3

The next day Sara visited the hospital's medical library. She read of a thirty-three-year-old railroad worker who had survived a spike driven through his frontal lobe by an explosion and had emerged with drastic personality changes. She read of a thirty-one-year-old car accident victim who woke up in an infantilized state and had to be taught to eat and walk again. She read of a twenty-seven-year-old boy who survived frontal lobe damage due to a plane crash who emerged with his mental facilities not only intact but measurably improved, as though he had been quietly studying all the while. She dug deeper, reading articles that attempted to explain why some brains recover from injury and some don't, articles that compared the brain to a computer hard drive, to a beehive, to an amoeba, articles that used the most erudite and complex scientific language to arrive at a conclusion as satisfying as a simpleton's rhyme: It happens because it happens. Some injured brains simply rewire themselves, rebuilding old connections or making new ones by using unused portions of nervous tissue. Collateral sprouting, the articles called it. Sara read and thought of the tall man, visualizing a tangle of seedlings, tender and white, taking root within the dish of his skull.

More usefully, she located a short article that detailed techniques designed to jump-start the vegetative brain by stimulating the senses. The prescriptives were appealingly low-tech: massage for his skin, salt and lemons for his taste buds, and ammonia capsules for his nose. At home, Sara was rooting around Tom's workbench in their garage when she heard the door open behind her.

"What's that?" Tom asked.

"Stuff for a patient," she said. He walked over and saw her pile of objects: several pieces of wood, two red and black patterned cards designed to be propped in an infant's car seat.

"I want to make a clapper," Sara said. "To stimulate hearing."

"For a baby?"

"Kind of," Sara said.

Tom hesitated, then smiled encouragingly. He located two pieces of maple the size of a deck of cards, tacked on a leather hinge, sanded them smooth. While he worked, Sara went to the kitchen and found a small yellow sketchbook, a wirebound volume with thick unlined pages that had been left over from a garage sale.

It was the yellow notebook more than anything else that eased Sara's mind. In its pages she began to record details about his seizures and vocalizations. She tracked the increasing flexibility of his limbs, the slight increase in his muscle tone, his decreasing weight, the persistent falling-off of his vital signs that followed each episode, a symptom that the doctors attributed to stress. The notebook contained little that wasn't in the chart, but it was not the information that soothed her, it was the act of writing it down, of placing these seeds of data into orderly boxes. It was not medically valid, she knew. But accuracy wasn't the point; it was a question of attention, of giving the tall man her unstinting effort. The tall man was lost; who knew what slender bit of information would help steer him home?

Over the next few days, Sara began to notice little changes in the tall man: the way he held his feet slightly canted toward each other, so that the big toes kissed. The way his hair seemed thicker, silkier. The slow, animal eye blinks that preceded a seizure. During the seizures, she would observe his face closely, watching how its musculature accepted the strain, watching his saintly appearance become ferocious and raptorlike, an image that frightened and allured her.

For the next week, to Tom's silent approval, Sara spent long days at the hospital, returning home well after dinner. She brought in a rubber bite guard for the tall man's mouth and a padded chair for herself. She began to identify footsteps by their rhythm: Josephine's pachydermic thumps, the papery slide of the housekeepers, the crisp heel strikes of the rent-a-cop, the syncopated creak-and-drag of stroke patients who did laps with their walkers. During those nights of that first week, Sara stayed with him, watching him seize, trying to imagine what the tall man was experiencing from within. In her readings, seizure victims had reported witnessing blue lights, buzzing rainbows, bright flares that held both pain and pleasure. During his seizures, Sara held him and peered into his eyes and thought that she saw something like pleasure, something that looked like *yes*.

On the Monday after New Year's a storm moved into the area, flooding low-lying streets and closing bridges. At eight o'clock that night Sara phoned Tom from the hospital and quickly told him she was going to stay the night. She brewed a pot of tea and sat next to the tall man, listening to the rattle of rain. The satellite map showed a large low-pressure area a hundred miles out in the Pacific. Sara smoked and watched. To her eyes, the storm possessed the chambered look of an ultrasound, a swirl of gray around a black, convulsing heart.

The seizure began as usual just after two A.M, but the tall man's tremors quickly amplified beyond anything Sara had previously witnessed. His body flung itself skyward like a puppet, smashing into the bedrails, upturning a table. Sara tried to fasten the restraints, but his hands were moving too fast. His right hand raked his neck as if he were trying to strangle himself, his fingernails drawing blood. He was respiring rapidly, his tongue quivered and extended, and a bubbling sound came from the back of his throat. She tried to hold him down, but a convulsion threw her off the bed. She lay on the floor, watching his hand clawing at his neck until droplets of blood arced around the room. The EEG stylus skittered. The twins looked on, grimacing, bespattered.

Sara crawled to the corner of the room and watched, horrified. He flipped onto his side and slid partway off the bed, then propped himself to his full height. He stood there a moment on ruined legs, tottering barefoot in his gown, his arms outstretched like a mad king. He reeled and caught himself, a bloody rope of saliva swinging from his chin, then he convulsed once more and fell sideways, his head hitting tile with a dull flat sound, and his eyes rolled back and his limbs shook down to quiet.

Sara waited, convinced that he was dead. She stood up and walked to him slowly and touched him with her foot, and saw his chest rise and fall. Straining, she tried to lift him, but her weak knee gave way and she fell to the tile. She propped him against the bed as best she could. She sat with him a moment, feeling the light warmth of his bones, the caged rasping of his breath.

She wet a cloth in warm water and knelt next to him,

washing tenderly behind his ears, wiping his head, his nose, his eyes. His neck was covered with flayed skin and blood; she silently chastised herself for letting his fingernails get so long. The blood had already started to thicken, so she gently daubed the worst of it away. His fingernails had raked deeply around his trach, raising curlicues of skin that were hardening in the cool air. She sponged it clean as best she could, wiping away the gore until she could see the broken alabaster of his skin.

Josephine arrived fifteen minutes later, wearing sneakers, jeans, and a madras shirt that did a poor job of concealing the fact that she had nothing on underneath. After snapping on a surgical glove, she traced the fingernail scrapes around the trach tube. She pursed her lips, seemed entertained.

"What are you trying to do, lover boy?"

She stood, hands on hips, waiting expectantly.

"Maybe some stim would help," Sara offered.

"Yes," Josephine said. "Stim is good."

Sara gently blew on his face. She took his hand and rubbed it gently. Josephine looked on amusedly.

"Finished?"

"I guess so," Sara said.

Josephine leaned in and squeezed the tall man's testicles. He arched his head forward and made a hollow, dual-toned groan.

"You home, lover boy?" Josephine shouted.

The sound came again. His lips parted, his tongue pushed blindly against the roof of his mouth. He sucked in a lungful of air and made the hollow sound again, more urgently. The noise continued for perhaps ten seconds, until Sara saw it.

"The trach," she said softly.

Josephine looked.

"We have to close it," Sara said, trying to be calm. "So he can talk."

They rooted around for a makeshift stopper. Josephine pulled out the plunger of a large syringe, a long, clear plastic wand with a fat black rubber tip.

"It'll stick out too far," Sara said.

Josephine's big hands snapped the wand cleanly in two, leaving the rubber tip attached to an inch of plastic. Sara took it, trying to ignore the flutter she felt inside. She braced her fingers on the top of his collarbone and, with her thumbs, worked the tip gently into the aperture like a stopper into a bottle until she felt it seal.

The tall man swallowed, and the wand twitched. Sara could hear the mechanics of it, the hushed wetness of muscle against muscle. He groaned again, but the groan had a shape to it, a definition that took a moment for Sara to recognize as a word. He repeated it.

Where.

"You're in the hospital," Sara said, conscious of the tremble in her voice. "You were brought here some time ago. You're safe now."

He repeated the word, adding more sounds with his tongue and lips. He could not control them well, and twin balls of foam formed at the corners of his mouth. He said it half a dozen times until Sara made it out.

Where is she.

The twins cooed as if in assent.

"What did he say?" Josephine said.

The tall man swallowed painfully, opened his mouth. His tongue lifted, a blind pink mollusk.

Help m-me f-find her help me.

His voice was faint and raspy, as if he were shouting across a great distance. His stammer was not the compressed frustration of most stutterers; rather, it was a gentle, experimental

35

prodding, as if the tall man had no idea what the word he was forming sounded like and so had to experiment until hitting upon the correct sound.

"How can we help?" Sara said, taking his hand. "Tell me what happened."

The man opened his eyes and stared at the ceiling. A jewel of sweat hung from his chin.

Where is sh-she?

"Good," Sara said, proud of the calmness in her voice. "You're doing a good job. Now tell us your name."

Where is she?

H-help me find her.

"Hey," Josephine boomed, causing Sara to flinch. "Answer the question."

Sara shot Josephine a severe look. Josephine shrugged innocently.

"Can you hear me?" Sara said, turning back to the tall man. "Tell me your name."

The tall man arched his neck and narrowed his eyes, as if he were trying to read something written in the air.

S-sam, he whispered. *Sam-you . . .*

"Samuel?" Josephine said.

"Is that it?" Sara said loudly. "Is that your name?" Her voice sounded cadging, motherly.

Y-yes.

"Samuel what?"

For a full minute, he closed his eyes and did nothing. From where Sara stood, she could feel his temperature rising. His heat enveloped her; he smelled clean. Then he spoke.

I d-don't know.

"Where are you from?" Josephine asked.

Don't kn-know.

"Birthday?" said Josephine.

No.

"Address, phone number, anything?"

No.

Sara bit her lip in concentration. "Do you know where you are now?"

Hosp —

"Yes. Tell us where you were before that."

He thought a moment.

W-water.

"Right, on the water." Sara fought to keep her emotions down. "In a red skiff. And where before that?"

The tall man closed his eyes, licked his lips slowly.

I-island.

"What island? What is the name of the island?"

The tall man's mouth kept moving steadily.

He m-made me.

"It's all right," Sara said, placing a hand on his shoulder. "You're here now, you're safe."

M-made me.

"Samuel," Sara said, "you said you came to the island from somewhere. Do you remember where that was?"

Him.

Sara stopped.

"Who is that?"

Broth —

"Your brother?"

His head moved — an almost imperceptible shake.

"Her brother?"

Yes.

"Is he the one who hurt you?"

My n-name is —

"We know that," Sara said with a touch of impatience. "But who is the one who tried to hurt you? The brother?"

Him.

Sara took a breath, gently touched his jaw. "Did her brother hurt you?"

W-watching me.

His voice grew hoarse and fainter. His eyelids began to quiver. Josephine looked on impassively. She reached again for his lap; Sara pushed her hand away.

"We have to ask simple questions," she whispered, trying to sound patient.

"We're going to start over now," Sara said loudly. "I'm going to ask you yes or no questions, so you can rest your voice. Okay?"

Yes.

"You know that you were on an island."

Yes.

"Do you know where were you before the island? Where you come from?"

The tall man hesitated.

Yes.

"Tell us the name of that place."

He tried to form a sound, and his lips failed. He tried again, and Sara heard.

"Chicago? Is that what you said? Chicago, Illinois?"

Yes.

Sara felt a white burst of exultation. "You're from Chicago. Samuel from Chicago."

Yes.

Samuel from Chicago. Sara felt a hot thrill move up her spine. This was it, the cracking of the vault door, the first stab of light into the dark room. There would be other words, other names, other places, each word magnetically linking to the next, forming a chain that she would use to pull him upward, to return him to his family.

"Now the girl," Josephine said. "Her name."

"One thing at a time," Sara said, "I've read about this – "

"The name of the girl," Josephine repeated steadily. "The one you want to find."

O.

"Her name is oh?"

Sara glanced at his bandaged leg. "Maybe it begins with an O." she said. "Is that right, Samuel?"

O.

"So what's the other guy's name, the one who hurt you?" Josephine said.

My n-name is Samuel.

"We know that," Josephine said. "Tell us his name."

At this the tall man seemed to grow upset. He took a shaking breath. He tried to speak, but his mouth spasmed.

"It's all right, Samuel," Sara said. "Tell me what you know."

"We're losing him," Josephine said.

"Tell me," Sara said, more urgently than she meant to.

Hel-help.

"I will."

The tall man's hand began to shake, and Sara took it.

"I will, Samuel," she said. "I'll help you find her."

He pulled away.

How l-long?

Sara hesitated and looked at Josephine, who shrugged.

"He's going to find out sooner or later."

Sara took a breath. "Eighteen months."

The tall man's eyes widened slightly; his nostrils flared. His mouth opened in a soundless cry. Sara watched, her heart pounding, desiring to embrace him, to hold his head against her, to stroke his cheek.

"He's had enough," Josephine said.

Sara smoothed his hair. It felt thin but strangely luxurious, like fur. "Rest now," she said softly. "You've told us so much, remembered so much, and I haven't even told you my name. It's Sara."

He made a final sound, then closed his eyes. It was a few seconds later, after Sara tucked the blanket up to his chin and turned away, that she heard what he had said.

I know.

4

Two days later, Sara returned to the house on Raven Lane at four o'clock to find Tom in his chair, beer in hand, his feet set wide on the floor as if tamping it in place.

"Hi, hon." Sara tried unsuccessfully to conceal the surprise in her voice. "Finish early?"

"Yeah," he said, rubbing a big hand through his hair, rearranging the tangles. "Market tanked, forecast's rain. Not a lot of meat moving."

Sara sat on the couch next to Tom, glancing not at her husband's face, but at his hands. They were long, almost delicate hands that seemed to have been transplanted from another body – a musician's, perhaps – and which did not seem to be operated by Tom so much as they operated him, anticipating his emotions through a repertoire of clenches, twitches, waggles, and oddly balletic poses. Now Sara watched them rotate some invisible object – an apple? a golf ball? Something was up.

"So the therapist tells me you can try some hiking," Tom told the dog.

Sara looked at the television screen, where Aviation Weather was playing. When had he talked to the therapist? That was just like him, uncovering the facts before she was ready for them.

"Maybe we could take a trip along the coast next weekend," he said. "Do a little nosing around."

His words filled Sara with black dread. A house by the sea was a long-standing dream of theirs, the rustic complement to their suburban life. Before the accident they'd made a habit of driving west on weekends, mooning over the burnished log retreats near Port Angeles, the picturesquely weathered salt-boxes along Clallam Bay. They'd even sketched a picture on a menu back that they kept in the glovebox: a plank-sided two-story place, picture windows overlooking a rocky beach, front porch swing, a small dock nearby with a rowboat.

"I don't know," Sara said, touching her knee lightly. "It's felt kind of stiff lately."

He turned. "Maybe a trip would do it good."

Tom had a broad, well-built moon of a face, a rather puggish nose, bright eyes, and incongruously full lips, all of it framed by a wild thicket of brown hair. It was by no means a handsome face. In fact, there were times when Sara thought him almost Cro-Magnon-like, an impression magnified by his chronically rumpled appearance. Still, slovenliness had always been Tom's greatest asset, since it camouflaged the silken intelligence that lay beneath, the intelligence that had helped him defy what seemed in retrospect to be fairly steep odds. How many other boys raised in that trailer park had ever made it out? How many could have run a three-hundred-acre ranch single-handed at eighteen years old? How many other men could have, when the ranch failed, relocated to the city and built a life selling that same beef to gourmet restaurants?

Even after eleven years Sara had no idea how he accomplished these things, except to imagine that Tom kept a tiny picture puzzle of the world in his head, an ideal version of how he would like things to be, and his life was devoted to making that picture as close to perfect as possible by swapping one piece for another. Are steaks better than cattle? Then go with steaks. Total a car? Buy a big truck. In the weeks after the accident, Tom had never been more reassuringly Tom-like. Squint eyed and sawdust haired, he had outfitted their home with an elaborate framework of handrails and ramps. He had made a project of understanding, in detail, the serotonin reuptake blockage process; he had balanced this household on his ample shoulders for several months. That first Christmas, in an attempt to cheer her up, he had constructed miniature ornaments to hang from the titanium rods that protruded from her knee. Rumpled and determined, he reminded Sara of those rescue dogs they use in avalanches: sloppy yet precise, unreadable in his exertions, digging steadily toward a goal only he could sense.

Not that Tom didn't have his difficult days. There were the two (or was it three?) times that she'd awoken to find him and a bourbon bottle at the kitchen table. Or the time last month when she'd found him asleep in the truck, the radio turned up to a heavy metal station. Tom never acknowledged these incidents directly but acted contrite and befuddled afterward, as if some rogue spirit had comandeered his body.

"Next weekend doesn't work," she said. "We've got a TBI patient who needs a lot of attention."

"Can someone cover for you?" he asked.

"Not really. It's . . . it's a special case."

His hands clenched briefly, then relaxed. "There isn't anyone?"

"No, no, there's not. They're short staffed right now."

On television, the announcer leaned forward, grimly excited. A 2,100-millibar low had moved in: a storm front sweeping across the coast; areas of high wind. A chance that the airport would be closed, he said. They sat silently and watched the rain begin.

Tom would have gotten the boy out. That was the thing they both knew, the unsayable truth. Those clever hands would have found a way, freed himself, pressed the square red button with his thumb, undone the clip, lifted the padded straps over that curly head. Once she'd tried to talk about it. It hadn't gone well. Sara's voice had sounded accusatory, and Tom had retreated, his voice choked. He'd said "I would never blame you, Sara" so many times that it seemed he was saying the opposite. They'd walked out of the room, Sara to one of her endless night drives and Tom to the kitchen, where she'd found him the next morning asleep at the table, his arm curled protectively around a half-empty bottle of Maker's Mark.

"I wish I could go," Sara said, hearing defensiveness tighten her voice.

"Fine." Tom ruffled the dog's ears in a precise and secret rhythm the dog loved. "It's fine. Do you want a cup of tea or anything?"

"No thanks."

"Hot chocolate?"

"No. But thanks."

"Cup of soup?"

"No thanks."

"You're welcome." Tom returned his attentions to the dog.

Sara felt an impulse to reach out to him – she felt the desire move through her shoulder and hand like a living thing, and then let the impulse ebb and disappear. They sat, and Sara looked at their reflection, two figures on a couch pushed farther apart by the convexity of the television screen. Between them, a pixilated darkness shifted.

They'd known each other at Big Prairie High; Tom was a year younger and lived three miles away, in the Cheatgrass Ranch, the local name for the dilapitated trailer park behind the water tank.

From the time she was small Sara had been warned about the Blacks. They were a notorious family even by local standards, a clan of aspiring felons presided over by Tom's father, Archie, an unemployed machinist whose solitary talent, it seemed, was persuading women to sleep with him. He had produced nine Black kids by four different mothers, each resembling the father so precisely that it seemed Archie was producing die-cut copies of himself (the only decent machining he ever did, local wags liked to point out). The previous eight Black children emerged onto the landscape like maniacal angels, all equipped with their father's bushy hair and propane jet eyes, poised to vandalize, dope, and ring down celestial havoc.

Tom's mother, the story went, was a soft-spoken geologist from Colorado who had the unfortunate luck to see those propane eyes glowing at her across a dim bar. After Tom was born, his mother stayed, teaching at the community college and setting up a separate house in Archie's spare trailer. The arrangement lasted three years, until she got fed up and moved out. Whether Tom remembered his mother or not (and he always claimed he didn't), the fact was the youngest Black child never fit in at the Cheatgrass Ranch. Not to say he didn't look like the rest — that was undeniable — but beneath that wild appearance resided an unusually organized mind. As a small boy Tom would stack his father's beer cans into elaborate structures, filling the cramped trailer with cathedrals of Rainier; he once landed in Archie's doghouse for employing his father's bong in a crystal radio set. Amid the Cheatgrass squalor, Tom grew up clear-eyed, alert, a straight-A student whom teachers always suspected of cheating. He learned to move through the world quietly, his eyes sharp behind the wild crown of hair he could never quite tame.

Sara, for possibly obtuse reasons, found him interesting.

They talked sometimes during high school, and during senior year he paid occasional visits. Though her mother made off-hand fun – the barbarian, she called him – there was something about him, a warm steadiness. It resided mostly in his voice, a slow, soft instrument that could utter the most mundane sentence – *This lemonade is good* – and make Sara wonder momentarily if she had ever really known lemonade, or goodness. Yet despite the attraction, Tom Black was a puzzle to her. During high school she thought of him often, trying to determine how much of her attraction was genuine and how much lay in the thrill of their unlikeliness as a couple. Because there was a thrill – a perceptible buzz, actually, that traveled through certain rooms when they walked in, not the least of which was the living room of her own house.

Senior year, when Tom asked Sara to the prom – his hulking body set uneasily on the porch, his brow held low as if he were storming a medieval castle – she had said yes without thinking. They had gone and had had a nice enough time. But Tom hadn't said much, and at the end of the night Sara had found herself standing on her front porch listening to the rain hit the roof and wondering if it had been a good or bad time. Nervous, she had teased him, asking if he knew how to talk.

"Not that well, to you," he'd said. "After all, we just started to get to know each other." Then he'd said good night and walked through the rain back to his truck.

After all, we just started to get to know each other. She had stood on the porch, vaguely indignant. What was that supposed to mean? Hadn't they just spent a whole evening – dinner and car rides and dance and more car rides – doing little else but getting to know each other? *Well*, she remembered thinking as she slammed the door and went inside, *glad* that's *over*.

Sara left for college, studied nursing, mostly forgot Tom

Black. Four years later her father fell dead in the fields of a heart attack. Sara had returned home to see Tom running her father's tractor. He had been attending a community college and running a friend's ranch when he heard. He hadn't said a word to anyone, just showed up and kept showing up the next day and the next, taking care of her father's fields and cattle as if he were a hired hand. She brought him lemonade and he drank it sitting in the tractor and she watched the muscles of his throat move up and down. The first time Sara touched him was the day they made love.

Vera summoned her considerable powers to undermine "this local infatuation." She teased and wept, fainted and laughed, bribed friends to lobby Sara. She faked a spinal injury, hinted darkly of joining her husband, and finally donned the blue Chanel dress and attempted to seduce him. By the end of that summer their union, once merely unlikely, had achieved heroic dimensions. They were the underdogs, the couple nobody thought possible. The world was conspiring against them, and with each attempt their bond grew stronger.

Toward the end, in an unexpected flanking maneuver, Vera resorted to the truth.

"He'll want you to stay here, you know," she said. "He'll want you to run the ranch together."

"We can make it work," Sara said. "Tom has a plan."

"I don't want you to make the same mistake I did."

"I'm not you."

"He's a hick, Sara. He's a nice enough boy, but he's nothing compared to you."

"He loves me. He's honest."

"Love fades, darling. And honesty?" Vera's red lips twitched in amusement. "Honesty is overrated."

Tom and Sara were married in the county courthouse, and

Vera, defeated but unbowed, swanned back to Philadelphia to live with her sister. Tom and Sara worked her father's ranch, and within months it was apparent that Vera had been right. The ranch failed, slowly, inexorably. As their money dried up, Sara found it easy, almost comforting. Her mother gone, it was easier to admit that she'd never truly wanted to be a ranch wife. This was not a failure, it was merely a prelude, a chance for her and Tom to bond in their slow descent, like brave musicians on a sinking ship. They stayed up late, plotting and planning, looking at maps, imagining themselves in different cities, doing different jobs. Then one day at breakfast Tom cleared his throat and said he'd been doing some thinking about the food chain. Two months later the ranch was sold, Sara was applying for hospital jobs, and Tom was reading up on portable refrigeration units.

They'd seemed like explorers at first, astronauts stepping gingerly about this unfamiliar landscape, growing accustomed to its crowds, its coffee-and-fish smells, the way the evening light shone through the rain. Sara landed a job at King County. Tom took out a loan and set up a beef-aging facility in Renton and began visiting restaurants. Barely two years later they were looking for a house, hauling their scuffed furniture into the miraculous geometry of its freshly painted rooms, exchanging cheery waves with their new neighbors, lying beneath the skylight listening to an unfamiliar symphony of squeaks and tics. Tom called it their dream house, and it had been a measure of their dreams that the house still needed a lot of work. But that was okay, because they had chosen the perfect place. MountainLake Hills was twenty minutes north of the city, with close-trimmed hedges and thoughtfully set trees and smooth concrete sidewalks that rang with the footsteps of smiling, healthy children. This house, and this neighborhood, was the proof of their clean, solid suburban life. No more apartments, no more moves, no more landlords, no more cobwebs to remind Tom of his Cheatgrass days. This was their life now: they would fix up this house, they would fill its rooms with shouting children, they would become fast friends with their neighbors, enter this world of sidewalks, barbecues, lemonade stands. Tom seemed to see it all as if it had already happened, and Sara saw it, too, at least she tried.

But as time passed, Sara found herself growing restless. It wasn't just that she missed the ranch or that it had all happened too fast. She couldn't – and she knew how strange this sounded – *believe* in the neighborhood. The houses looked nice from the outside, but once you got inside they were boxy and thin walled, the type of construction her father used to disdain as "Japanese." The door frames were made of plastic; even the streetlights would tremble if you tapped them. The mothers were too well dressed, the children too attractive and too precocious. The neighborhood reminded Sara of a movie set where everyone had lines they had to speak or else it would upset the timing of the entire production. She fought the feeling, quelling it with the clutter and bustle of working on the house, distracting it with work. But the sensation always returned, the floatiness, the feeling of being suspended between worlds.

The problem, as Sara saw it, was partly structural. The MountainLake Development Company offered homes in several models and three different floor plans. However, beyond slight variances in molding options (natural cedar posts for the Santa Fe porches; scrolled corinths for Victorians), each model was essentially interchangeable. The result was that to Sara, every house appeared to be the same house, and every family appeared to belong to the same gigantic extended family, of which Sara was a distant in-law. Invisible threads of intimacy seemed strung beneath the blacktopped streets, connecting each house to the next in a finely articulated network of PTA meetings, play groups, and car pools. Even her next-door neighbor Mrs. Wooding, a stern ex-Bostoner with a velour sweatsuit wardrobe and a bottomless obsession with her flower beds, seemed to locate her place in the flow with mysterious ease, attending cookie exchanges, hosting crowded piano recitals, and, according to the neighborhood newsletter, manufacturing 1,500 chocolate truffles to help raise money for the local arts council. These women were nice enough, but they radiated a certainty that made Sara uncomfortable. When she tried to explain her feelings to Tom, she found herself floundering. Tom responded in his Tom-like way, by looking her in the eye and stating questions that were simple, honest, and utterly unanswerable. Didn't she like the house? Wasn't this what they had wanted?

"Yes," she had told him one night at dinner a few months before their son was born. "Yes and no."

Tom regarded her carefully. "What's that mean?"

"Sometimes I feel like we aren't meant to be here. Like we just picked it out of a map, and we could just as well be somewhere else, living another life."

"Where else should we be?" the voice wondered patiently. "Tell me, and maybe we'll go there."

"I don't know," Sara said, frustrated. "Not the ranch, not an apartment, not anywhere, really. I just don't like this narrowing. The feeling that this is all there is, for a long time."

"Life can't help but narrow as you get older — what else could it do? There are fewer choices than when we were seven, than when we were seventeen. You choose a path."

"You see it that way, Tom. I see it that way, but life here

seems so . . . scripted. So boxed in. It makes me wonder if this is where we should be raising our family."

Tom steepled his fingers. "Slow down, honey. You're over-thinking this."

"Is there even such a thing as overthinking? Could it be possible for just one second that everyone else is underthinking?"

"You don't know these people very well. Underneath, they're all muddling through, just like us."

"I know them well enough."

He persisted, his voice laying out bricks of undeniable truth. "No, you don't. It takes years to get to know people, to really know them. Maybe they secretly have the same kinds of doubts you do."

Sara siphoned her tea through tightened lips. Her belly shifted, and she put a hand on it.

"Maybe you're right," she said, giving in. "Maybe I just need to give it time."

"Time," he said, reaching over to pat her expanding belly. "That's all anything takes."

When the boy arrived, Sara's restlessness had seemed to evaporate. For long months she had felt at home, sated by the clamor and busyness of a new mother's life. It would return to her sometimes, standing at the kitchen sink or late at night during a feeding. But mostly she was at peace. She and Tom worked well together, sharing with equanimity, keeping a light tone, avoiding the businesslike edge they sometimes saw in other rookie parents. They enjoyed themselves with their neighbors; they developed some friendships. The scrubby spruce around the neighborhood started to grow. Occasionally Sara caught herself visualizing them as ancient trees, she and Tom silver haired and content beneath them, watching their grandkids on a swing, arcing through the blue dome of some future sky.

And now. Sitting alone in the room, listening to the rain on the roof. Waiting for something. Accompanied by the absence they can neither acknowledge nor ignore.

"I started fixing up the back room today," Tom said, his eyes still on the television.

It took a moment for Sara to figure out his meaning. He had never called it by that name.

"I moved some things," Tom said. "So we can build a desk and some bookshelves. We can use it as an office."

Sara blinked slowly, like a dull child. She should have known. In recent weeks Tom had developed a passion for rearranging – of the medicine cabinet, for instance, or the laundry room, or the garage. He folded his socks and stacked them by color; he arranged the spice cabinet alphabetically. He'd never mentioned the boy's old room, but Sara felt the inevitability of the progression.

"Hon," Tom said softly. "It's time."

Sara could picture him now, with his tool belt and putty knife, methodically scraping the purple giraffes and koalas from the wall, efficiently disassembling the little wooden bed, unscrewing that astronaut light fixture and putting in something quiet and normal. Rehanging those awful Remington prints he had brought from the ranch – blade-faced cowboys leaned out over straining quarterhorses, lariats a-whirling, manes rising like flames in the wind, a vision of an America that never was. Those cowboys, with their poised, false drama. They never existed anyway, not like that. They were essentially a myth, a bald-faced lie of history that everybody agreed to believe for the sake of . . . of what? Of having something to believe.

52

"This is an opportunity," Tom said. "It means some doors are closing, others opening."

"I don't want to adopt," Sara said.

"I didn't say adoption," Tom said.

"What other doors are there?"

"Me and you kind of doors," he said, smiling. "Trip-down-the-coast kind of doors."

Sara felt a burst of fondness and pity. He was so transparent in his maneuverings, so determined.

"Maybe we'll go," she allowed. "After work calms down."

"Well, here's some incentive," Tom said lightly. "Brenda and Derek invited us for dinner a week from Friday. If we happened to be out of town . . ."

Sara turned.

"You didn't."

Tom looked closely at the television. Sara knew that he didn't like Brenda any more than she did. Yet he still tolerated her. Perhaps, she suddenly thought, even conspired with her.

"Tell me you didn't accept. Please."

"She's been asking for months, Sara. Literally months. You know how she is."

Sara did know. The whole neighborhood knew, owing to the success of Brenda Oliver's teddy bears, a cancer research fundraiser. The project had begun three years ago, after her daughter died of leukemia, and expanded so efficiently that there were now hardly any checkout counters in King County unadorned by the halo-shaped display case. Sara's initial admiration was gradually eroded by Brenda's insistence that Sara's accident had transformed them into soul mates. Each day during Sara's hospitalization, Brenda had brought a different-colored bear to her hospital bed – tangerine, plum, ivory. "A gift, from my angel to yours," she would say.

Sara didn't tell Brenda, but she had in fact tried some conventional approaches. She'd attended mass for two solid weeks before all the body and blood got to be too much. She'd tried reading some of Brenda's books, trudging through saccharine deserts in search of an oasis of fact. She'd even given therapy a second try, traveling in secret to a renowned psychologist in Tacoma. But the doctor was an unreconstructed Freudian who stank of tobacco and tweed; all he'd wanted to talk about was her father and mother, and she'd quit after three sessions. When Sara heard Brenda talking about redemption and healing, there were times when it seemed almost tempting, this notion that there existed an apparatus, a gently whirring machine into which your soul could be inserted, swabbed with healing drugs, scrubbed of its pain, and returned intact to your body.

But though she tried, Sara couldn't bring herself to believe in such a thing. Brenda's way was too false, built on the principle that recovering from the death of a child was in some essential way not any more complex than fixing your vacuum cleaner or toning your abdominals. Sara suspected Brenda was in fact deeper in denial than Sara, the only difference being that Sara at least *knew* it. Besides, Sara was all too conscious that dear departed Katrina – that perfect angel who taught us so many lessons about grace and courage – had in fact been a difficult child with a habit, even when sick, of bullying smaller children. So Sara had played along, putting off this dinner invitation for months, inventing increasingly outlandish excuses about work and travel in the hope that even Brenda would eventually get the hint and give up. Now she began to sweat.

"I don't think we can commit to a whole dinner," Sara said evenly. "This patient's been having seizures, and we never know when one might hit."

"It's every six hours, isn't it?"

"Yes," Sara said, wondering how Tom knew. "Six or seven."

"We could keep it quick, just dessert or drinks."

"Besides," Sara persisted, "she's the one who keeps sending me those flowers every month and pretending she's not. What am I supposed to say about that?"

Tom patted the dog, spoke in his new, cheery voice. "She means well, Sara."

"Everybody means well," Sara said. "That's the problem."

5

Sara was surprised how easy it was to keep the tall man's ability to speak a secret. She rolled his bed into the far corner of the room, out of sightline of the door. She considered posting a quarantine sign until she decided that the sign would attract more attention than it deflected. She kept the scrim around the tall man's bed halfway closed, so that someone passing by would not chance to see his mouth moving. She tucked the stopper in a plastic bag and taped it inside the cabinet like a spare key.

Checking her reading, Sara tried techniques that, as the books authoritatively put it, could "activate the patient's circuitry." She read him lists of place names from maps of the Northwest, naming every island from Alaska to Oregon and all the suburbs of Chicago. Much to Josephine's bemusement, she toted in Tupperwares full of scents and textures that might be familiar – a bucket of sand, a pine branch, a clump of seaweed, a baseball cap. She tried different persons: stern, jokey, soft, cajoling, each one designed to deliver the same essential plea: *Tell me who you are.* But no matter how hard she tried, he kept murmuring the same handful of semi-intelligible phrases, each of which she copied dutifully into the pages of the yellow notebook.

He will not stop.

He knows, he always knew.
He watches me and her. Waiting.
Stop him. Help me stop him.

On repeated hearings, Sara was able to extract shards of information: The girl's name was Oceana Spero, Oshie for short. She had blue eyes and reddish hair. The brother's name began with a K. The tall man did not seem to remember anything about a pistol, or a red skiff, or anything else.

Grimly enthused by the prospect of detective work, Sara spent hours telephoning people with the surname Spero, first initials O or K, with no luck. She broadened her search to all Speros in the Seattle area. She spent several pricey hours with a people search specialist who, three days later, delivered the brick of truth: There was no Oceana Spero to be found in the United States or Canada. Sara asked the tall man repeatedly if this was the correct spelling, asking if there was anything else about her that he could recall.

Oceana Sp-spero, he whispered with slurred, fierce precision. *Find her.*

So Sara kept looking in ways that were less effective but still satisfying, paging through outdated phone books, poring over the hospital's visitor log. She found herself watching redhaired passersby, comparing them to the imaginary portrait she'd begun to construct.

"I'm trying," she told the tall man. "But you have to tell me more. You have to remember more."

O is alive. Help me, Sara.

"What did she look like? Tell me again."

Beautiful, he said. *She was b-beautiful.*

"That doesn't exactly help, Samuel," she said stiffly. "How tall was she? Tell me what her face looked like."

Find her find her find her.

57

"Why, Samuel?" Sara said. "Tell me why."

His lips pulled back as he pronounced the sound.

K.

"You're afraid he'll find her?"

Y-yes.

"What will happen if he finds her first?"

He did not answer.

The seizures continued, maintaining their frequency and intensity. The doctors prescribed phenobarbital, to little effect, and then Valium. They noted a persistent depression in heart rate and respiration after each seizure, which they attributed to stress, and recommended a 15 percent increase in his calorie intake. Sara marked all these things down carefully in her yellow notebook. She studied the tall man's face during the seizures. She saw the muscles flex and tense, saw expressions move across it like wind. She could see a silken core of ecstasy beneath the violence of those moments, a trancelike state that lingered long after the seizure had passed. *Those are the memories fighting to get out,* she thought. She felt a pulse of unreasonable optimism. *There are things we can sense but can't touch,* she told herself. *There is a world beneath the world.*

One day Sara asked the tall man what he saw when the seizures came.

Lights, f-faces.

"Do you see Oceana?"

Us together.

"What else do you see, Samuel?"

Island.

"What does it look like?"

Rocks. T-trees. Waves never stop.

"Is Oceana on the island?"

58

Yes.

"What else?"

Green w-water. Starfish.

"What else?"

Old man.

"What's he doing?"

Lying n-next to the water. Eyes open.

"Who is he?"

D-don't know.

"Is he dead?"

Yes.

"Who hurt the old man? Who does this?"

I did.

Sara hesitated. "Are you saying that you hurt the old man?"

K m-made me.

"Tell me more, Samuel."

Made me.

"Who is the old man? Why does K want to hurt him?"

Don't kn-know.

"What do you see? Take me there."

Can't. Too much.

"Tell me what you see."

Beautiful, he said. *T-terrible.*

That Sunday Josephine said, "Maybe you ought to talk to him more."

Sara turned. Josephine shrugged.

"You're always asking him questions – who is she, where is he, what does she look like. Tell him stories. Maybe the more stories he hears, the more his brain will grow. Like with my plants at home."

"He hears stories on TV."

Josephine rolled her eyes.

"I already talk to him," Sara said defensively. "I talk to him a lot."

"Good morning, good morning," Josephine mimicked. "That's not going to cut it, darling."

"Well, what story am I supposed to tell him?"

"How should I know? Read a book. Talk about sports."

"I don't think it could make a difference," Sara said after a moment of hesitation. "A voice is a voice."

"Stories are different. Besides, he already likes your voice."

Josephine gave a lascivious wink and tilted her head toward the tall man's lap.

"Don't be ridiculous," Sara whispered fiercely, closing the scrim.

"Am I blind now?" Josephine said.

Sara blushed. Josephine's big hand patted her back.

"Don't sweat it, hon. It happens with a lot of my patients. It's like a weather vane, that's all. It just means he likes being with you."

"I'm not going to talk just to . . . you know, turn him on."

Josephine smiled. "I thought that's what we were doing — he's turned off, and you're trying to turn him on."

After Josephine departed, Sara sat awhile in awkward silence. Then she busied herself with the twins. Sara bathed them and changed them and talked to them, newly conscious of her murmurous singsong. *We're washing your legs now. That's a good girl.* She dressed them and leaned them back into their beds. She dimmed the lights, clicked off the TV, and closed the door, looking warily up and down the hall. Then she sat at the foot of the tall man's bed. Cleared her throat.

"Well then, Samuel," she said. "How are you doing?"

She was disappointed at the sound of her own voice. She had meant for it to sound breezy; instead it sounded teacherly, the voice of a bossy older sister. She took a breath and tried to locate a brighter tone, something like she imagined hearing at a cocktail party.

"I don't know if you noticed, but it's raining out," she said. "That's the sound you hear against the window. It's supposed to clear up later, and a high-pressure is supposed to move in for the weekend. At least that's what they're calling for."

Sara looked down to see a triangle rising in the blanket. She watched it and thought, *Why not?* She shifted her chair, conscious of his blank gaze. She ran her fingers through her hair, ransacking her brain for other stories – happenstances, nosy neighbors, petty workplace operas – and could find none. Other people told stories, didn't they? Josephine was always telling stories, about her dickhole neighbors or about her piranha, who seemed to possess a more complex and singular personality than most people she knew. But Sara, Sara didn't have anything. She sat quietly, pressing her fingertips against one another as Tom would have, hoping the tall man didn't sense her embarrassment.

The clock ticked, and as it did a sentence came to her. It was a simple sentence, just five words. She said the words silently to herself. She felt calm and exhilarated at the same time.

"I have a little boy," she said.

The tall man looked at her. Sara had not meant to say that. She had meant to say, "I had a little boy," but when the time came to say it, she could not put him in the past tense. She kept going.

"He's four and a half years old," she said. "His name is Luke."

*   *   *

61

Sara hadn't enjoyed her pregnancy. She had given it a game try, patting her expanding belly with feigned contentment, pursuing as many cravings as she could dredge up, but in truth she found the feeling of something growing inside of her a little unnerving. The birth itself had been a battle royal, twelve hours of hard labor, episiotomy, IV tubes, finally a suction cup – a toilet plunger! – fitted around the baby's pinioned head. When the doctor handed her this stunned, dripping, blue-eyed infant, she was consumed by an overwhelming aura of warmth combined with a quiet disbelief that she was being allowed to keep him. The whole thing seemed ludicrous, a prank that would be rectified any second by smiling authorities. A few hours after the birth, when the nurse came in the delivery room to check on things, Sara remembered sleepily loosening her grip on the baby, preparing to give him up to his real parents.

Everyone was taken with Luke from the start. He was an unusually attractive infant – fat as a baron, with his father's poetically tangled hair. The nurses fussed over him with competitive fervor. Neighborhood mothers she barely knew cornered her on the street so they could point out the way Luke would tighten his feet into tiny fists or the way his tongue snaked out of the corner of his mouth when he smiled, and when they did, Sara would smile and silently wonder why she hadn't noticed the same thing. Perhaps, she theorized, because she was too busy dealing with the the never-ending calamity of her new existence. She seemed to spend each moment buttoning and unbuttoning outfits, wiping up fresh messes, searching frantically for diapers, and unknotting the Gordian straps of the old plaid car seat she'd got for $10 at a garage sale. The other mothers witnessed her struggles and thrust catalogs at her filled with gear she simply had to buy – a Swedish front pack, a portable crib, a video baby monitor, a musical blanket.

But out of sheer stubbornness she refused, and the mothers humored her with arch smiles. *You'll catch on*, they said. But she didn't. Sara watched in envious awe as other mothers soothed their newborns with a touch, a sound. Luke began to cry more frequently, and Sara would resort to simply guessing what was wrong, like a losing contestant on a game show. Are you hungry? Thirsty? Sleepy? Wet? Overtired? *What is it?* After six months, a dark tendril of doubt began to take root.

"So you're not June Cleaver," Tom said. "Who is?"

"Everyone. They all know this stuff, and they're so in tune with everything."

"You'll get the hang of it, sweetie," he said, kissing her cheek. "If it's worth getting a hang of."

To an extent, Sara did. At home with Luke she was able to perform well enough, to say the right thing with the right motherly assurance in her tone. But out in the sylvan streets of MountainLake Hills, Sara couldn't concentrate. She felt like an unprepared actress, missing her cues, stumbling through the motions. Her ineptness, of course, only increased her child's ardor. Luke adored Sara and cried whenever she left the room — hard, piteous cries that lasted until she picked him up, until she held his tiny face next to hers, transmitting her warmth to him. What he wanted, it became apparent, was to taste her, so she would let him. Luke would feast greedily on her cheeks, her ear, her eyes, and it was at those moments that Sara felt most at ease. *This is love*, she would think happily, feeling his tiny mouth gnawing on her. *This is real.*

One Saturday morning Sara decided to join the cadre of new mothers pushing their jog strollers and talking about their babies, their toddlers, their preschoolers. They chatted blithely — *Oh, he loves playing on the computer. Only two, and he can already put the DVDs in by himself.* Sara tried ineffectually to join in, and though the mothers listened with hungry smiles, her stories fell flat. After a few moments she abandoned her efforts and decided instead to take in the spectacle of the neighborhood. It was a beautiful spring morning, and MountainLake Hills was readying itself for the day: its lawns neatly clipped, its flowers rising attentively, its garage doors purring upward. She saw helmeted squadrons of kids biking down the street. She saw gleaming minivans deploying in formation for karate class, dance recitals, and SAT workshops. She heard the bleat of cell phones, the chirp of the video games, the preemptive singsong of mothers standing near the monkey bars – *not too rough now, not too rough.* She watched a soccer team of seven-year-olds outfitted in professional-quality green satin jerseys exerting themselves silently before the frozen smiles of their parents. Everywhere she sensed the great and urgent river of the modern child-raising meritocracy, watchful parents steering children through a never-ending maze of improving activities, each moment observed and accounted for, each decision propelled by a never-slowing rhythm of hope and desire: *This! This! Now this!*

Turning away, Sara's eyes were drawn to a group of three boys sitting on a bench near an empty baseball diamond. They were ten years old, maybe eleven. They had baseball caps and blue jeans and pleasant, freckled faces bobbing in gentle syncopation. Sara looked more closely and saw the reason: They all were plugged into headphones, each retreated into his own world. She looked into their eyes and a word slipped unwillingly into her head: *Never.*

Sara watched the boys, and as she did something happened inside her. It wasn't a decision; it happened on a reflexive level, like the knotting of a muscle. She vowed that Luke would be, above all else, an original kid. He would not be swept under by a dizzying wave of entertainment and overscheduled activity; instead he would learn to live self-sufficiently. It was simple, really. If childhood had become a rushing river, then it was her task to build Luke a boat. A strong boat made of discipline and independence to bear him through until he was old enough to make his own choices.

Sara felt her scalp prickle; her heart whammed against her rib cage. She knew that she was being hopelessly idealistic, but she could not stop herself. This was what she'd been missing. This was the kind of love she was built to give – a love that hollowed out a safe space and granted her son the means to become whatever he wanted to become. Room – that's what it was about in the end. Room to grow, room to think, room to create. Even her mother, Vera, normally not a wellspring of parenting advice, had been eloquent on the matter. "The open road isn't for everybody," she used to say with a shrug. "But what other road is worth taking?"

She began with little things. When Luke fell – and he fell with a ski jumper's spectacularity – she would count to five before comforting him, so that he'd learn that it wasn't the end of the world. When he dropped his bottle, she lifted him out of his high chair so that he, not her, could pick it up. When he began to crawl, she sewed Christmas bells to his outfits so that she could know where he was without having to check on him constantly. Other mothers, coming over for coffee with their children on their arm, were at first taken aback. But after a while, the women saw how Luke handled himself and they began to make admiring noises – *Quite a little trooper you've got there*, they would say – and Sara would say yes and try not to notice that tingle of pride she felt.

Energized, Sara began to add other features to her repertoire. She made Luke clear his dishes as soon as he could walk. She made him clean up his room shortly after. She made it a habit to leave him alone in his room for a couple of hours each day – quiet time, she called it. She developed a voice, a neutral, businesslike, thoroughly adult voice, that she used to talk to Luke. A voice that, she couldn't help but notice, cut like a scalpel through the buttery pleas she heard on the sidewalk. *Time to go, Luke,* she would say quietly, and he would stand up and go.

By the time he was two, Sara noticed other mothers asking her about things that she did. Scraping corporate decals off his toys. Her no television rule. Books she read or avoided. It was all made up on the fly, but Sara had a way of making it sound at once more organized and more vague, as if this were some mysterious curriculum that she had formulated. *Oh, he's just a good boy,* she would say.

Though she didn't admit it to herself, Sara took to her role with a gusto. Luke was blossoming. He wasn't a perfect kid, not by a long shot. He wasn't a good sharer, and a tad serious, perhaps. But he was not like them; that was the bottom line. He was tougher, he was more self-sufficient, he had a way of looking at the world that showed he was seeing it, not seeing just what his mother wanted him to see. Sara thrilled to hear an echo of her own voice in his piping tone, a cool neutrality. As he grew older she added other elements: Luke earned his dessert by singing a song at dinner, he set the table, he hauled laundry. When he hurt himself or fell, part of her rejoiced. *He will learn to be strong,* Sara would say to herself. *He is his own individual, he must learn to live in this world.*

There were occasions, of course, when things did not go so well, moments when Luke got frustrated or angry, or when he would come to her and hold out his arms, desiring nothing but her touch. She would indulge him, hug him warmly, and set him on the ground again, facing the world. There were times, though, when a hug was not enough, when Luke would attach himself to her leg, linger underfoot. Sara would find herself ashamed and angry at this clingy, obstinate child. The other mothers didn't seem to mind – *Having a tough day*, they would intone sympathetically – but that only made it worse.

There was that neighbor kid's birthday party when Luke was almost three. All the guests were gathered photogenically around a pink birthday cake while Luke sat beneath the table with a silver jet airplane. He wasn't playing with it, he was examining it with ferocious concentration, placing his fingers along the wings, spinning the tiny black wheels, while a few inches above him, a carnival of games and party favors spun, far off as the surface of the moon. Another mother sidled up to Sara – an ex-lawyer, Sara recalled, who had traded in her courtroom suits for Jil Sander outfits. She aimed a cable-knit elbow at Luke.

"Your little guy's sure good by himself, isn't he?"

"Yes," Sara said, looking the woman in the eye.

Jil Sander sighed elaborately. "I wish I could get my kids to play like that."

"You could," Sara said without thinking. "Don't be their best playmate."

"Don't you ever worry," Jil Sander said, her voice heavy with concern, "that he won't be, you know, social?"

"Not really, no."

The woman's eyes grew cartoonishly wide. She actually cupped a hand to her ear, as if unsure she had heard correctly. Sara, taking the bait, continued.

"I think you have to get along with yourself before you can get along with others."

"Really," Jil Sander said, and as she did, two other women turned, sharklike, wedges of cake glinting in their hands. Sara felt their eyes on her, but she continued. She tried to lighten her tone.

"I mean, there's no point to being friends if there's no substance to be friends with. I mean, if it's not built on something real."

That sounded wrong.

"What I mean is," she said, blushing, "some things in life are more important than getting along with people."

"Really?" Jil Sander tried to hold back a smile, not having expected her cross-examination to be so fruitful. "What things would those be?"

Sara tried to cover, but it was too late. The game was up, all was ruined. The women tilted their heads, glancing furtively under the table at Luke, now suddenly the friendless, airplane-fixated boy. Sara wanted to hold her ground, to tell them that they were wrong. But she didn't. She panicked.

"Come on, Luke," she said in her cool voice. "Time to go."

Luke looked up from under the table, his eyes round. There was still cake. There were still presents. Ice cream. The other children fell silent, aware that one of their own was being asked to do the impossible.

"It's time," she said quickly, holding out his coat. "I just remembered, we've got someplace we've got to be."

"No."

"Pardon me?"

Luke lifted his face to hers. She could feel his nervousness, but he didn't back down.

"I want to stay."

Sara felt the mothers shift. This was what they secretly desired, sweet comeuppance.

"Get your coat, hon," Sara said calmly. "We're leaving."

Luke sat down beneath the shelter of the table and picked

up the airplane again. Sara stood there for a moment, calculating.

"Tell you what, I'll count to three," she said, injecting cheer into her voice.

Luke, his head down, spun the airplane's wheels.

"Oh, let him be," one of the mothers murmured. "We'll start with the cake now."

Sara felt something steel within her.

"No thanks," she said, leaning over and picking Luke up below the arms. He barrel-rolled away from her, farther beneath the table.

Sara went after him, engaging in a noiseless karate battle. He was strong, landing a series of quick, soft blows. She told herself she had no choice, but in the depths of her heart, she knew better. And Luke did, too. The irony was unmissable, even to a three-year-old: She had raised her son partly as a rebuke to overprotective mothers, and now she cared more about the opinion of those mothers than she did about him.

Luke, thank God, finally gave in. She said her awkward good-byes and walked out the door and down the sidewalk. Sara put the key in the car door, but Luke kept walking past the car and into a neighboring park. She was going to follow him, but instead she let him go, watched him take furious, stiff-legged steps across the wet grass. He went ten, then twenty yards, not headed anywhere. Sara decided to let him go, let him burn off steam. She put her bags in the car and then turned to find him standing with his hands at his sides, watching her. Not just watching – looking with a deep concentration. She had trained him to see, and now he seemed to be seeing right into her, at that dark root of fear still growing in her heart. The fear that had never quite been vanquished, not by all the high-minded parenting, not by the ladderwork of systems and rules, not by the praise from her friends and Tom. The fear that Sara did not love her son enough.

Sara looked up from her reverie, surprised to see the tall man sitting there, his eyes wide.

At first, Sara felt guilty about pretending that Luke was still alive. So she rationalized: she told herself she wasn't pretending; she was merely omitting a fact that the tall man might find upsetting. She was simply rearranging time, and what was the harm in that?

For the next week she told the tall man more stories — birthdays, trips to the zoo, first time riding on a bike, stunningly average evenings at home. Sara had no idea if these reconstructed days were true, strictly speaking, but they felt real. She told the tall man tiny, idiotic things: the strange bristliness of Luke's eyebrows, the hammerlike shape of his second toe. She described the theatrical way he ate, inserting gigantic bites of food, then pulling the empty spoon from his mouth as if he had performed some marvelous feat of magic. How he would stare at things for hours, how his attention span seemed limitless, awe-inspiring. How a toothless old man in the park once smiled and rubbed Luke's head and said that he was one of those, a watcher — Sara liked that. She told the tall man about how Luke's big eyes and quiet manner sometimes caused people to mistake him for a girl, a fact that had caused Tom concern but that Sara had rather enjoyed. After all, what would be the difference? One chromosome? A few genes? A race won by a different sperm cell? We all come so close to being someone else.

Sara told the tall man about Luke's favorite bedtime story, *The Golden Egg Book* by Margaret Wise Brown. She remembered many nights when Luke would come to her with that book extended in his hands. She tried warm milk, blankets, cuddling with him to get him to bed. But the only foolproof guaranteed solution was that story of a lonely bunny who finds an egg and wonders what's inside.

Luke would always want to be the egg and ask Sara to be the bunny and throw Legos at him to make him hatch. He loved pretending he was asleep, monitoring her through flickering eyelids to make sure she was playing her role with proper sincerity. Then he'd wake up and jump into her arms and she would press her nose into the shampooey tousle of his hair.

It was easy to talk to the tall man for the same reason it was easy to talk to Josephine. There was no nodding, or sentimental posing, or sympathetic touches. He was absent except in the most vital way. She imagined his voice: soft, scratchy, marked with quiet inflection. She filled in the silences with his questions: *I see. How did that turn out?* With pillows, she adjusted his head to the proper inquiring angle.

As she drove home one night after a day of telling the tall man stories, Sara suddenly remembered the name of the children's song that was playing when her car smashed through the guardrail. The strange thing was that she could actually feel the memory arrive. Her heart started to beat faster, and she began to sweat uncontrollably. Then the memory arrived whole, a completed image delivered into her mind at tremendous velocity, as if it had been pushed through a pinhole. She closed her eyes and she knew. "Here We Go Loop De Loo," that's what the song was.

6

"Have you seen my yellow notebook?"

Sara was standing next to the front door of their house, attempting patience. Tom sat on the couch, reading a magazine. He had watched Sara root through her backpack, the pockets of her coat, the unopened pile of mail on the hallway table. Now he and the dog looked up at her with identical blank expressions.

"That yellow one?"

"Yes."

"No."

"Goddamn it," Sara said, then softened her voice when she saw Tom's face. "I could have sworn I had it."

"You had it the day before yesterday," Tom said carefully. "Did you bring it home yesterday?"

"Yes," Sara said, although she had no idea if this was true.

"Checked the bedroom?"

"Yes."

"Bedside table?"

"Yes, yes, yes. It's not here."

Tom remained cemented to the couch as Sara limped through the house, fighting down a rising feeling of panic. Without the notebook, she had no record of the tall man's condition, his words. Nothing.

"Could it be in the car?"

"Already checked."

"Bathroom?"

"No."

Sara watched Tom's mind work through the possibilities and churn steadily toward a verdict.

"It'll turn up," he said.

"It better," she said, more harshly than she intended. Tom picked up his magazine, and Sara looked away, ashamed to be so touchy.

Tom returned to his magazine. From the door, she could see the article he was reading: "How to Build a Scandinavian-Scribe Log Cabin." Perfect: just the sort of muscly know-how he loved. Watching him, Sara found herself idly wondering if he had stolen the notebook. Wouldn't it have been natural, even logical, for him to do a little covert information gathering? Tom could have removed the notebook from her purse and tucked it inside his magazine; he could be reading her entries right now. There was nothing embarrassing there, she told herself, just records of his vital signs, a few meaningless phrases, a daily log of his progress. But still.

Trying to be unobtrusive, she walked behind him, but when she got there she saw only the magazine. "Each scribe must be precisely made or the log will not seat properly against its mate," the caption read.

"I probably left it in the truck," she said, cheerfully, she was sure. "I should be back in time for dinner."

A stir of activity surrounded her departure. Tom pressed a sack lunch into her hand – leftover Chinese – and kissed her quickly. He was polite and a little distant, and when Sara started the car she had a moment of regret, seeing her husband standing alone at the doorway. She watched him in the rearview, diminishing, waving as if he were sinking into clear water. *Each scribe must be precisely made or the log will not seat properly against its mate.*

When Sara opened the TBI ward's heavy door, she was happy to find the tall man alone. She couldn't yet think of him as Samuel. She had no logical reason for this, except that the name was too soft; his face seemed to require something harder. He sat propped in his bed, his neck erect as a ballerina's. She studied his hawklike profile, felt the rise and fall of his breathing.

"He missed you."

Sara turned to see Josephine standing at the door, watching her. Sara scratched her cheek to hide her blush, smiled.

"It's good to see you."

Josephine walked to the closet. She ignored conversational niceties; it was one of the things Sara liked about her.

"One time in San Bernardino I had this old Hispanic lady who thought I was her dog," Josephine said. "She kept petting me, scratching behind my ears, rubbing my nose. Of course, I had longer hair at the time."

Sara smiled.

"Another time, I took care of this old queen named Gabriel who became convinced I was his boyfriend. He wouldn't let us touch him unless I sat on his lap and called him Sergeant York."

"What did you do?"

Josephine's eyebrows soared in comic protestation. "What am I going to do, keep correcting him? I felt stupid at first, but after I started, the guy's recovery went a lot smoother. It kept his spirits up – and not only his spirits, you know?"

Josephine put on her coat, tapped her beeper with a red fingernail. "You've got everything, then?"

"Yes. I'll be fine."

Josephine eyed her a long moment, then extracted the yellow notebook from her purse. She held it wonderingly before them, as if she were performing some sort of magic trick.

"I left it on his bed, didn't I?" Sara said.

Josephine's hands went to Sara's shoulders, and she held her at arm's length. "Just remember, whatever he talks about, it's all made of bullshit anyway. What do the docs call it with kids . . . cannon . . . ?"

"Babbling. Canonical babbling."

"Of course. He probably read too many mystery stories, that's all."

Sara tried for a reassuring smile. "Probably."

"So say it."

"Say what?"

"You won't go and freak out on me."

"I won't go and freak out on you."

Josephine scrutinized her, then patted Sara's cheek with her palm, like a Mafia don. "I know. Because I won't let you."

They kissed good-bye on both cheeks, old-world style. The door closed. Sara stood there for a moment, allowing Josephine's presence to evaporate. She swiveled the twins' beds to face the window. She rearranged the tall man's covers, placed his hands outside so they lay comfortably, palms down and slightly raised as if poised on a keyboard. They were small, unremarkable hands, the fingers thick with blunt, square nails on them, the fingers of an old man.

She leaned over and placed her mouth next to his ear.

"It's Sara," she said. As gently as possible, she went to work, turning him and cleaning him, moving the washcloth over the ruined landscape of his body. She noticed the scar on his leg had begun to weep, so she applied some antibacterial balm. She

75

cleaned his teeth, then ran the brush over the pink buds of his tongue. She thought about Luke and the stories she was going to tell tonight. Perhaps she would tell about the time he got lost at the state fair. Or perhaps the time he rode with training wheels for the first time. She considered each as if she were regarding a menu, anticipating the feel of each possibility.

The seizure arrived earlier than expected. Sara held him tightly, surprised as she always was by the strength of his slender muscles. His eyes were closed this time, and he held his head back, his face raised to the fluorescent light. His body seemed looser, more flexible, and Sara had to cradle his head slightly to prevent it from whipping back and forth.

When it was over Sara prepared herself, trying to think of different ways to approach the questions she'd already asked a hundred times. She located the trach plug and nervously set it into place. She positioned him and waited.

But the tall man did not speak. He lay back, a stunned expression on his face. Sara worriedly took his numbers, and when they were normal, she looked at him again. He didn't look injured or debilitated. If anything, he looked almost blissful.

Sara.

"I'm here."

Sara . . . I –

He inhaled, and Sara leaned forward to catch the words.

The island it has thick trees it is rocky and by myself . . . plane gone someone watching can't see them . . . watching . . . alone in cabin and don't see. Come on, I'll show you. Come on show.

He kept talking. A torrent of words, images, dialogue, snatches of conversation, all of it scattered, impossible to follow and yet somehow whole, flowing in a continuous whispering exhalation. Sara snatched the yellow notebook and wrote down what she could.

Left me they left me . . . didn't see sign and she kept lucky boy lucky boy Alaska boy and then left and watched them go and gone and walk up beach and he's watching . . . all closed, no kids, nothing and trees and rocks and watching me waiting and watching figuring watching me and knowing what to do he always knows.

Closed. Not here, somewhere else . . . but I am here and him here and he knows hey hey hey hey wait.

Not actually Chicago, actually. From forest lake this a mistake forest lake.

K-J-E-L-L . . . J is silent.

Not from here city boy fat boy city boy, city boy.

At first she tried to steer him, inserting questions – *Is Oshie there?* – but it quickly became apparent that his mind was moving at a velocity she could not enter. His eyes fluttered, his voice kept dropping away in midsentence and starting up again in a new one. The tall man reminded Sara of a bird trying to build its nest, snatching and weaving with a quiet fervency.

Lucky boy, Sam's a lucky boy. Might drop couple pounds this summer, lucky boy . . . you'd like that, wouldn't you?

Me, I would take you. Father won't, no no way. Needs it for his projects, the project, the project. It's always the project with him.

Watching me. All the time.

Three pages of the yellow notebook were overflowing with notes. On the fourth, Sara wrote down the facts, as best as she could determine: Samuel had come to the island from Forest Lake, bound for some sort of camp. He'd arrived in his father's plane, and there had been a mix-up and he'd been left there alone. He'd met a boy by the name of Kjell, who was Oshie's brother. They'd talked, and Kjell had led him into the woods. The tall man's memory seemed to stop there, looping around and starting again, repeating the details in varying intensity and order. He talked for twelve minutes in all and then stopped suddenly. His pulse and respiration returned to normal, and he drifted into a shallow sleep.

Her heart thudding against her ribs, Sara dialed the Forest Lake Police Department, which could not have been a busy place but took great pleasure in acting like it. The receptionist put Sara on hold for five minutes, then transferred her to the Records Division, who transferred her to a beat patrolman, who transferred her to a cheery desk sergeant in charge of missing persons. Sara repeated her inquiry in a stage whisper: any missing persons, first name Samuel, last name unknown, reported in the last three years? She waited nervously, debating whether or not to hang up the phone. Then the sergeant returned. "One Steve and two Scotts," he announced. "No Samuels."

Over the next three days the tall man continued to talk. His communications fell into a clear pattern: they occurred after seizures, and they always began with Samuel on the island, with Kjell watching Samuel from a window. From there, the sentences would break loose, rushing through the dry canyons of his memory. The tall man would describe an incident a dozen times, from several different angles; he reversed sequences, he would perform long stretches of semi-intelligible dialogue. Sara listened raptly, playing detective. When he was done talking, she would ask pointed questions about other parts of his past – questions about Forest Lake, his house there, what his bedroom looked like, what his mother looked like, trying to use the question marks as tiny grappling hooks to lead him into new territory. But though she asked hundreds of questions, the hooks didn't catch. He kept whispering.

He talked for only a few seconds one time, another for nearly twenty minutes. He talked about walking into the woods with Kjell, about seeing the Speros' cabins for the first time, about meeting Oshie. Sara tape-recorded his voice and played it back to herself, trying to decode the unintelligible sections. She incanted his phrases, building them, reordering them, trying to connect their threads. As she did all this, her detective self fell away and she began to sense something solid, to feel a momentum beneath the words. His low, scratchy voice intoxicated her; she felt like a traveler catching glimpses of a distant coast. Each night she returned home to lie next to Tom beneath the dark slab of the skylight, still hearing the searching rhythms of that voice.

The island it has trees and rocks
His eyes on me all the t-time eyes
You're the one, he says. You're the one.

*   *   *

He's watching me. That's how it begins, Sara. An island, a cabin in the trees.

Me, curled on the floor, asleep. Then waking up. To my feet, panicked.

Hey.

On one side, Kjell. Long hair. Muscular arms. Sharp face, pale eyes like a cat's. Then me, soft in city clothes. He's the hero, the wild island boy. I'm the exile, the misfit. We look at each other, and know.

I'm from Chicago. This is all a mistake.

Kjell not moving. Not blinking.

Not actually Chicago. A suburb. Forest Lake.

His face hard to read. Eyes cold.

Dad dropped me off at the dock by mistake. Left before he saw the sign.

Kjell pulling a branch from a spruce tree, spinning it in his fingertips.

So anyway, I was just wondering, is there, like, a phone around?

No reaction. Thinking he's mute, deaf, an idiot.

Telephone? Holding hand to my ear. You know, to call?

Kjell smiling, me seeing I'm the idiot, he already knows. Was here yesterday. Watching like now. Saw the shiny float-plane, buzzing in out of the blue. Saw Dad, silver haired, satisfied. Saw stepmom, chesty and jangling. Saw me, squinty and nervous. Looking around, trying not to seem scared. Heard them talk. Saw them hurry, saw them leave without checking. Without checking anyone was here.

Watched it all.

So is there, you know, a town on this island?

Kjell raising his eyebrows. Something mechanical about his expressions. Like he has to work hard to smile or frown.

Not unless three people is a town.

So you live here?

Gesturing with his eyes.

South side of the island. Not far. With my father and sister.

His voice soft, knowing. I mirror his way of standing, the way he holds his hands.

If you don't mind, I'll need to use your radio. If you can't reach him directly, I'll just call for another plane to take me. It's no problem – we can afford it.

Antenna is down. A storm. Last month.

Well, then, how far to the nearest –

Sitka. Forty-nine miles.

That's not far. How often do you go –

80

Don't. Got everything we need here.

Do you have a boat?

Father has a skiff.

Great –

But he won't take you. Too busy.

My voice, still calm. I could pay. Money's no problem.

Not worth it. Won't risk the skiff, not for that trip.

What about supplies, fuel? Does someone deliver them?

Every four months.

So when is the next –

They came three weeks ago.

Frustration. I stammer, ask about fishing boats, planes,
ferries. Kjell shakes his head. Eyes like blue stones.

Reality sinks in. The truth that has been in those eyes all
along: I am marooned on an island three thousand miles from
home. I pretend to tie my shoe. Tears hitting the laces.

Then, his hand on my shoulder. Me, sobbing, pulling away,
but Kjell taking hold, his hand, this strong force raising me up.
Handing me a red bandanna, waiting. A small but definite
smile, a spark.

Come on, Samuel. Follow me.

Wait. Tell me your name.

Spelling it. The J is silent.

Kjell leading me out of the clearing and into the woods.
Dark, cool space. Moss and fern. Cathedral light, the clean
smell of spruce. Him moving like a shadow, me scrambling.

Then out of the trees onto a rocky beach. Kjell walking into
the shallows, water boiling at his feet. Walking far from shore,
up to his waist, but not sinking. A hundred yards. Then I
understand: a land bridge, leading to the next island.

Me hesitating, breathing deeply. Following in tiny steps,
arms like a tightrope walker's. Nearly falling, making it.

81

Climbing up the bank and looking for his praise, but he's gone, down the trail.

Trailing Kjell through the forest, finding a rhythm. Ducking where he ducks, jumping where he jumps. A playground game, follow the leader. Then something ahead. Through the leaves, a dome of sky. Crossing a final mossy log and then feeling it open up. My stomach prickling – the feeling of entering a hidden room.

A lagoon. Several football fields long, kidney shaped, walled off by tall stands of spruce. On its far shore, some buildings and docks set on pilings. Next to the buildings, a small slice of ocean through the trees, a passageway.

Is that a river?

A door, Kjell says. To the ocean.

Is this where you live?

Kind of.

Pieces of ships: old wheelhouses, sailing masts, landing crafts, steering wheels, flaked plywood. Door handles made of shackles, windows of ancient portholes, orbiting wind chimes made of fishing line and shells. Boardwalks and ladders. Bunched bouquets of pink and orange fishing buoys, blue plastic drums to catch rainwater. Crab pots rebuilt into a chicken coop. A large wooden pole over the water, for hoisting things from boats. A stream with a wooden paddle wheel creaking softly. Thick black electrical cords like snakes.

Who built this?

Dad did the electric and the plumbing, the design. Mom did most of the framing work, the decking, and the siding.

So your father, he's a carpenter?

Kjell smiling.

He builds good walls.

The story coming in bursts as we walk down the boardwalk:

His father a marine biologist. Came here from Massachusetts for a research project that was supposed to last three years. That was thirteen years ago. He's out on a collecting trip right now.

Your mom?

Drowned. I was six.

Sorry.

Don't be. If your mom's going to die, six isn't a bad age.

Kjell moving, talking in his soft voice, laying out the rules of the place as if I've come to stay. Everything divided into two categories, things you can touch and things you cannot touch. Solar batteries, you cannot touch. The paddle wheel, you can touch but need to be careful because you wouldn't want to get snagged. The winch and boom, you can touch but you shouldn't undo the knots because Father likes to have them a certain way to bring his specimens from the boat. The herring net, you can touch — and should touch, particularly when it fills with fish, which are pulled from the net and put into the yellow bucket and buried in rock salt.

Then a building separate from the others. Square, trim looking. Painted metal roof and a door, a brass padlock as big as my fist.

My face against the window. A desk, a microscope, and tall stacks of books and three-ring binders. A rumpled cot and a carved wooden cabinet. Walls covered with sketches of strange-looking organisms, anatomical drawings. Octopus, shrimp, crab, other creatures. Stacked on shelves, dozens of large-mouthed jars with pale, shadowy shapes inside.

Specimens, Kjell says. He draws them while they're alive and then keeps them in the jars. He doesn't trust photography — says the light is different every time.

I rattle the door.

Keeps it locked when he's on collecting trips. Worried somebody might tamper with his big project. He's trying to locate and preserve specimens of every organism that lives around this island, Kjell says. Every worm, every clam, every minnow. For a biomap. Every year he says he'll be done. Every year we stay here.

Kjell's throat tightening.

I try to chime in.

My dad always promised to take me on this big trip to the Grand Can –

Don't tell me about your father.

I was just –

If he cared about you, would he have brought you here?

His voice hardening.

It's for babies and fuck-ups. They pretend it's for the kids' good, but that's a lie.

My voice squeaking – I helped choose the camp.

Who told you about it? Who paid the fee? Who do you think got on that plane and celebrated because they were finally alone? That's the honeymoon, Samuel, don't you see? Leaving you here.

Me looking at the ground. It's true. It has to be.

Kjell's voice, gentle.

Fuck them. They wanted to trap you here, and that's what's happened. Except that you're not trapped.

Kjell touching my arm, almost smiling.

You're here, Samuel. Your dad doesn't know that, and my dad doesn't know that.

Here.

Yes.

Last stop on the tour, at the end of the boardwalk. A small

room, drafty and small. A sheet of plywood and a mattress for a bed. Spare clothes hanging in a small hammock; a wood stove. Wide-set floorboards, lagoon water below. Threads of light traveling across the ceiling and down the wall. My room, Kjell says. About to say more.

Padding footsteps down the boardwalk.

Oh, she, Kjell says turning. A slender red-haired girl carrying a coffee mug.

Seeing her in stages: bare feet, tanned legs, slim waist, oval face. Short auburn hair. Eyes the same pale blue as her brother's, but set at a slightly Oriental angle.

Her, Sara. The curve of her. The way her hair tucks behind her ear. The coffee steam on her face, her body. Only a girl — thirteen? fourteen? — but something older in the way she stands, in that voice.

Who are you?

Her toenails bloodred. The board moving as if it were breathing.

Samuel is from Chicago.

Finding words — not the fat city kid now. Now the traveler, now the big shot. Acting casual, as if I chose to come here. As if I talk to beautiful girls all the time. Hoping she can't spot the nervousness behind my smile.

Oshie talking — eager for company, willing. She's home-schooled, likes the island, can't wait until they move back to the mainland. Her voice teasing.

Prom *was* a little boring this year.

Okay, sweetie, Kjell says, a hand on her shoulder. Don't bore our new guest just yet.

How long are you here for? she asks.

A while, I say casually. We'll see.

Let's go, Kjell says. But Oshie will not. Her eyes bright.

I just want to talk to him.

Now now, Kjell says. Samuel just arrived. We don't want to be rude.

He turns her toward the house, nudges her in that direction.

See you later, I say helplessly.

Yes, she says over her shoulder. You will.

So I realize: Kjell's sister is one of the things not to be touched.

7

"It's bullshit," Josephine said pleasantly.

Josephine picked up her chocolate milkshake and took a hydraulic slurp on the straw, then centered the glass on its lace-rimmed coaster. She patted her lip with the corner of her napkin.

Sara looked across the table at Josephine, trying to figure out how to respond. The women were seated in a corner booth at a diner near the hospital, a former greasy spoon whose new owners were trying to transform it into a fashionable hangout. They had gutted the interior and brought in studded leather booths, chrome tables, Italian espresso machines. The changes were invisible to the restaurant's patrons – purposefully cool software types and roving-eyed college kids, carelessly attractive mothers and their carefully attractive children, all of them moving and talking and beaming quick, ascertaining looks at one another, lending the air a shimmer of desirability – but Sara noticed them. She could sense the presence of the old place beneath the new, hidden but still tangibly there, and it made her uneasy. While Sara had told Josephine a sketched-out version of the tall man's story, she had gazed around, making sure that no keen-eared nurse slid unseen into a nearby booth. Now she spoke, trying to keep her voice down.

"So you mean . . ."

"That it's bullshit." She tapped the table with her index finger three times. "It's a good story, I'll give him that. But bullshit."

"So you don't believe it happened?"

"Maybe it happened. Maybe not. Either way." Josephine leaned back, regarding Sara with catlike satisfaction.

"So you think he's making it up?"

"No no no no." Josephine extracted the straw from the shake and gestured professorially. "You have to understand – the person always remembers something – a license plate, an address, some number. That's how it gets solved."

"This isn't a soap opera," Sara said, trying for patience.

"Exactly. Where's the story about the gun that shot him? Phone number? Birthday? He needs to tell you something real. Not just words. Not just these"—she searched disdainfully for the word—"*stories.*"

"I've been calling every Spero west of the Mississippi."

"How many?"

"Twenty-seven. I've reached twelve so far, with no luck. I've also got a call in to the police and Coast Guard in Sitka. I'm doing everything I can think of."

Josephine had a large person's habit of eating delicately. Her front teeth excised the tail of a French fry, and she leaned back.

"His numbers?"

"Still dropping. The doctors upped his cals and put him on low-dose dopamine. Seems to be doing better now."

This was partly true. The doctors, puzzled at the small but perceptible drop in blood pressure and respiration, had recommended the changes a week ago, but the improvements had been short-lived. They had scratched their heads, called in specialists. At rounds the other day, several residents had gathered around the bed, clipboards poised. They'd invoked the possibilities: brain infection, clots, vascular damage, viruses. They'd peered in his eyes, manipulated his limbs as if they were divining rods. The tall man was becoming one of those dreaded "fascinating" cases, a chessboard on which to test stratagems. Sara had watched, silently willing them away.

"So," Josephine said, interrupting Sara's reverie, "want to hear my theory?"

"Sure."

"It was the girl," she said. "Lover boy tried to kill himself over the girl."

"That doesn't fit," Sara said. "He said it was this Kjell fellow. He's trying to find her."

"Perhaps," she said, enjoying her air of mystery. "But he loves the girl. If you want to find out who he is, find her."

"How do you know?"

Josephine shrugged. "I know," she said, applying her lipstick in jabbing strokes. "These things are not so uncommon."

Sara looked at her doubtfully. "Has it happened to you?"

"Couple times," she said, smacking her lips together.

"Really." Sara could not conceal the contemptuous bend in her voice.

Josephine capped the tube neatly. "Dmitri tried to throw himself off a bridge, but lost the nerve. Timmy tried to use a razor. They both told me they did it because it will make me have sex with them again. No way, I tell them. To kill someone else for me, that is a little bit sexy. But yourself?" She laughed. "Not sexy."

Sara spoke, unable to help herself. "His name was Timmy?"

"His name was Zbignew, but he looked like Tim Hanks, the movie star. So he is called Timmy."

"Tom."

"Exactly."

"No, it's Tom Hanks. His name is not Tim."

"Yes, yes," Josephine said impatiently. "Of course."

The women sat in silence for a while, Sara feeling foolish but relieved. If Josephine had taken the story seriously, she would have felt half-compelled to notify the doctors. But seeing Josephine's skepticism let her dismiss the idea. His words were simply audible seizures, mere static.

"Larch came by the other day," Josephine said. "She said it was routine, but she acted a little bit funny."

"Really?" Sara leaned forward, slightly alarmed. Michelle Larch was the head floor nurse, an attractive wisp of a woman who, for reasons Sara vaguely comprehended, was deeply feared throughout the hospital.

"I guess just to check on things." Josephine shrugged. "She does that sometimes."

"Do you think we should tell – "

"No," Josephine said without hesitation. "We shouldn't tell those dickholes a thing."

Sara felt a surge of gratitude and started to smile. Josephine extended her hand like a traffic cop.

"Let me ask you a question," she said deliberately. "How much have you been home in the last three days? Eight hours a day? Ten?"

Sara's cheeks burned. In the six days since the communication began, she had remained in the ward sixteen hours a day. Tom hadn't seemed to mind; she darkly guessed that he was relieved. But the truth in Josephine's remark still hurt—even if Tom had minded, Sara still would have come to the ward.

"Tom wants me to work," Sara said.

"Right."

"Besides, how else are we going to get him back to his family?"

"Of course," Josephine said archly. "His family."

"I don't know why you're being this way. I'm just trying to help return him – "

"Don't get me wrong," Josephine said. "In a lot of ways Sammy's the perfect man. Never talking back, not going out late at night, not running around behind your back. Body's a little thin, you know, but he'll fill out."

"That's ridiculous," Sara said, reddening. "It's not like I'm in love with him."

"On the other hand, I'm sure he would also make a fine son. Quiet. Obedient. Always polite. Plays well with others."

"We talk. That's all we do. We just talk."

Josephine gave an audible snort. It had been she who suggested telling the stories in the beginning, and now she was ridiculing the idea as if she'd never heard it. This was typical of her, part of her rights as a nation-state.

"It's a conversation," Sara said. "I tell him things, and he tells me things."

"About Luke."

"Yes."

Josephine nodded knowingly, and Sara felt a pulse of rage. Josephine, Tom, the psychiatrists, the nurses, they were all alike – wanting to view everything in Sara's life through the prism of the accident.

"I'm not crazy, Josephine," she said steadily. "I'm not trying to replace Luke. I'm just trying to help this patient."

With dainty forbearance, Josephine rearranged her bulk in her seat, knitted her fingers.

"Okay, let's say for a second you're right. Why not just tell him a bunch of made-up stories – tell him you're from Chicago, from Alaska, whatever propaganda you wish? I mean, if you're right about this, then that might help him remember."

"That won't work. I have to tell him the truth."

"How do you know?"

"I just do."

"You. Just. Do."

"This is about helping someone. I'm a nurse, it's what I do."

Josephine shrugged and regarded the napkin holder. "I just want to make sure you don't get in too deep, that's all."

Sara flashed anger. "What makes you think I'm your responsibility?"

"Nothing, it's just – "

"Why don't you do your job, and I'll do mine, and we'll leave it at that."

Josephine smiled. This was a type of warfare to which she was accustomed.

"So what do you want? To be by yourself? To take care of him by yourself?"

"Yes."

"Ah, but it's not that easy, darling. You see, you and me, we are stuck with each other. Marooned on an island, you might say."

"Go to hell."

Josephine's smile grew.

"With you, I will."

The package was wrapped in plain brown paper, weighed eleven pounds, and was waiting at the TBI ward when Sara returned from lunch. The return address was Forest Lake High School, Forest Lake, Illinois. Sara placed her hands on it, feeling an electric tingle of guilt and anticipation. She began to tear into it, then stopped.

Sara had faxed a letter to Forest Lake High School – along with four like it to the Forest Lake Police Department, the

Missing Persons Division of the Chicago Police Department, the Sitka Police Department, and the Coast Guard. The letters were written on administrative letterhead and spelled out, in politely bullying language, the hospital's request for assistance in a search for the identity of a John Doe, first name possibly Samuel, last name unknown. When she was typing the letters, she had felt bold and clever, but, she realized now, she'd never truly expected anyone to actually respond.

She peeled off the first strip of tape, then another. She had imagined many times how she might feel when the break-through arrived, when she linked Samuel to his family. And now that the moment was possibly before her, she was afraid. It wasn't that she hadn't tried to prepare – she had. She'd looked at maps of Forest Lake, visited the Chamber of Commerce's Web site, seen the expansive homes with the prairie roofs. She'd tried to picture the tall man in one of those houses, set amid the stolid American elegance of the place. Had tried to picture his face among those amiable midwestern faces, to make him a college student, a kid on a basketball team. But those were just games, harmless imaginations.

She stared at the box and heard the sound of familiar footsteps moving toward her. She slid the package under her desk and looked up in time to see Tom walking into the ward, darty eyed and uncomfortable. He gave her a hasty peck on the cheek.

"You working alone?"

Sara nodded, straightened her desk. It was disorienting seeing him here, now. He'd dropped in before, but always down at the nurses' station. Sara tried to look pleased. Tom explained, saying that he had a new restaurant client in the neighborhood. He strode toward the tall man, and Sara was suddenly aware of her heartbeat.

"How's this fella doing?"

"Fine," she said quickly. She was aware of the change in her voice, aware of the tall man's eyes on her. "How's work?"

Tom jingled the change in his pockets and stretched, his big back heaving, establishing himself a comfort zone. He flexed his hands. It occurred to Sara that he could, with little effort, break the tall man in half.

"Looks like we might be adding a couple Pike Street restaurants."

"That's great, hon."

Tom shook his head. "Might be more than we want – they're big tourist places, hundreds of steaks a night, and they want to be able to go up to a hundred and twenty-five filets and two hundred sirloins. Anyway, it's between us and another outfit."

Like many rural folk who move to the city, he regarded his profession with frank and open suspicion, and that was one of the reasons he was effective at it. Moving meat, he liked to call it, glossing over the dozens of intermediary aging steps that made his steaks so desired. Not that he couldn't talk about those things with clients, in passionate detail. But out in the world, Tom had the ability to ignore them. He was a meat mover, period.

"You'll get it," Sara offered.

"Maybe we will," he said, all caution.

"You will. You always do."

But Sara had no evidence to justify her confidence, because in the last two weeks Tom had seemed more interested in tending the house than his business. After his makeover of Luke's old bedroom, he'd gone on to reorganize the basement, the crawl space, the garage, the guest room, never quite finishing one room before he moved on to the next. Clusters of boxes had begun to sprout in hallways – plastic bins,

94

buckets, and totes that were meant to hold the belongings according to whatever private Dewey decimal system Tom had devised. Sara had watched him as he worked, poring through old record albums and books, bins full of toys, sorting old jackets into piles for him, her, and the Salvation Army. With his wild bush of hair and focused manner, he reminded her of an archaeologist sifting through the remains of an ancient city.

When he wasn't doing that, Tom was spending an undue amount of time hunched over his computer. He had gotten a new one as a job perk, a shapely silver-colored laptop. He had learned quickly – it was just another piece of equipment, after all – and within no time he was an expert, his piano player's fingers plying the keys late into the night. Watching him, Sara had found herself offhandedly wondering if he was having an affair, and was surprised when the notion both frightened and pleased her. Tom had done nothing to discourage this theory. Whenever she walked into the room, he would hit a button and the screen would transform into tropical fish – an image that struck Sara as an apt symbol of their home life: gliding, underwater silence.

And now he had come here, to the TBI. Phonied up some excuse and just dropped in. Sara knew his visit was meant to serve some larger purpose, and her job was to wait for it to reveal itself. Which it did a few seconds later, when Tom walked over to the tall man and gave his foot a stern shake.

"Wake up, buddy."

He shook it again. His hands looked knobby and gigantic against the delicate flute of the tall man's foot.

"Come on now, wake up. You'll be late for work."

"Stop that," Sara said, too loudly. "You'll hurt him."

Tom looked at her, his face a mixture of childish surprise and bemusement. "I'm not going to hurt him."

Tom never meant to hurt, he only wished to inspect their clockworks, to buff and improve them. To him, a broken thing was an insult to an orderly universe; it must be fixed or cast out, lest its disorderliness prove infectious.

"I know," she said. "It's just that . . ." She stumbled. "He's real vulnerable right now. To infection, I mean."

She sensed her heart hammering against her rib cage, her facial expression tightening as she looked at each of them in turn. The idea that Tom could shake his leg and wake the tall man had frightened her – what if he had? What if the tall man had sat up, what would she do? She felt as if she would split in two.

Tom gathered his coat, gave an untroubled yawn. "I guess you'll be sneaking out early, too, huh?"

Sara tilted her head questioningly.

"It's Friday. The Olivers, remember?"

Sara's heart sank. Dinner with Brenda and Derek. She'd planned on spending most of the night here, going through the Forest Lake package. She couldn't go into that perfect yellow house, not like this. She couldn't bear the pressure of those soulful blue eyes, not tonight.

"I might be a little late."

"Don't blow this off. We promised."

"*You* promised. I just said I'd try."

"So please try," Tom said. He said it flatly, without sarcasm. Sara found herself wishing that he'd be sarcastic, that he'd give her something to push against. But he didn't.

"How's your leg feeling?"

"Better." Sara flexed it to show him. "It's getting close to eighty percent."

"Great."

He paused, his long fingers playing with the edge of the door.

"Want to knock off early? We can go get a drink before."

Caught off guard, Sara hesitated, and Tom quickly held up his hand.

"Okay, I understand. But I'll leave my phone on, just in case."

"I'll try," she said, and as she said it she knew she'd said the wrong thing. He averted his eyes and picked up his case again, masking his hurt feelings with briskness.

"I'll try, really I will," she said, hating the condescension in her voice. Why couldn't she have teased him along? Why couldn't she have playacted, pretended an interest that would in time grow into something real? Without that, there was no future. They knew each other too well. They had been through too much.

Sara and Tom stepped in unison toward the door, and Sara deftly backhanded the scrim closed, so that their good-bye kiss would take place out of the tall man's gaze. She didn't know why she did this, but she was certain that to do anything else would feel strange.

Hearing Tom's footsteps disappear down the hall, Sara felt herself relax. She waited a moment, then walked to her desk and opened the box to reveal the Forest Lake High School yearbooks 1995–2000, along with a sympathetic note from the school librarian.

Sara picked up the yearbooks. She felt their smooth, dark exteriors and their embossed, hopeful lettering, and they seemed miraculous. Books with children in them, hundreds of children. She began to page through their indexes, marking each Samuel. She clipped out their pictures and taped them neatly on separate pages of her legal pad, a tidy stack of Samuels: Brisson, Schneider, Reinemer, Freeman, Wetzler, Bryant, Lamendola, Keller, Sella, Hughes, and McAteer. English, Jewish, Irish, a world of Samuels.

She pulled out a small magnifying glass and studied their faces, particularly the eyes. She quickly ruled out eight, leaving three possible Samuels from Forest Lake: Keller, Bryant, and Hughes. In each boy's face there was something that resonated with possibility: the nose, the shape of the head, the angle of the eyebrow. She gazed at the tall man, trying to mentally rebuild his scarred face. She took the photos to the copying machine in the nurses' lounge and enlarged them several times, until they were nearly life-size.

Sara walked to the tall man, raised his bed to the sitting position, and propped the photographs on his chest one by one, comparing. She spoke each of their names loudly in his ear, watching the EEG machine as she did it. The stylus wavered but did not move.

8

Sara never saw it coming. She was watching Brenda Oliver so closely that she never noticed Derek stand up from the couch. When she reconstructed the moment later, she knew Derek must have stood up, must have flashed some Masonic gesture to Tom, uttered a magical phrase: *lawn mower, drive belt.* But by the time Sara noticed, Tom was gathering himself to stand, his mouth set in soldierly determination.

"Where are you headed?" Sara said, resisting the impulse to grab the back of his belt and rein him back to the couch.

"We'll just be a sec, hon," Tom said. "Derek's got something he wants me to take a look at."

"Darn drive belt's looser than a goose," Derek said, shaking his head at the unfathomable mystery of it all. "I'd haul it to the dealer, but then they probably don't know any more than ole Tom does."

Tom chuckled and shook his head humbly. He enjoyed playing this role, ole Tom the omniscient handyman, the garage superhero. He stood up, flexing his hands, preparing them for manly reparative action.

"Don't sweat it, gals," Derek said as he fetched two fresh bottles of beer from the fridge. "We won't be gone long, nosiree."

Though Tom possessed no discernible drawl, Sara had

noticed that her husband's presence caused the men of MountainLake Hills to talk in ranch-speak. Sara also suspected that Derek, a chunky, balding account rep type, would be sipping Shiraz if not for Tom and that he'd have chosen to wear khakis instead of the jeans he now hitched practicedly, although the effect of his pants was considerably lessened by the chalky creases down the front of each leg. Now, beer bottles clinking like spurs, Derek clapped a brotherly hand on Tom's shoulder and steered him toward the stairs that led to the garage.

"Good luck, boys," Brenda sang in falsetto.

In a barely controlled panic, Sara watched her husband depart. Brenda smiled ruefully. "Isn't that just like them? They pretend to want to be with us, and then as soon as they eat it's off to the garage."

"Yes," Sara said. "Maybe if we stopped feeding them."

Brenda laughed, a glassy cascade of sound. Her laugh, like her hair, was two shades brighter than could be considered natural. When they'd arrived, Sara had observed with satisfaction the asterisks engraved at the corners of Brenda's eyes, the parenthetical furrows around her mouth. Yet she still looked good. Brenda was one of those women whose every feature was unremarkable, but who nevertheless achieved a striking beauty. She acted attractive, so she was.

"Right," she said, still giggling. "Why *do* we feed them?"

"I don't know," Sara said, sending Brenda into another paroxysm of laughter.

Up to this point, the evening had been slightly less excruciating than Sara had feared. Tom and Sara had arrived forty-five minutes late – purposefully, on Sara's part – hoping the predinner socializing would be rushed. But Brenda had trumped her by making a turkey tetrazzini, which simmered while they had a long chat in the living room. Tom had carried most of the load by talking about his favorite subject: cutting steaks. "It's got to be done by hand, and you can't skimp," he'd said. "All these butchers – and they are butchers – they're trained to get the absolute maximum out of every cow. But cows are like people: no two the same. If the steak doesn't look perfect, then grind it up, sell it to fast-food restaurants. You want the best steak? Make the best cuts."

"Amen," Derek opined. "And that philosophy doesn't just apply to meat, if you know what I mean."

Tom kept rolling, holding forth on his theory of demand that he used to stock his various restaurant clients. It was quite involved, a calculation that took into account the NASDAQ, the weather, the fortunes of local sports teams, municipal holidays, and the tourist season. "The way I work, I can't afford to be off my forecast by more than thirty percent," he said. "Though I always keep a backup supply in case of emergency. Like natural disasters – did you know that people eat a lot more steaks when there's a big earthquake or tornado somewhere in the U.S.? Particularly filet mignons."

"Primal instincts," Brenda said sagely. "The urge to strengthen yourself for a crisis."

"Have you ever considered writing a software program?" Derek asked. "Something that could automatically download all the pertinent numbers and give you a stocking number?"

"Hmm," Tom said, looking thoughtful, though in fact, Sara knew, he had looked into it. "I sorta like operating by gut feel. Besides, if it could get put on a disk, I might be out of a job."

"So you could say," Brenda interrupted, "that you have a barometer on the male appetites. I wonder what else varies predictably like that? Liquor, I expect. Cars, maybe? Condoms?" She nudged Sara.

"You're not far off on that last count," Tom said. "I got talking once to a guy who stocks the machines in the rest rooms of these places. He told me that his varies a lot, too. The most get sold around holidays – Christmas, Easter. But there's one holiday that beats them all, and I bet you can't guess it."

There was a burst of guesses – Thanksgiving, New Year's Eve, Fourth of July.

"Mother's Day," Tom said, shrugging off the shocked protests with a grin. "It's true."

Seeing Tom like this never failed to be a revelation. He seemed able to click a switch and, depending on the personality of the room, deliver endlessly subtle variations of his straight-talking, ranch-hand self. What he really had, Sara thought, was a direct barometer on people's appetites for Tom, along with an ability to serve it up exactly as it was desired. Sara felt stirred, her stomach pulsing. How little she knew him, even after all these years. How exotic he still seemed.

But now Tom had disappeared to the garage, and Brenda was fixing her cobalt eyes on Sara's and reaching out to cup her knee.

"I've been meaning to ask you, how are things at the hospital? You're taking care of coma patients now, right? Three of them?"

Brenda belonged to that breed of midwestern women who choose to address the world through a grid of attentive questions asked in rapid succession. Brenda fastened her bright eyes on Sara, and the bombardment began. As Sara answered, Brenda began to nod sympathetically but mechanically, as if within her some laser were scribing the answers onto the grooves of a permanent record (which, Sara realized, it was). Brenda's head tilted watchfully, and for a moment Sara was reminded of those hungry yellow-beaked birds that had invaded her house after the funeral, the ones that fed on the flowers.

Sara took a deep breath and reminded herself that Brenda was insane. With Tom gone, this was her fallback: to persuade herself that all this normalcy was merely a thin camouflage for the fact that this woman was singularly and ebulliently crazy. *Brenda is crazy because she denies the reality of the world. She is crazy because she secretly sends sunflowers to me every month telling me that somebody loves me. She is crazy because she thinks she can keep her dead daughter alive through teddy bears and frilly books.*

"Right, three of them," Sara said, using a voice that one would use to talk to a large and possibly dangerous animal. "I get to set my own hours."

"That's great." Brenda beamed. "But the work must be difficult, no?"

"Not too bad. It's mostly baby-sitting, if you want to know the truth."

"And do you work closely with the doctors?"

"Not really. We do our job and they do theirs."

"My cousin Peggy is a nurse. She hates all the doctors in her hospital; they get in the way, she says, and I believe it. The doctors were almost no help with Katrina; we found the nurses were the ones who gave us real help."

So here was the transition: the time when Sara was expected to ask Brenda questions; the time when, if Sara wasn't careful, the conversation would be steered toward the looming rocks she'd been trying to avoid – Brenda's daughter, all the humble, life-affirming work Brenda was quietly doing.

Sara fiddled with the stem of her wineglass, stalling. The Olivers' house was immaculate, nicely if not too expensively decorated, with an abundance of tchotchkes and family photos. She pretended to study them, thinking of the tall man.

"I like what you've done with this room," Sara said, and winced inwardly. Not only was this patently untrue, it was not a question and therefore broke protocol. But Brenda didn't seem to notice this. She was all too eager to get back in the role of questioner.

"Sara, Sara," Brenda said, rearranging her knees so they were aimed at her guest. She opened her eyes slightly, as if she were seeing Sara for the first time. "Something about you looks different."

"Really?"

"Yes. You look . . . prettier. Full of life." She delivered the compliments with a doctorly graveness. "Is that a new hairstyle?"

"No." Sara actively resisted the temptation to touch her hair. "I don't think so."

"Hmm," Brenda said. Sara shifted uncomfortably.

"Lost weight?"

"No."

"Then there's only one thing left," she said after a moment. She tucked one slender leg beneath her and leaned forward playfully.

"What's that?"

"You're having an affair."

Sara laughed, too loudly, she realized immediately. She took a sip of wine and tried again, with better results.

"Hate to disappoint you," she said.

Sara felt herself blushing. *Don't be foolish,* she told herself. She had no reason to blush. Yet Brenda, the idiot savant, had caught the whiff of something. She leaned forward, homed in on it like a retriever.

104

"So you're not?"

"No," Sara said, flustered. "I mean, yes. What I mean is, I'm not having an affair."

"Are you sure? Sometimes you're the last to know."

"I'm sure," Sara said, belatedly recognizing Brenda's meaning. She tapped the arm of the couch, took the bait. "Have you?"

"Yep," Brenda said, glancing at the door and leaning forward, her voice dropping to a childlike whisper. "With the mailman. You know, Bill."

At first, Sara did not believe it, but as Brenda unspooled the story, Sara recognized it for truth. The handsome, newly divorced mailman, the lonely mother, the workaholic husband who shut himself off. According to Brenda, this wasn't the first time Bill had made after-hours deliveries to the women of MountainLake Hills. Listening, Sara experienced a warm, disconcerting burst of fondness for this woman. She felt slightly but pleasingly disoriented, as if the living room had tilted a few degrees and had begun to spin.

"Then it ended," Brenda said. "I realized it was just a stage I was in, kind of in between two and three, you know, denial and repression? But it gave me someone to talk to, helped me get out of my funk, made me less dependent on Derek. I realized that I was in charge of my own feelings, that I didn't have to depend on Derek or Bill or anybody. And I think it helped Bill, too. Of course, he had to change routes and all."

Brenda smiled a toothy smile, and Sara felt her good feelings evaporate. Brenda viewed her love affair as if it had been a new pill, as if it were just another happy skirmish in her triumphant therapeutic journey. A trip to the mall: One affair, please, hold the complications. But could it be dismissed that easily? After all, it had to be something. There had to be something messy, some burst of heat and moisture beneath that unruffled surface. Didn't there?

"Sara, I must confess," Brenda was saying, "I have an ulterior motive for bringing you here."

Sara felt a pulse of fear.

"Well, I'm not going to tell you that quickly," Brenda said, apparently mistaking Sara's expression for interest. "That would take all the fun out, wouldn't it?"

Sara followed Brenda up the stairs into the dormered second story. Sara glanced in the doorways as she passed: the bathroom, a closet, the Olivers' king-size bed. The rooms were more tasteful than Sara had imagined, as if whatever style virus had infected the living room had been contained by the stairway. She noted the plush of the red velvet bedspread, not at all the kind of thing you'd expect Brenda to own. Sara stood at the door and had a flash of imagining Brenda lying naked next to someone on that red bed – was it Bill the mailman? Derek? Sara shook it out of her head.

"I'm working on a kids' book now, with KB as the main character," Brenda was noting, in a sisterly tone that implied that Sara had somehow been integrally involved in this project from the ground floor and therefore knew that KB stood for Katrina's Bear. "He's just a regular old toy bear most of the time, but when kids are having troubles he comes to life and helps them. All the proceeds will benefit the Cancer Society, of course."

Brenda now took Sara's hand and led her into the last room, the dormered space that overlooked the front yard. Katrina's room, Sara guessed, partly converted to an office. The horseshoe-shaped desk stood in front of the window like a captain's bridge, its surface covered with correspondence and book designs. Around them, the side walls of the dormer were festooned with ribbons and memorabilia and photos. There were teddy bears, letters, heart-shaped cards, and a poster-size montage of Katrina photos – falling in the leaves, licking a grape Popsicle, riding a pony, running on the beach. There were unbound pages from the memory books Brenda made, lacy, elaborate scrapbooks that she had begun to sell door-to-door (this time to benefit leukemia research) that provided a matrix in which memories of still ticking loved ones could be created and preserved. They were frilly books chock-full of brief, probing questions, nothing so much as two-dimensional versions of Brenda: *What's your favorite color?* the opened page inquired. *Your favorite smell?* This was the command post from which Brenda governed, from which her loyal army of magical bears fanned out into the world, healing the sick, curing the lame, conquering death.

Brenda moved toward a bin, still holding Sara's hand, an inscrutable smile playing on her lips.

"What do you think?"

"It's quite a room," Sara said.

"I like to be surrounded by her," Brenda said. "To feel that she's here with me, you know? Working alongside."

They stood in silence. Sara's leg ached. Brenda's hand reached for Sara's again, and though Sara tried to evade it, the hand was persistent, pinning her in its iron grip. The moment held a therapeutic air, as if Brenda wanted her to stand here as long as possible, as if she thought merely inhaling the stray ink molecules from the photos might have some healing effect.

The moment ended. Brenda released Sara's hand and stepped quickly across the room toward a large pink bin. She reached into it and plucked out something small and furry – Sara could not see what it was – and tucked it behind her back. She stood, schoolmasterish and pleased, against the far wall.

"Do you mind if I ask you a question about Luke?"

Sara swallowed. "Sure."

"Okay," Brenda said. She readied herself, setting her feet and throwing her shoulders back as if she were about to launch into a cheer. "What was his favorite toy?"

"What?"

"His favorite toy? Did he have one?"

Sara's heart beat fast. She should have known this moment would come. She should not have started to like Brenda, insane Brenda. She should not have relaxed her guard.

"I don't remember."

"Oh, come on, Sara," Brenda said, her hand still tucked behind her back. "There must have been something. Something he never wanted to be without."

"Well," Sara said hesitantly. "There was this lion."

"Did the lion have a name?"

"Larry."

"What did Larry look like?"

"He was small," Sara said. "Kind of ugly, really, with these gray paws and beady eyes. His mane was made of yarn. He had a long face. Sort of like Richard Nixon."

Brenda opened her hands, and Sara felt a steel weight drop into her stomach. Brenda walked over and pressed the lion into her hand.

"Take him, Sara. Hold him."

Sara held the lion in her fingertips. She saw that the pink bin was brimming with a tawny sea of Larrys, dozens of them. Possibly hundreds.

Brenda raised her hands like a holdup victim. "True confessions, Tom gave me a photo of the original," she said. "It took some time, but the factory finally got it right. You can't imagine how tough it is to work with these Chinese. Anyway, I designed this label. Do you like it?"

"Luke's Lions," the label said, the Ls interlocked and set on their points to form a heart. Sara held it in her hand, not quite believing.

"I figured it was time that Katrina's Bear got a playmate," Brenda said. "Everything's all set up. They will be sold in the same outlets, and they're working on a new design for the display box. I've even started working him into the books."

"They're, uh, nicely made," Sara said, touching the mane.

"The best," Brenda said. "Same factory that makes the Beanies."

"Wow."

Brenda extended the label toward her, all business now.

"I've left this part blank. It's where you can write something about Luke, and why this lion is important. There's room for about fifty words, sixty if you use short ones. I think it would be nice if the label sort of matched with Katrina's, you know?"

Brenda stood frozen, her eyes radiating blue beams of pure goodness.

"So what do you think?"

"What do I think," Sara said slowly.

"Right."

"Well," Sara said. "I think this is all a big surprise. I think you went to a lot of trouble."

Brenda covered her eyes with her hands. "I know, I'm terrible. I'm terrible and sneaky and presumptuous. To tell the truth, I was afraid Tom would tell you. But now that you've seen it, I want to know what you think."

"What I think is thanks," Sara said carefully. "Thanks, but I don't think that's something we want to do."

Brenda betrayed no disappointment. "Are you sure?"

Sara held the lion, rolled its plastic innards in her fingers. "Yes. I'm sure."

"Okay," Brenda said brightly. "Nothing ventured, nothing gained."

For a moment it occurred to Sara that perhaps this was precisely the ending Brenda desired. After all, she couldn't have believed that Sara would actually participate in such a scheme, could she? By raising the stakes so high, she was forcing Sara's hand, asserting herself as only Brenda could, in some sort of perverse showdown. Sara looked at Brenda, and as she had before, Sara sensed something beneath the surface, a glint of steel beneath the soft exterior. They stared at each other, each one unwilling to talk. Sara was first to crack.

"I'll bet those guys will be hungry for some cake by now, don't you think?"

"Yes," Brenda said, effortlessly finding a natural tone. "What kind did you make?"

"Pineapple upside-down cake."

"Yum."

"My mother's recipe."

"From Big Prairie?"

"Yes," Sara said, surprised that Brenda had remembered the name.

"Well, anything from there has to be good."

They turned to leave, and as they reached the door Brenda stopped and turned.

"You think I'm a fake, don't you."

"No, Brenda, I – "

"Don't worry, I don't take it personally. You think I make up all this stuff to make myself feel better about Katrina. Don't you?"

Sara stammered, could say nothing.

"You know, maybe you're right," Brenda said, setting her hands on her hips and looking around the room as if with new eyes. "Maybe it is all silly and meaningless, all these things. Maybe it's just decoration. Whistling in the graveyard."

"No, Brenda," Sara said. "I appreciate all the work you did with the lion. It's just not me."

Brenda put her hands on her hips. "Sara, I can't begin to guess what is you and what's not you. I don't know what your life was like before, or who hurt you. But you know what? I like the memory books and the teddy bears, I like the way they make me feel. They make me feel like Katrina's still with me."

Sara, stung, couldn't resist. "But she's not. With you, I mean."

"That's true," Brenda said, tilting her head in that infuriating childlike way, as if considering the matter for the first time. "You think it matters?"

"Yes," Sara said, fighting to keep her voice calm. "I think it matters. I think it matters a lot. What use is all this if you're making it up?"

"I'm not making it up. It's just how I see things. The bears are fake, but the feeling behind them is real."

Sara struggled with this for a moment, conscious of Brenda's eyes on her. *She is not crazy,* Sara realized. *She is tough and smart, and she knows exactly what she is doing.*

"Fake is fake," Sara said. "Nothing can be fake and real at the same time."

Brenda closed her eyes. "I'm sorry, Sara. Here I am trying to help, and I'm only making things worse."

"You're not making things worse. You just go where I'm not ready for you to go."

"I hear you. I do, I really do. In the future, I'll mind my own business. We all have to do things our own way. If we don't, then they're not really ours, are they?"

"I couldn't agree more."

Sara saw Brenda smile and felt the argument closing off too neatly. Brenda took a small step toward the doorway.

"As long as we're talking about this sort of thing," Sara said, unable to resist, "I'd appreciate it if you'd please stop sending me the flowers."

Brenda's brow creased.

"The sunflowers," Sara continued patiently. "The ones you send each month?"

"No," Brenda said, a smile crossing her face. "That's not me."

Sara stood in silence, embarrassed by her puzzlement.

"Well, I'm glad I know that."

Brenda put a hand tenderly on her arm. "Me too."

Then Brenda took her hand away. "So is it serious?" she asked.

"What?"

"With the guy. And don't tell me there's not a guy."

"It's not what you think. He didn't send the flowers, I'm sure of that much."

"Not the romantic type, huh?"

"No," Sara said. "Not quite."

"Well," Tom said, lobbing his keys on the hallway table. "That wasn't so terrible, was it?"

"No," Sara said. "Not really."

She set down her purse and looked around their house. The streetlight glowed through the gauzy curtains, washing the living room with snowy light. Sara thought of the tall man. He could be waking up now, as he often did in the night. Would he be trying to talk? She saw the spare key hanging on the door frame and involuntarily pictured the stopper in its hiding place. She experienced a nearly irresistible urge to leave, to drive back to him, to lose herself inside his voice. She took a breath, forced herself to take off her jacket and hang it in the closet.

Tom rummaged a beer from the fridge, sat down expansively on the couch. "Actually had a good time, sort of. That Derek's a good guy."

They talked harmlessly awhile, Sara struggling to keep her mind focused while Tom chatted on, not noticing her distraction. Or perhaps just pretending not to notice, Sara thought. Then Tom stood abruptly and walked to his office, emerging with his laptop. He plugged it in at the kitchen table.

"Come here," he said, pulling a chair next to his. "I want you to see something."

The screen flickered and formed a postcard-size image of a two-story log cabin backdropped by tall spruce. He clicked, and it grew. She could see a mothering swoop of roofline, a fat stone fireplace, and a covered porch with a rocking chair. Missing shingles gave the roof a gap-toothed appearance; the porch railing needed mending; the logs were gray with age. Mildly decrepit and charming, it stood wavering on the computer screen, which reflected their faces: Sara tilting her head skeptically, Tom's face quietly alight.

"It's cute," Sara said after a moment. "Whose is it?"

"Could be ours."

Tom explained. A client friend had turned him on to a real estate broker that handled state auctions for seized property. This one was out west, five acres near Port Lucy, an old inholding in Olympic National Park. A creek, a small meadow. It was assessed at $32,000, and nobody had bid yet.

"The land itself is worth twice that. At least."

"I thought we wanted to be near the ocean. Not deep in the woods."

"It's fifteen miles from the ocean. A quick drive. Besides, this is an *inholding*, Sara. An old homestead. You know how rare those are these days?"

"So it's a convict's house or something?"

"My friend says it was owned by an old-timer who rented it to some hippies then died. No family, no nothing. It needs some remodeling, but hey, that'll be the fun part."

Tom put an arm around her waist. "What do you say," he said, threading a finger through her belt loop and drawing her close, "we take a peek at it this week. I'll take the next couple days off and we'll scoot down the coast."

Sara stiffened. She glanced down – he didn't seem to notice.

"I don't have any clients anyway," Tom continued smoothly. "We could head down tomorrow, be there by noon."

Sara watched his lips move. A couple of days? The dinner at the Olivers' had been bad enough. There was no telling what two days might do to the tall man. He was fragile, she reminded herself sternly. Sara had a professional responsibility. She cloaked herself in these excuses and more, knowing in her heart the real reason: that she could not bear to go a day without hearing his voice.

"I can't."

Tom looked up slowly.

"I'm sorry, hon," she said, trying to soften it. "There's just too much going on at the hospital right now. I can't get away."

"You can't."

"No."

Tom chuckled, a high, dry sound. He unthreaded his finger and pulled his arm back. "Well, if you can't, then you can't."

114

He sat looking at the image of the house.

Sara said nothing. The laptop closed with a metallic *snick*. Tom studied the label on his beer can. Sara was about to walk out of the room when he spoke.

"I got a question."

Sara turned. Tom sat at the center of the table, his hands folded.

"Explain to me why this person sees more of you than I do."

"He needs me, Tom. I have to be there."

"And I don't."

"No, it's just that . . . it's where I have to be right now. He needs me, and nobody else. I know it sounds stupid, but that's how it is."

Tom's voice was tight, controlled. "No, I don't know. Tell me how it is."

"He's waking up," Sara said after a moment. "Remembering things. About a crime, I think. He's trying to tell me his story."

Sara glanced up. She'd hoped that the word *crime* would pierce his calm, but he remained composed, eyes narrowed, facial muscles locked firmly into laconic rancher mode.

"This story," Tom said. "Is it for real?"

"Yes."

"How do you know?"

"It's consistent," she said. "It all fits together. And it feels true."

Tom rolled his eyes, and Sara felt a flash of anger.

"You have no idea, Tom. No idea who he is. Of what he's been through."

"Neither does *he*, Sara. He's lying there like a goddamn two-by-four, babbling God knows what. I'm right here, right now. Your life is here, and you don't see it because you don't have the guts to try."

"Try? You mean like Brenda tries? Should I tell myself some happy story that makes everything better? Should I hug my teddy bear and make everything all right?"

Tom looked down, his fingernail working the edge of the tabletop. Sara saw a dark space where the lamination was giving way. The old glue stretched.

"You're hard on people, Sara. Hard on me."

"You have to admit, Tom. What she does – what all of them do – it's not honest. It is not real. It might make them feel good, but it doesn't work for me. So I'm sorry if that's hard, but it's the truth. And I don't know any other way to live."

"It's not right, Sara. You're not this way. You weren't this way, not before it all happened. Think about it, Sara. What we had – did that not exist? Was that fake, too?"

"People change."

"People get changed, you mean. They let themselves be changed and they don't fight."

"Is that what you think? That I don't fight? That I lie back and let all this happen to me?"

Tom closed his eyes. "You want to know what I think when I look at you? *She's still down there.* Still underwater, two years now, inside that car. Every day I wait for you to climb out, but after a while I start thinking, Maybe she likes it down there. Maybe she wants to stay down there. Maybe she's found someone to stay with."

"So I should do what, exactly? Smile for the camera, have a couple beers? So I can shake everybody's hand and smile and feed them what they want?"

"Is that what you think?" Tom said quietly. "You think I trade on Luke?"

Sara said nothing.

Tom stood. "At least I'm trying, Sara. At least I'm not hiding out in some room by myself. Because that's where you are, even if he's there. You're by yourself. You can be with people or not, that's the choice, and I choose to be with people."

"I'm with people."

"If you can call a brain-damaged freak a person, then yes, you are with people."

"Don't say that."

"It's true."

"He is a human being and I'm helping him and I don't see what is wrong with that."

"Truth, Sara – isn't that what you want? He's not a whole person, and never will be."

"Fuck you."

Tom didn't blink. "Go deep enough and you never find anything too pretty, do you? It's all messy and ugly underneath. Half-truths and lies and bullshit and people trying to get by. All of it. Except for you and that clean little room. You and your new son."

Sara shook her head, but his voice kept coming.

"It's a choice, Sara."

Sara felt tears on her cheeks. She turned away and could feel Tom's eyes on her. When she turned back, he was looking at the wall.

She thought, This is how it will be. Tom will pack up and leave, I will stay in the house. We will divide our possessions into piles. We will cry, and then one day we will stop crying. Neighbors will wag their heads and say they saw it coming. There will be lonely nights, but they will become bearable in time. Tom will start over, find a new wife, start a new family. I will live in this house, grow older, become known in the neighborhood, the cautionary tale: the woman who could not love, who was trapped by her fears. People will walk by my house and see my shadow in the window and be warned.

This kind of thing happens, Sara thought as they walked upstairs, as they brushed their teeth, as they slipped silently into the far sides of their bed and stared up at the dark skylight. Happens all the time.

9

Early morning. Mist moving through spruce. Nothing moving. Except me, Sara. Walking through the forest along the path, finding my way to the beach.

Arriving, looking around. Trying not to be nervous – but where is Kjell? Walking toward the water, intending to shout, and then stopping.

A boat. Tied off by the land bridge, nosing onto the beach.

Short and fat, like me. Wood gone papery in the sun, hull warped. But a boat all the same, oars tilted and ready. Me stepping in shakily, trembling ripples. Testing the oars, waiting until the bow is pointed toward Spero's island. My heart beating fast. Pushing my hands forward. One stroke. Another.

It's been a week now, every day the same. Wake at the cabin, walk to the land bridge, and find Kjell. Him showing me things. Predators and prey, animal tracks, leaf-shapes, the makeup of soil. The curl of a snail's shell. How to walk – lean forward on the balls of your feet, to walk only on the mounds – the remains of tree stumps, he said. How to eat a clam – dig it with hands and rinse it and slip a knife into the opening, scrape it out, and pop it into your mouth. How to tie a bowline. I work at it for an hour, wrestling with a short piece of line, my soft hands working it into a tangle.

Not quite, Kjell said.

I can't.

His hand on my shoulder. Like they say, if you can't tie a knot, tie a lot.

I can't –

First time I tied a bowline, Father made me do it five hundred times.

Gently taking the line from my hands, starting over.

See?

Every day, showing me things. But never Oshie or his father. Keeping them to himself, or until I'm ready, or for some other reason he will tell me – for he will tell me everything when I'm ready. That is the promise.

So now, in the boat. Rowing carefully, like he would. Turning around every few seconds to check my line. Keeping close to the shore, hearing the waves. Feeling the keyhole entrance, the velvety rush of a rising tide sucking me toward the dark tunnel, and then through it into the quiet of the lagoon.

The lagoon. Calm green water, trees tall and close, reflections wavering. Lamplit windows. A white wooden skiff at the dock – Spero's skiff. Paddle wheel creaking like an opening door. I pull the boat onto shore and tie it off onto some alder. Moving quickly along a little cliff above the shore, forearming branches out of my way, feeling stealthy and cool.

Hey.

The voice close, from the bushes on the lagoon side of the trail.

Kjell? Hating the hopefulness in my voice.

Bushes parting like a curtain. Him eyeing me with a brother's pride. Me fighting down a smile.

How was your crossing?

Not bad.

Kjell takes a few steps toward the lagoon, then vanishes, dropped out of sight as if through a trapdoor. His hand, beckoning.

Here.

Two ancient spruce trees, their roots like praying hands.

Come on.

Then I see: the cliff eroded, but the roots remain, forming a chamber the size of a living room. A canvas hammock. Candle lanterns, a few books. A milk crate, a deck of cards. More roots, white from the salt, making a screen from the beach. And Oshie. Sitting straight on the hammock, feet on the ground.

Kjell's voice, pleased – See? I told you he would come.

Me, lowering myself into the cave, nervous. The air moist and nutty. My skin prickles. Then a cup, filled with dark blue liquid. I choke, and Oshie laughs.

Didn't you study fermentation in Chicago? She takes the cup from me and tips the rest into her throat. Jittery, animated.

This is the apartment, Kjell says. Our place.

The rest of the day flowing into one moment: Swinging on the hammock, Oshie and me shoulder to shoulder. Droplets of dew falling into our drinks. Kjell showing off, swinging like Tarzan, doing acrobatics. Playing cards, Kjell beating us both soundly at poker.

He's simply too good, I say. He is the king.

She laughs, a sound like water.

Feeling a desire to embrace her. I reach out to touch, grasp Kjell's shoulder instead.

Does your father know?

About this place?

Kjell looking at my hand. Smiling, but not a smile.

Then a burst of motion in the thicket. A bird on the roots, a bluejay. Chattering, fearless. Beak sharp and tilted, eyes like wet pebbles.

Oh, he knows. He pretends not to know, and we pretend to believe him, but we all know that he knows. There is nothing that escapes him. Not the fishes of the sea nor the birds of the sky, for he hath dominion over all that moves.

Smart-ass, Oshie says.

He shall see all the creatures, and he shall count them, and he shall name them, and it shall be made good in his eyes. And woe be to those who oppose him, for his strength is mighty and his wrath is great.

Kjell lunging at the roots, a rustling noise. Standing, right arm outstretched, the bluejay's leg pinned between his thumb and forefinger. The bird fighting, digging its beak into his wrist. Red lines tracing down his forearm.

Stop.

He will count this. He will count it and it shall be made real.

Kjell . . .

Oshie, touching him on the shoulder.

Her touch calming him. He stops talking and looks at his hand, as if surprised to find the bird there, and lets it fly. It circles the space three times, then vanishes.

It's true.

The only true thing is that you're drunk.

I'm drunk and it's true. That's two things, and you shouldn't argue with your elders.

You're not my elder.

I'm more than that.

Silence. Kjell setting his cup down. He reaches to remove a stray hair from Oshie's cheek, and she flinches. That's all – a movement of his hand, the touch of a finger and a thumb, a turn of the head. But it is there. Everything there at once, and I see

Kjell fully for the first time, the hidden part suddenly alive, and I know he is in love with his sister.

Now Oshie standing. Stretching theatrically.

Well, I don't know about you two, but I feel like taking a walk.

Parting the root curtain, walking next to her. Hearing each wave in parts. Water. Foam. Underneath, pebbles rearranged.

Look.

A wall of mist pouring like milk through the trees and filling the lagoon. Wrapping around us, inside us.

Oshie touching my arm.

Smell.

I do.

No. Close your eyes and really smell.

Inhaling the mist, feeling it brush my face, fill my mouth. Salt and berries and musky dirt and something else.

Dad says the fog carries the scent of oranges. But no oranges grow for a thousand miles. It's sort of a mirage, really. Real, but not real. Do you know what I mean?

I know.

*   *   *

Each morning, Sara would depart the house at five, walking into the darkened ward well before first light. She would purchase a can of 7 UP from the vending machine and set it on the table next to the tall man's bed. She would click on the light, careful to keep it out of his eyes. Then she would give him the 7 UP, nesting the blankets around his chest to provide a place for the can, placing the straw between his lips. His mouth was too weak to chew, but he could manage a few sips while she took his vitals, the bubbles ascending through the straw.

When he had finished the drink, Sara would stopper his

123

trach tube and wait. Sometimes he began talking immediately; other days it took several minutes, as if some inner part of him were slowly waking. But he always began at the same place: *He is watching me.* From there, he would move fitfully forward, retelling the story he'd already told, occasionally venturing into new territory. He spoke slowly, sometimes inaudibly, sometimes in lucid bursts. Sara pictured the sentences twined within his skull, a great knot slowly loosening as each was pulled free. He told of other visits to the apartment cave, of using the boat to explore the island. Sara began to discern individual voices. There was Samuel's soft, slightly ethereal voice, bumbling and stuttering. Then there was Oshie's, which was hoarse and musical. And Kjell's, flat and whispery but carrying a pressure behind it, like a blade. She felt the voices moving against one another, and it made her fear for Samuel. Hearing his voice against Kjell's was like watching someone slowly lose his balance and fall. Sometimes she felt the urge to shake the tall man, to tell him, "Don't listen." But the tall man kept speaking.

She disliked watching him speak. He looked in such pain, his features twisted and shook, the words came with such difficulty. Sara closed her eyes and tried to listen purely, to concentrate on what lay behind each word. It was not hearing so much as feeling, and the more she did the more she grew to love the sensation. She began to identify familiar passages, to anticipate words and images, to unearth connections that had been hidden. She began to inhabit the story as one would inhabit an abandoned mansion, slowly moving from room to room, learning to see despite the darkness.

When he finished talking – and he usually wearied after half an hour – Sara pulled the stopper and gave the tall man his massage. She looked forward to this, working her hands into his scant flesh, unknotting his ligaments, cupping the taut fruit of his calves. He had continued to lose weight despite the increased feedings, and it was Sara's hope that the massage would help activate his metabolism. She spent hours working on the tightwires of his hands, finger by finger, and was gratified when they showed some flexibility. She moved his limbs alone and in tandem, rotating and stretching through an increasing range of motion.

Sara fed the tall man at noon, uncapping his stomach tube and hanging 800 cc of Nutri-Gel. She talked to him as the milky liquid dripped into his stomach, describing sirloin steaks and soft baked potatoes, strawberry pie with amaretto ice cream. The doctors usually showed up around one to perform their Socratic mullings about the tall man's decline (latent epilepsy seemed to have caught fashion, causing a fresh round of proddings and brain scans). With each passing visit, however, Sara could sense their interest waning. Without an obvious infection to fight or a clot to dissolve, the mystery of the tall man's condition was becoming unsatisfyingly murky.

The housekeepers, on the other hand, seemed unusually attentive. They worked in tandem, two whippet-thin Korean women who held their graying heads resolutely to the floor so that Sara could tell them apart only by the brand of their sneakers: Nike and Converse. They seemed quiet and polite, but Sara knew better. These two were the most accomplished gossips in the hospital, and they had a close relationship with Nurse Larch, the feared head nurse. Each day Sara watched their eyes rove over the tall man. Had they heard him speak? Seen the stopper? If Larch found out that Sara had been keeping aspects of this case to herself, Sara would be transferred and the tall man would be exiled to the Greenland of the psych unit. So Sara sat at her desk as Nike and Converse worked, ice coming to her teeth, and she didn't breathe until she heard their footsteps fade down the hall.

When things quieted, she would rotate his bed toward the window and tell him what Luke did today. She told the tall man that Luke bit into a lemon for the first time and believed it was alive and threw it across the room. She told him that Luke got a haircut – a buzzcut, like a tiny marine – and he kept looking at himself in the mirror for the rest of the afternoon, unconvinced that it was him. She told him that Luke spent a day on the driveway, hammering the concrete. There were still little C-shaped dents there, where he had thrown up sparks that smelled like gunpowder. She told him about the way he stood against the wall and measured himself each day. It never stopped feeling strange, telling stories about Luke as if he were alive. But the strangeness was what she began to enjoy. Sara's voice changed as she told the stories, became lower and more intimate. *It will help,* she told herself. *He'll hear himself, his own boyhood, the life he lost.*

One afternoon Sara began telling the tall man about her mother. She wasn't sure how it started. She was replacing the tall man's coverlet and found herself describing the color of her mother's hair. That hair – thick and curly and blond – ranked as Vera's prize possession. She wore it a dozen different styles, always keeping up with the magazines (which came, she noted ruefully, a full two weeks later to Big Prairie than to the civilized world), but it always looked the same in Sara's eyes: movie star hair, the exact color and texture she saw on starlets on the big screen at the Main Street Theater. Knowing her mother, she figured that the color flowed from a bottle, but it didn't matter. Her hair was like a living thing: blond, but more than blond, deeper and shinier somehow, the hollow of each curl holding luminous pools of honey and ocher. To Sara, it looked like you could drown in it.

Sara's own hair had grown in drab and disappointing. A vaguely nutty noncolor, not brown, but not quite red, either. Her mother tried to dye it, but the color looked thin and false. "Oh, well . . ." Her mother laughed her musical laugh. "Better not to have two blondes in the family."

Truth be told, Sara didn't know that many hard facts about her mother's past, aside from Vera's cocktail party patter: *Philadelphia, wealthy family, came west for love and adventure – not necessarily in that order.* Mostly she remembered how the air seemed to change when her mother walked into a room, how she had the ability to make the commonest activity – driving a car, mowing the lawn – seem unbearably fun. She remembered the way people would remark on her dresses, the ones she'd picked up at a boutique in Los Angeles, or San Francisco, or Seattle – all places, to the people of Big Prairie, that might as well have been Venus. Sara remembered the way her mother would pack her red suitcase and take her field trips for days and weeks at a time. She remembered how she'd invent stories about where her mother had gone (the most popular one was that she was on top-secret government work). She remembered her mother's returns: that slender form floating toward her through the blurring mesh of the screen door, that hair in some new golden confection, that skin emanating chemical-sweet traces of smoke, cologne, and the molecular intrigue of faraway rooms. Sara never knew why, but she always knew, without any corroborative evidence whatsoever, that her mother had been with men. "Well, hello there, my fabulous darling," she would say, looking at Sara with sly admiration, as if Sara had been the one who had gone away.

Her father never seemed to mind. Of course, the chief characteristic of his personality was that he never minded anything. In later years, Sara thought of him as the human analogue of the ranch itself—flat, quiet, and dry, though prone to short, brief thunderstorms whose chief effect was to reinforce the sense of immovable calm that came afterward. He was above all else a hard worker, a man who poured whatever misgivings he might have had about his spouse's absences into his endless workdays. When she was around twelve, Sara asked her father why her mother went away so often. He lit a cigarette, inhaled deeply, and looked at it as if it might answer the question.

"She just does," he'd said finally. "The country isn't the place for everybody."

"But she promised she would take me with her."

Her father took a long draw on his cigarette.

"There's something you should understand, Sara." He looked her in the eye. "Your mother has a way of . . . bending the truth a little."

Sara looked at him blankly. She'd never thought of truth as something that could move, much less bend.

"She lies?"

"Yes, I guess she does a little."

"But it's wrong to lie."

"That's true," he allowed.

"But why does she do that?"

He leaned back. "It's not lying, exactly. More like pretending. Like the people in your books – they like to pretend, don't they?"

"Yes. Lots of them. That one king does, who wants to meet the milkmaid."

"I guess in some ways your mom is like that," he said after a moment. "Making stuff up, like the king."

"But they do it because of love."

He took a last sip of his cigarette and crushed it out. "You

128

could say that's what she's doing. She loves a lot of different things, different places."

He saw the hurt shining in Sara's eyes. Touched her cheek.

"Don't worry, hon," he said. "These things have a way of squaring up."

"What's that supposed to mean?"

"Well, the way I look at it, your mother sorta evened things out by making the most honest person in the whole world. The person that always tells the truth, no matter what. Who never, ever pretends to be someone else."

Sara understood. Her father smiled and pulled her on his lap. He smelled of leather and tobacco.

After her mother died (Christmas dinner, stroke, two years after Sara and Tom married), Sara had gone to Philadelphia for the funeral. Her family turned out to be well-off, but not nearly as wealthy as her mother had suggested. The famous childhood mansion turned out to be a well-kept brick house on a middle-class street. She and Sara's father had met not at a glamorous Hollywood jazz club, but at Bob's Big Boy off Cienega Boulevard, where she waitressed. It turned out her mother's fiancé – an Italian heir to a shoe company, they said – had just broken off their engagement, and her mother had fled to Los Angeles with a friend to recuperate. Her father was finishing up his agricultural degree at Cal. He told her about his plans to go north and start a ranch. They'd eloped three weeks later, and Sara was born within the year. The wedding had apparently caused quite a scandal back in Philadelphia (enough that her parents never came to visit), but Vera had always maintained to them that she was happy. And not just happy – extraordinarily happy. "She used to go on and on about the beauty of the wide-open spaces, the wonderful people," her aunt told Sara solemnly. "I guess that's the blessing, that she found a place she could truly call home."

They left the coffin open, partly for tradition and partly for her mother, who, thanks to the suddenness of the stroke, still looked good. Her hair was curled in some new style that Sara hadn't seen. Her body, Sara couldn't help but notice, still retained its golden youthfulness. Her cheeks were soft as peaches, untouched by the dry prairie wind. Her face looked almost triumphant.

10

Want to see something?

Maybe.

Kjell and I, in the apartment, nighttime. Weary. Days filled with seeing now, all I do is see. Don't look, he says, see. That spiny plant is good to eat. This red urchin is poisonous. These birds' eggs are narrow on one end so they roll but do not fall from of the rocky ledges where they're laid. On and on.

But this, sensing something new. Kjell standing, stubbing out his joint, sniffing the air. Following quietly into the woods. Running through the forest, feeling faster than I've ever felt, leaping in the dark.

The boardwalk rising in the mist, flat and slick. His father's lab.

Shhhhhhh.

Rooting around in a pile of rocks, finding one, pressing fingers behind it. A key.

Found this yesterday.

The click, twist, and inside now. Dark chemical smells. His flashlight roving, showing a cluttered nest: books, drawings, binders. A shelf of shadowy jars.

You be the lookout.

The flashlight, cold in my hand.

What are you looking for?

Remember how I told you Dad leased this island? The tribe wants to buy out the rest of the lease. To sell it to the government – for some wildlife reserve. But Dad won't do it. Seventy thousand dollars and he says no.

Shaking our heads, sharing disbelief. Then Kjell shuffling papers, opening drawers. Me waiting, poking around. This place like a cave.

Bolder now, exploring, shining the light on the drawings, on the shelves full of books, diagrams. Seeing the jars on the far wall, moving closer. The flashlight going out, then on again.

Goddamn batteries, I say. Walking to the shelves, trying to see. Light clicking off.

Clicking back on, the jars next to my face. Pale flesh, twisting in the light. My insides lurching. Brains. Penises. Intestines. Faces.

Boom boom boom.

Kjell pulling a piece of paper out of the drawer, slamming it closed, moving toward me, whispering go go go its him, its him.

Boom boom boom. Footsteps on the boardwalk.

A beam of white light passing through the room. Kjell climbing the shelves like a ladder, reaching for the window. Opening it, pulling himself out, reaching back for me.

The footsteps, closer now.

Come on.

Climbing clumsily, reaching the top shelf. But the window is too high. I pull and thrash, boot toes striping the wood. Sliding back down.

Kjell, calm. The letter in his hand.

Jump, he says.

Pull me up.

I can't. You've got to jump.

The shelves shifting beneath me.

They'll fall.

They're nailed in.

Come on. One, two . . .

Bending my knees, launching upward, feeling the shelf fall away. For a moment, believing I made it. Then crashing formaldehyde and glass shards. The sound of liquid spilling through the gaps in the plank floor. Kjell disappears.

A big hand on my leg. Then another. Pulling me down.

Well, he says. Who do we have here? A stray? An orphan? Something the cat dragged in?

Me staring at the floor. Feeling his cool gaze behind the flashlight beam. His sharp eyes moving over me, calculating. But not angry. As if my presence were an unexpected treat.

Don't feel like talking? I'll take that as a sign of intelligence.

His voice high, strangled, vocal cords pickled by salt water. His hand on mine, sinew.

Stand, lad. We have business to conduct.

Him writing on a legal pad, black fountain pen moving swiftly. Did he already know of me? Did Kjell or Oshie tell him?

Leaning over, seeing his words: *Six hours each day, minimum. Locate, collect, and preserve. High-quality samples. Grids and markers.*

A contract. To collect specimens. To replace the ones I've broken.

Name?

Samuel. From Chicago.

His eyes taking in my muddy corduroys, the baseball hat. Sign.

Looking at his face in the light: large, craggy, white. Veined

133

cheeks. Short beard, battered nose. Eyes like deep water, knowing everything.

You must be staying at the lodge. But it's closed, no?

Yes.

You'll be staying here from now on, in the boathouse with Kjell. It was he who put you up to this little adventure, then?

No, I say. I came alone. Just curious.

His eyes on me, pressing.

I'll replace whatever I broke.

Yes, you will, my boy.

Showing me a map, grids drawn in red wax pencil. The thumb and index finger of his right hand cut off at the last joint, the skin folded over the stumps.

These are the areas you'll be focusing on. Nowhere else. The waters around here can be hazardous. Understand?

Then I see. Over Dr. Spero's shoulder a shape moving behind the glass, a face. Kjell. Standing there, listening, and I understand. He meant to get me caught. The break-in, the botched escape, the smashed jars, they build to a purpose. Kjell has a plan.

Do you understand, boy?

Yes.

Handing me a small white notebook. Then turning away and making more notes. Me, growing bold. Knowing that Kjell is listening.

So what are you, making a map or something?

Exactly.

That shouldn't take long.

He stops.

How hard can it be? Take samples, mark it, move on.

He turns and faces me. His voice light, dangerous.

No, it wouldn't be hard. It wouldn't be hard if this were the savanna or the rain forest or anywhere else on earth. But it's not. Here, every rock is its own city, its own set of inhabitants. My job is to figure out the web of relationship. You must understand, my boy. What we're talking about is a complete rendering of a pristine habitat. A place with no pollution, no hunting, no fishing, no scuba divers, nothing except what's been preserved exactly as it has been for millions of years, and when we do that – well, it doesn't matter that you grasp the details, Samuel, but you need to know that your work is important. I need to know what you find, and exactly where you find it. Is this clear?

So that makes you like Noah.

This makes him smile.

No, my lad. It makes me like Noah's supervisor.

Spero turning away, tidying up some papers. He waits until my foot touches the sill before he speaks.

You'll stay away from Oceana, of course.

He checks my face.

You need not question me. She is fifteen years old, and I am her father. That's all you need to know.

Finding my tongue and courage.

Maybe you should've built better shelves.

Spero moving in close, his eyes closing me in. Tapping my pounding heart with his cut-off finger, his voice soft.

Maybe your mother should have taught you not to touch your friends' things.

*   *   *

It was at the MountainLake Hills playground, on a Saturday, when Luke tried the big swings for the first time. A ridiculously sunny Seattle spring day, the park brimming with new mothers and their children. The mothers were glorying in the freshness of their roles, engaging in bright conversations with other mothers and their children. Sara stood with Luke on the fringes, who looked on for some time before deciding that he wanted to try the swings. Not the little ones that he'd been riding, that every other kid his age was riding. The big-boy ones, without the leg holes.

Sara sat him in the swing, a slinglike piece of rubber, and put his hands on the chains. His fingers wrapped around tightly. He bit his lip – he was nervous, but not so nervous that he couldn't do the usual play-by-play commentatary.

"Now I'm going to swing on the big-boy swing."

"Yes, you are," Sara said in her matter-of-fact parenting voice. She drew him back, felt the eyes of other mothers on them. Knowing the other mothers were watching always lent her an extra sheen of confidence. "Ready?"

Luke nodded.

Sara pushed and immediately realized she had pushed too hard. The swing arced outward, and Luke's hands let go at the top of the arc. He flipped and fell and hit the cedar chips face-first. Sara rushed over – no time for counting now – and saw a bright wash of blood through his fingers.

"You're okay," she told him.

Around them, Sara heard the footsteps, looked up to see the faces of the neighborhood moms, the expressions of shock and sympathy.

"He's okay," she said, fighting to keep her voice in control. "He's fine."

The doctors sewed him up, two stitches subcutaneous, three on the outside. The nurses had straps ready to restrain him – standard procedure, they said, for someone so young – but the straps remained unused. Luke sat perfectly still, staring at the ceiling, a thousand miles away. He had a way of holding in his emotions when he had to, a deep concentration he would focus on other things — a wall, a bird. People assumed it was something that Sara had taught him, but that wasn't entirely the case. It was a coolness, a reserve that was his inheritance as surely as the freckle on his nose. This was what he'd learned from her, Sara thought, how to float above himself.

On the way home, Sara bought ice-cream cones and they ate them sitting in the car by the Sound. He had a Band-Aid on his lip — not the one with the cartoon tigers, like they'd offered, but a plain one.

"You know, it's okay to cry sometimes," she said.

He gave his ice cream a careful lick. "I know."

"If something hurts a lot, or even if it doesn't hurt. We all feel like crying sometimes."

"You never cry."

"Not that I'd show you," she said teasingly. This was a reliable way they talked, jokey. "But if I have to, I do."

Luke thought about this. "What would you cry about?"

"Oh, I dunno. If my ice cream falls out of its cone."

Luke smiled slyly. "No, you wouldn't."

"Well, if something ever happened to you or Daddy, then I would cry."

"You would?"

"Yes," Sara said, a little insulted. "I would."

"Oh."

"You think I wouldn't cry?"

"There's no bad things, there's only bad attitudes."

He had already begun quoting some of her platitudes back at her — a bad sign for the future.

Sara regarded her cone carefully. "Well, sometimes there are bad things."

"Yeah?"

"Yeah. Like today. I shouldn't have pushed you so hard. I should have been more careful. That was a bad thing."

Luke mulled this piece of information.

"But didn't you learn from it? Doesn't that make it a good thing?"

"I learned from it all right," Sara said, struggling with the logic. "But I still shouldn't have done it, so it's a bad thing."

Luke licked his cone thoughtfully. "What other kind of bad things are there?"

"Just things," Sara said helplessly. "Things in the world. Problems to figure out, problems that no one can help us with."

Luke's tiny brow furrowed, and he looked for a moment like an old man. Sara yearned to have raised a simpler child, one not aware of the darker possibilities. She gently plucked a shard of cone from his chin.

"Can we always solve them? The problems?"

"As long as we do our best."

"But what if there are bigger problems? I mean, really big ones."

"Then we'll do our best, and that will be enough."

He wasn't buying.

"Don't worry, big guy," she said, sliding her arm around his slender shoulders. "We're lucky. Nothing will ever happen to us."

A lie, but what other choice was there? When Luke had been a baby, the choice had seemed so simple: You can raise your child either in the real world or in some safe dome. Sara had chosen the real world, but now that parts of that world loomed dark and threatening, she wanted to go back and start over. *As long as we do our best* – was that enough?

"How do you know we're lucky, Mom?"

"We just are. I can feel it. Close your eyes. Can you feel it?"

He crinkled his eyes shut. "Nope."

"Try harder. Do your best."

He sat still for a long time, concentrating. A thread of chocolate ran down his fist.

"Yeah," Luke said. "I think I can feel it now."

11

One afternoon just after a seizure, Sara heard the doorknob click behind her.

"Hey hey," said a voice that reminded her of a late-night disk jockey's. "How's everything in this neck of the woods tonight?"

"Fine," Sara managed, fussing with the blanket, her heart rising to her throat.

Michelle Larch was a tall, lean woman with a mane of blond hair. She wore leather sandals, jeans, and an unbuttoned lab coat that revealed a flash of tie-dye beneath, an ensemble no enlisted nurse would dare attempt. The woman eased herself across the ward with an elaborate saunter, clipboard tucked under her arm like a surfboard. She gazed bemusedly around the room, as if surprised to find herself there.

"Is Josephine on tonight?"

"No."

"Huh." Larch looked bemused.

"What's that?"

The head nurse smiled. "I thought I heard you talking to someone, that's all."

"The television," Sara said, pushing the remote button. "The volume is on the fritz."

The head nurse was the daughter of an air force colonel, a

woman whose doelike eyes concealed a razory mind. Sara had not had much direct contact with her, but the stories about her were common currency around the nurses' lounge. Larch went to elaborate lengths to appear disorganized but in fact kept elaborate files on each nurse, which she downloaded from the PalmPilot she kept hidden inside the Bolivian grass purse she wore around her neck. She wandered the hospital greeting the staff in her blissed-out voice, then retreated to her office to author cogent efficiency memos. She was mildly notorious for her habit of hugging nurses whose jobs she had terminated – a deep, sincere, full-body hug that Sara had witnessed several times. Hospital administration adored her, the nursing staff feared and despised her.

"I just have to tell you, Sara, it's so great to have you back with us," Larch said, her eyes locking onto Sara's with almost unbearable earnestness. "When you were gone, I mean, it was like losing a member of the tribe. You've shown us all so much courage, Sara. So much heart."

Sara looked down, embarrassed. Larch sidled toward the tall man, leaning on the chrome rails of his bed as if she were at a singles bar. Sara could see the lump of the notebook beneath the covers next to the tall man's hand; she held her breath.

"The better to see us with, I guess," she said.

"What?"

"His eyes. There's something about the eyes that reveals their true selves, don't you think?"

"I don't know if you heard," Sara said, trying to regain some semblance of a professional tone, "we've had some strep loose in here, so we're trying to minimize any – "

"Cool," Larch said, effortlessly snapping out of her reverie. "It's strictly routine. I'll just be a sec." She extended the word *sec*, made it sound exotic.

141

Her heart quaking, Sara stepped aside. Nurse Larch moved first to the twins, taking their pulses and blood pressures, checking their pupils, testing reflexes. The tall man lay still, his eyes locked on the wall.

The examination took an eternity. Larch peered in the tall man's eyes and ears, took his temperature, blood pressure, listened with a concentrated, wary expression. Sara bit her lip, waiting for the inevitable sequence of events: the tall man would speak, Larch would call the doctors and the tall man would be whisked away to the psych ward.

"Looks like it might storm," Sara said, looking at the window.

Larch took no notice. She lifted the tall man's arm and rotated it gently. "Wow," she said.

"How's that?"

"A lot of TBI patients, they get so stiff. But his tendons are fairly supple, his muscle tone is good."

"We do a lot of movement therapy," Sara said.

Larch touched the scar on the tall man's leg. "This looks almost fresh," she said.

"He's had it since he came in," Sara said, pulling up the covers. Larch stepped back.

"I understand you two have been hanging out a lot together," she said easily.

"Yeah," Sara said. "I like the quiet, I guess."

"He still having the seizures?"

"Pretty regular."

"Any changes in heart rate, breathing?"

"No."

The head nurse wrote a few things down, then something seemed to catch her eye. She moved toward the tall man and looked again into his face.

"That's funny," Larch said.

"What?"

"Well, it probably isn't anything," the head nurse said, chuckling. "It's just that I thought I saw his mouth move."

Together they stared at the tall man. Sara pressed her fingernails into her palm.

"Probably nothing," Larch said after a moment. "A little seizure, that's all."

Nurse Larch tapped the clipboard against her leg, leaned against the bed frame. Tucked a snake of yellow hair behind her ear and looked at Sara in a mischievous way.

"I've got one more question for you, Nurse Black. If you don't mind."

Sara's insides trembled. "Yes?"

"You wouldn't happen to have a cigarette, would you?"

Sara laughed, a nervous explosion. She located a cigarette and handed it to the head nurse. Nurse Larch cupped Sara's hands around the lighter.

"We used to use condoms over at General," Larch said, aiming her cigarette at the glove-covered smoke alarm. "They'd rip sometimes. So much for safe sex."

"Safety is overrated," Sara said, surprising herself.

They smoked and watched the rain fall against the glass. In another world, Sara realized, they might have been friends.

* * *

Why don't you just leave?

Sitting at a driftwood fire, Kjell and I. Him looking up, surprised.

Go. Take the boat to Sitka, I say. Get off this rock.

Kjell snapping a branch, prodding the coals. His voice quiet.

I could leave. But I'm not going to leave with nothing. And there's Oshie.

143

She could come, too.

Kjell shaking his head, stirring the fire.

Haven't you seen? How he keeps us apart. Keeps her on his side. Besides, what would we do for money?

Me, studying the coals. Seeing it.

The letter, I say. The offer from the native association.

So?

Your dad. When he pays for fuel and food – does he have a checking account?

In Sitka.

Could you get the account number?

The stick stops moving.

My voice, rising, laying out the plan: We write a letter, accept the offer, they deposit it in the account. Then we go to Sitka and withdraw the money.

Kjell watching, eyes alight.

He owes you this.

Make this happen, you're in for a share.

Oh no, the money's yours. I don't need it.

No. Your idea.

Me, wincing.

It won't work.

Why?

Oshie won't go. It won't change her mind.

Kjell taking a stick from the fire, twirling it in his palms, an O of fire.

We'll figure something out.

The next day, typing the letter, signing Spero's name to the offer sheet. Taking the skiff to the mail shed on the north side of the island. Ocean calm. Light rain hissing. Feeling confident now.

Opening the mail shed. Setting the letter in a box.

144

How long?

Mail boat comes on Friday. Takes a day to get to Sitka.

Every Friday?

Yes.

Slowly realizing. Blinking.

When I got here you told me there was no way off.

Kjell's eyes, steady. Lips sealed. Gulls diving behind him.

You lied to me.

Him not denying. Opening his arms, pointing to the ocean.

You want to go, then? Go back?

Rain coming harder now, like cold rocks. pummeling.

Say the word.

Looking away from him. The rain deafening on my hood, finding pinholes, irresistible. His eyes on me, brotherly, pressing.

No. I'll stay.

Later. Night. In the boathouse. Pretending to sleep. Wanting to slip away, to get away from Kjell. To have time alone. Maybe see Oshie again.

An hour passes. Kjell breathing, steady and deep. Rising slowly, praying the mattress doesn't creak.

Standing on the edge of the dock, breathing cool light. Moving nervously toward the house.

Practicing the words I'll use: Hello, Oshie? Oh, just taking a walk.

Stopping to watch two otters in the lagoon, their teeth cracking on clamshells. Rolling and diving, shadows beneath green water. Waiting for them to surface.

Someone behind me. The chemical smell of his oilskin coat, magnifying glass on a black string around his neck. A stubbed finger, aimed.

The male lives in the lagoon. The female is passing by and found her way into his territory, and now the chase is on.

Me nodding. Clouds of insects over the water, slanted light. Otters diving again.

He's playing possum. He shows her the food and waits until the tide goes out, and then the female can't escape.

Then what?

A pause, a smile rising.

He'll have his way with her, of course. Don't look so surprised, boy. Did you think he was interested in good conversation?

Trailing him into the shadowy warmth. Spero shaking off his coat, hanging his hat by its ivory bead. Formaldehyde smell. Rolling his sleeves, muscular forearms.

Hungry?

Ladling something pink and meaty to my plate. Cutting it in half. Watching me.

How long have you been here, lad?

Three weeks.

Not long enough.

Eating. Spero loud, ferocious. Shaking his head to tear meat off his fork. Specks of food collecting in his whiskers. Red wine, a glass lifted.

Kjell was born right here, you know. I'll bet he didn't tell you that.

Shaking my head.

On that couch. We had wanted to go to Sitka for the birth, but the weather came in and we had him here. November 11. Eleven pounds, one ounce. All ones. Different, right from the start. So we trained him, my wife and I.

What do you mean?

When he was three, he could read. When he was five, he was

146

running the outboard. When he was six, he shot a black bear and hauled it back to camp. When he was seven, he spent a week out on his own with nothing but the clothes on his back.

Spero taking another drink, pouring me one. Watching me closely.

We taught him survival skills. Extraordinarily receptive. He developed more quickly than we were prepared for. Very natural.

You make him sound like an animal.

Not like a single animal, but like all of them together. Call it a web or a chain or what you like. All the animals here are connected so closely that you can view them as a single interconnected being. This being – this beast with claws and antennae and tentacles – this is what I mean when I say natural. An old Greek idea. A single resourceful organism, not thinking but reacting according to appetite.

Leaning back now, drifting in thought.

My wife was the one who made it work. When she died, I tried to raise him on my own, God help me.

Spero, studying the tabletop.

Things . . . didn't go as I had planned. Having that kind of power can be too much for a young mind to handle. They want to go too far, too fast. The only rational choice is to try to direct that energy toward something productive, to channel it away from other . . .

Him catching himself, glancing up.

What's the matter, lad? Don't you like your dinner?

Him trying to cover, but too late. It's there, the tremble in his voice, the shamed glance. The Noah project is part counterfeit, an artifice designed to keep Kjell on the island. Spero made a mistake – he did his job too well. He built a boy whose appetites could not fit in the larger world. So the old man

147

remains here, filling in his grids and maps, letting months and years flow past, waiting and hoping that things will change.

A noise by the window. Spero and I looking out, feeling it at the same time. Kjell standing there, listening. Seeing his eyes, the wildness of his presence, knowing he's been there all along.

*   *   *

Sara and Tom's fight after their visit to the Olivers eased the day-to-day tension between them. Not that they drew closer; the opposite was true. Their argument removed ambiguity, freed them from politeness. They moved around each other briskly, passing in and out of doors, nodding across rooms. Sara worked twelve-hour days, occasionally adding nights when Josephine was off. Tom worked shorter days trolling for new clients but spent most of his free time burrowing into his increasingly ambitious house projects – cleaning out closets, reorganizing the laundry room, chiseling out broken back-splash tiles, replacing ventilation ducts. They spoke to each other with glancing care, as if from two vehicles passing at high speeds. Sara felt the danger of intimacy rise beneath the surface of each word, until each moment together felt as if they were balancing on a precipice. When they said good morning, Sara didn't know if they were going to kiss or collide in blows.

For ten days, they did neither. There were several nights when Tom slipped away to the couch or, as he sometimes did, the easy chair. Sara would wrap a blanket around his sleeping form, careful not to let the doorknob catch as she slipped out. The bouquet of sunflowers arrived on their appointed day, propped carefully against the door frame as usual. After two days Sara noticed that Tom had put them in a vase.

Each night, Sara returned from the hospital as if from a long oceanic journey. She stepped inside uneasily, trying to adjust her mind to the new reality. She saw piles of old clothes, sports equipment, toys, clothes, and board games with missing pieces. She heard the sounds of hammering and sawing, metal on metal, echoing from the catacombs of their house. Tom was still working on the rooms, re-creating them according to a vision she could not decipher. Whenever she opened a door, she hesitated for a moment, wondering what she might find.

12

Riding aboard the *Leira* on a wild plain of ocean, miles from anywhere, and Dr. Spero has no idea that we've gone. Kjell driving, me up front, big waves heaving beneath. Pointed toward Egg Rock, eleven miles away. A final lesson.

Kjell driving fast, skimming wave tops, showing me the power, the way to move through a hostile ocean. Me, nervous.

Isn't this outside the grid?

Exactly.

Ocean, endless and wrinkled. No birds, no fish, no boats. Wind booming, spray drying white on our raingear.

Then a low black shape, like a house. Rising slowly, until we can see it: forty-foot-high chunk of black rock, frosted in guano. A hive of birds. Reeling, screaming, long necked, blood footed, strafing us with shit.

Pulling up on the east side, in the lee, Kjell killing the engine. A thousand eyes watching. The hiss and gurgle of waves, kelp slurping. Kjell rigging the dredge lines.

Come on. Little bouncing never hurt anyone.

The dredge comes up overflowing with huge pink urchins, tiny brittle stars, crabs, striped worms, a large eel. I see, and understand the plan: Spero wants specimens? We'll give him specimens.

Let's try the west side, Kjell says. It should have better stuff.

Better than this?

Come on. Who's going to stop us?

Pulling out of the lee, feeling this is a mistake. Waves fat and fast, green sun glowing inside. Wind snapping our hair, pulling tears from our eyes. Kjell working the tiller, edging his way in, dodging rocks. His hand level, pointing to a pool separated by a picket fence of rocks. Inside, calm water.

Kjell circling, approaching the rock fence with the waves behind us. Me leaning out, seeing rocks black and shiny and studded with barnacles, rising and dropping like a jack-in-the-box. Kjell idling the throttle, looking back, over his shoulder.

Then a wave. Fat and fast, a nasty smile of foam on its crest. Kjell gunning the motor, me grabbing, bracing for the crash. We rise, the boat a surfboard. Seeing the rocks pass beneath, fixed in green glass. Kjell waiting, throwing the engine into reverse, the wave sliding forward, booming on the rocks.

We're in. A horseshoe cove, a broad, rocky beach strung with driftwood, rimmed in grass. A runty tree leaning into the wind.

Looking down, seeing the soft motion of flesh beneath. Colors and tentacles. Waving hello.

Pulling up pink-spotted crabs and whelks and an orange sea cucumber; a foot-long centipede-looking thing and a white rose anemone. Yelling as each set comes up, reaching over the sides to catch escapees, dumping out buckets to make room. Counting seventeen species we haven't seen before. Dumping and sorting until we can't feel our hands. Drunk on harvest, on fooling Spero. Kjell starting the motor.

One more set, I say. There's still room.

No. We're heavy enough as it is.

Looking at the gunwales, seeing he's right. Feeling the wind pick up. Closing my eyes, the spray prickling my hands. My heart thumping. Retying the life jacket.

Kjell idling, watching a gap in the rocks. Waiting for a break in the waves.

The waves come. And come. And come.

We could hang out awhile, I say.

Kjell looking out on the horizon, as if my voice has come from there.

His hand twisting the throttle. Moving toward the opening, me bouncing slightly on my knees, urging us faster. The buckets sloshing, settling. A red crab grasping a bucket rim, beginning to climb out.

Almost. Then, between the rocks, the engine cutting out. A silence, a sick hollow in my belly. Turning to see Kjell standing, looking at me with a faint smile.

He means to do this. He means for us to wreck.

Me lunging for a paddle, too late. The boat sideways now, pushed onto the rock, then dropping with the wave, skidding down its face, scraping, and tilting.

The next wave. Feeling the boat lifted and turned, then catapulting into the water. Tumbled, driven down, pressed on my back. Salt water painful in my nose, my eyes. Seeing.

An oar rising past me, twitching slightly.

A cormorant flying beneath the water.

Barnacles feeding, their feathers moving in and out, in and out.

Trying to rise, can't.

Then release, rising to the surface, the boiling rush, sweet air.

The boat flipping sideways, jackhammering on rocks as if it is trying to crack them. Another wave, pressing me against the rock, barnacles biting my cheek.

Gasping, flailing, watching birds watch me with black eyes, giving up. Then something pushing against the back of my head. Grabbing me with cold hands.

My leg, Kjell says.

Pulling ourselves on the rocks, rolling the boat over for shelter, crawling inside. Helping him with his boot, feeling the warm blood pour out.

Fucking dredge.

The cut, long and to the bone. Its center bleeding, flecks of rust and bits of shell along its pink edge. Kjell leaning forward, touching it, tracing it.

Lucky seven. Perfect.

Yeah.

Take my lighter. We've got to get warm.

My hands shaking. The dried seaweed smoking, then catching. Adding twigs, then larger pieces of driftwood. Kjell watching, not speaking. Approval in his eyes.

The warmth. Sleep.

His voice in the dark.

Sun star versus king crab.

What?

Sun star versus king crab, Kjell says. Who wins?

Big king crab or little king crab?

Medium.

I'd have to go with the sun star. The crab is stronger, but the star has lasting power. Hungrier.

Right.

My turn. Moon snail versus dogwinkle.

What do you think?

If it's not a big moon snail, I've got to go with the dogwinkle. They can drill through anything. Their shell is thicker.

Wrong.

The moon snail, then? You think it can take a dogwinkle?

Wrong again.

Who, then?

Hermit crab. They kill each other, leave two empty shells, hermit crab wins.

I didn't say hermit crab.

I know you didn't. But it still wins.

Morning. Kjell not able to walk, tends the fire and waits. Watching me, waiting. Me, hesitant.

So what now?

You tell me.

We've got no gas tank and one oar. What are we supposed to do?

Kjell poking the fire, eyes down.

Okay, I say finally. Okay.

I stand up, go to work. Finding one of the shovels among the rocks. Gathering rainwater from small pockets on the rock, picking mussels to eat. And talking, in a new voice, an expeditionary voice. Feeling a strength within me.

Saying, We'll leave at low tide, let the incoming carry us back.

Saying, Eleven miles should take half a day at the most, depending on the wind.

Saying, Here's more firewood.

The shovel's handle too thick for the oarlock. Starting to say something to Kjell, thinking better of it. Taking my knife, shaving it down so it fits. Sliding it into place, feeling his eyes on me.

Harder to fix the hole in the hull. I try using a life jacket, but it's too bulky. Then cutting it open and stuffing some of the fill

154

in my raincoat, shoving the package in the hole from the inside, stomping it until it's tight.

Kjell's eyes on it. Saying nothing, but I can feel his approval.

Then rolling the boat, loading. Feeling the oar and shovel in my hands, finding the balance.

Leaning, feeling the skiff jump forward. A faint wake feathering behind us. Turning, seeing the jagged gap and the waves. My arms quivering. My voice steady.

Moving a few feet with each stroke. Nearing the gap, hearing the waves slap on the rocks, popping in unseen hollows. The feel of the wood in my hands, Kjell's arm as my compass.

Steady.

The spray on my neck, the sizzle of foam.

Steady . . .

Pulling as hard and fast as I can, the cords in my shoulders stretching.

Harder.

Entering the passageway against a large wave, we're thrown nearly vertical. My arms frantic, paddling air then water, air then water, losing ground.

Now, now, now.

Digging hard, advancing to the edge of the entrance.

Hang on.

A wave pitching us back again, but not quite as far as the first one.

Now, now, now.

Inching forward, reaching the entrance a third time. Seeing the barnacle-covered rocks, instinctively bracing the oar and shovel against them.

Don't.

Kjell reaches for the oars.

Too late. The wave hits, and I feel the handles bend, feel the wood fibers popping, separating. But not snapping. Then feeling the wave pass beneath. Leaning on the oars and levering us through into open water.

Ten more strokes, then ten more. Kjell's voice.

Good work.

Rowing. Rowing. Rowing. Clouds scuddy and small. Spitting rain. The noisy silence of the ocean. My body, perfectly constructed for rowing. Arms swinging, legs braced, body rocking back and forth with power. Fat boy lucky boy.

The clouds lowering, the wind blowing cold. Lines of snot hardening on my cheeks, the seat biting into my legs.

How much farther?

Six miles.

My body rocking, pulling us slowly, steadily. Waves hunched and hard, spraying. A pod of porpoises rolling, blowing mist. I stop feeling my hands, watch them move the oars.

Spero is waiting, as Kjell knew he would be. Standing on the dock in his battered hat, his big head raised slightly, nostrils testing the air.

His hooded eyes on us: the battered boat, Kjell's bloody leg.

Hel-lo there, my boys.

His tone infuriatingly even, as if we'd just returned from a picnic. He smiles.

Pleasant evening for a row, no?

We rolled, Kjell says evenly. Lost the gas tank.

Where did all this happen?

At Egg Rock.

Me, feeling the need to sit down. Spero seizing my hands and staring at them. His thick hand finds my cheek, thumbs down my eyelids.

Dehydrated. Perhaps you should've brought more supplies.

Then Kjell limping past. Spero stepping in his path, placing his fingertips on his son's chest, pushing him down.

He needs stitches, I say.

I don't care, Spero says, reaching into his coat pocket.

My chest filling with fire. Doesn't he know what we've been through? But Spero talking, lifting his arm in the air. Then I see. He's holding the letter, from the mail shed. He sees us notice, and marks us with his eyes. He slowly tears the letter apart, lets the pieces fall to the water.

Tie on, boys, Spero says. Tie on.

A cold white sphere of hatred rising inside me.

13

Josephine's face appeared at the door frame, bearing a flushed expression that made Sara think something had gone wrong. She watched as Josephine entered, closed the door portentously, and held up a sheet of paper.

"Paging Madame Sherlock," Josephine whispered. "Looks like you've got your man."

Sara grabbed for the paper, but Josephine pulled it back teasingly. "Hot off the fax machine, from Chicago's finest," she said.

"Wait," Sara said. She was not ready for this, not now. She stood, smoothed her shirtfront.

Josephine fairly writhed in agony. "Come *on*," she said.

Sara took a breath. This wasn't about her, she reminded herself. It was about the tall man and his family. His latest murmurings had been marked with a fever and delirium that had left her frightened and unnerved, convinced more than ever of the delicacy of his condition. If there was news, she would tell him – she would, she promised herself. But that news had to be delivered gently and not through the foghorn of Josephine's voice.

Sara checked the tall man, saw that he was asleep. She swung the scrim around his bed. She and Josephine stepped to the corner of the room.

"Okay," she said, trying to steady her voice. "But quietly."

"Lake Forest Boy Missing in Alaska," Josephine whispered, affecting a newscasterly tone. "Samuel Lawrence Gapp, seventeen, a recent graduate of Lake Forest High, has been listed as missing by the Coast Guard after his parents failed to locate him at an Alaskan wilderness camp where he had been spending the summer. William and Yvonne of 634 Briarwood Park Lane . . ."

Sara snatched the article from her hand. The photo was fuzzy from multiple copies, warped slightly from the microfiche, and possessed of a grainy, hasty quality that made her think of a surveillance camera. It showed a young man with a moplike profusion of light hair that shadowed his eyes. His jawline was uncertain, and his lower lip protruded with a boxerly pugnaciousness. It was an oddly unattractive choice to submit to a newspaper, as if the parents did not care to take the time to find a better photo. Sara looked closer, trying to see the outline of his eyes, staring until the pixels seemed to fall apart, then reassemble themselves. Josephine looked over her shoulder.

"So that's him?"

"It was Lake Forest, not Forest Lake. No wonder we couldn't find him."

Sara read: "Mr. and Mrs. Gapp were traveling to Sitka to assist authorities in attempts to locate their son. Mr. Richard Connor, president of Alaska Wilderness Camps, said that due to unforeseeable financial events, the camp had been temporarily closed. Anyone with information about Mr. Gapp's whereabouts is encouraged to contact his parents, who are the owners of Lake Forest's largest and most reputable insurance business."

"Gapp," Sara said, trying out the word in her mouth. "Samuel Gapp."

"Looks like the parents are not exactly peasants," Josephine said, taking the article.

"Samuel Gapp," Sara said, feeling tumblers clicking into place. He had a name. He had a mother and a father. A room, with posters on the wall, clothes piled in the corner. To Sara it was as if a troupe of strangers had suddenly materialized in the room.

"Ahh, Mr. Gapp," Josephine said. "Now you get to go home. To have a party, do a little dancing, get a decent picture in the newspaper . . ."

But Sara wasn't listening. She was looking at the photo.

"What's the matter?" Josephine said.

"He looks different."

"What?"

"I mean, from the photo," Sara said. "His eyes."

Josephine tipped the photo to the light. "A bullet will do that," she said. "Besides, he's probably thirty pounds lighter now. This looks like it was taken when he was in eighth grade."

Sara put her hand to the tall man's face, covering all but his eyes. Then she squinted at the photo.

"Everything matches," Josephine said. "The date, the island, the name of the camp, the airplane, everything."

They stared in silence at the photo, then at the tall man.

"It's the light," Josephine said. She adjusted an elbow lamp so that it shone on the tall man from below, throwing his eyes into dark shadows. "See?"

Sara looked.

"You might be right," she said.

"Might be?"

"Okay," Sara admitted. "You're right."

Josephine handed Sara the telephone and plucked the photo from her hand.

"Make the call," Josephine said. "No dickhole theories. You've got a missing kid. He has a father. He has a mother. Not complicated."

"Tell you what," Sara said. "I'll write a letter. No mother wants news like this over the phone. A letter makes it more official. More real."

Josephine looked on doubtfully.

"I'll overnight it. They'll have it in the morning, then I'll call."

Josephine shrugged. "Suit herself."

"Yourself."

"What?"

"Suit yourself. That's the saying. Suit yourself."

Josephine made a dismissive popping sound with her lips. "These sayings of yours, they make no sense."

Sara sat before the battered typewriter she'd scrounged from the ER, regarding its black plastic body as if it were an undefused bomb. She'd been trying to write the letter for an hour now, but the phrases that came to mind seemed at once too casual and too melodramatic: *This news may come as a shock . . . your son who has been missing for two years . . .*

She pulled the sheet from the roller and balled it up. She looked over at the tall man, whose head was tipped in the orange wash of sunset. His arms were at his sides, palms up. The fringe of hair glowed halolike around his pale skull. He looked to Sara's eyes as if he were about to ascend, bed and all, into the cool evening air.

This was how it was supposed to happen, wasn't it? Wasn't this the idea, to reunite him with his family? To watch his mother take him in her arms, to see the grateful expression on

161

her face? To feel what it is like to bring someone who was dead back to life?

Yet Sara could not bring herself to type the words. She wrote ten letters and tore up ten letters, each dismissed as too brusque, too sentimental, too clinical, too personal. She tried to picture the mother and the father in the room and figure out what she would say to them.

Your son is alive.

He wants to see you.

He has a story to tell.

Sara stared at the white paper, tried to concentrate. She'd readied herself for this, hadn't she? Hadn't she played the scene out in her mind? The parents would arrive, jittery and breathless, and Sara would greet them warmly but professionally. She would take a moment to prepare them – to inform them about the infection, the trach tube, the sobering extent of his injuries. The hospital would try to make a fuss, but Sara would not permit it. This was a family matter. She would answer all questions, conduct herself with dignity. She would bring the parents into the room, and she would pull back the scrim and place his hand in theirs and step back. *Here's your son.*

And then . . . good-bye.

Or perhaps not. Sara's thoughts leapt forward eagerly. The tall man was in no condition to travel. William and Yvonne would have to stay here for a few weeks until he stabilized. And if he ever did improve enough to go home, a wealthy couple like that would opt for professional assistance. Sara wouldn't move out there permanently, of course, but perhaps for a few weeks, until they got someone trained.

And after that? Sara soothed herself with images of their future relationship. She would stay in touch. The Chicago doctors would figure out the key to the infection, beat it. He would get better. She would visit often, help oversee his rehab. She would be there when he rose from his wheelchair to take his first steps, when he spoke his first clear sentence. Years would pass. Sara would play the role of distant but beloved aunt, a keeper of secrets, their destinies corded in an unbreakable knot. She closed her eyes and pictured a scene a few years from now, a figure walking toward her along the shore of Lake Michigan. Not in hospital garb, but in jeans and a T-shirt. His body filled out, lean and strong. Limping, but a noble limp, an athletic limp that matched her own. Behind him, she could see the sky's reflection in the water, all the clouds merging to this point. In her imagination he was walking toward her from the water, the sun at his back. She waved to him. The figure drew closer until the light revealed his face.

Tom. She was picturing Tom's face.

Sara's frustration bubbled over. Why did the fax have to arrive now? Why couldn't it have waited another day? Another week? Let him keep talking, let him get to the end of his story, and then she would be ready to face anyone. But she kept hearing Josephine's words.

He has a father. He has a mother.

She turned and watched the tall man sleep. His chest rising and falling, his mouth partway open. His lower lip shiny and pink.

Sara typed out a single page informing the Gapps of Samuel's condition and inviting them to Seattle at the earliest possible date. She included her home phone number. She folded and sealed the letter before she had time to think and set it in the outgoing mail at the nurses' station.

When she returned she conducted an experiment, attaching the EEG and measuring the tall man's response to his own

163

name, his parents' names, and his address. She read the words in a loud voice, her lips next to the tall man's ear, and watched the needle. It didn't move much, but it did move.

He turned fitfully, murmuring something inaudible. Sara put her hand on his lips.

"Be happy," she said. "Somebody loves you."

Sara arrived home to a terse message from Tom that he'd be working late. Relieved, she ate dinner quickly, cleaned up, then walked across the first floor to the living room. She enjoyed the echo of her shoes on the wooden floor. She sat on the couch and looked around, luxuriating in the silence. She heard a car approaching, then felt herself relax when it passed by.

Sara looked at an old photo of herself and Tom at the beach. She permitted herself to dwell on his face for a second, seeing forgotten details. That isosceles triangle of freckles just above his right eye. The way the blues and greens in his irises seemed to swap places in the light. The nearly invisible chip in his front tooth that his tongue always found when he smiled.

Now, in this empty house, she found herself drawn to Tom's office. She stepped in warily, feeling like a trespasser. She walked slowly around his desk and sat down. On the left-hand wall hung a stylized diagram of a cow showing the position of each steak, on the right an Ansel Adams print of the Wyoming prairie. From this vantage the kitchen island was framed perfectly in the doorway, the spot where she stood to chop vegetables or make bread. From the desk Sara could take in all three sights at once – beef, land, wife: Tom's holy trinity.

Sara opened the drawers, paged through his call sheets, flipped idly through his Rolodex. She wasn't looking for anything; she simply wanted to pretend, to use this as a substitute for closeness. She imagined him seated at this

164

captain's chair, managing the flow of well-cut steaks from slaughterhouse to spotless restaurant plate. A man who was able to expertly gauge the appetites of thousands, but whose own desires went unspoken. Sara poked at his day planner, thumbed through his files. She found index cards with the name of each restaurant, filled in with the name of their owner, their meat buyer, and their maître'd. She found a file labeled "Backup Suppliers." Then, toward the back of the drawer, she found two files marked "PL #1" and "PL #2." She opened them and saw what looked like blueprints.

PL. Port Lucy.

She hesitated, then spread them on the desk. They were pencil drawings on graph paper, two floor plans. At first Sara thought they were copies, for the exterior dimensions matched. Looking closer, however, she saw that the drawings were different. The first called for a big kitchen and two bedrooms. Tom had penciled everything, as was his habit, even adding the queen-size bed, the bureau, the cupboards. Sara smiled at his perfectionism. Tom had done the same with this house. "Why should I build a room without knowing what goes in it?" he'd said in that low, irrefutable voice.

When Sara examined the second plan, she saw he'd drawn something far simpler. Stark, even. The cabin was divided into a woodshop and a spartan living area. She looked closer and saw one bathroom, a kitchen efficiency, and a bedroom furnished with a bureau, a sink, and a single bed. A narrow rectangle, drawn neatly on the graph paper, set beneath a window in the corner of the room. He'd used a ruler. Tom always used a ruler.

Sara looked at that single bed for a long time, feeling the walls faintly warping around her.

So this was his project. Preparing, getting things ready. Did she really think he would be caught without a backup plan? No, this second cabin was for him alone, a place at least until he could locate a new Mrs. Black, which would happen eventually, wouldn't it? Plan number one or plan number two. Clean, straight, bisecting lines. Good cuts make good results.

It's a choice. That's what he'd said. But he wasn't going to wait, was he? He was already working on his choice. He'd been building it right here, behind this door, laying it all out so that when the time came he would be ready.

When Tom arrived home an hour later, he planted a brotherly kiss on her cheek. Sara waited awhile before asking if he'd gotten any word on the cabin lately.

"Yep," he said flatly. "Couple other bids in. We'll have to see how it shakes out."

"So what do you have in mind? If we get it, I mean."

Tom opened the fridge and took out a container of Chinese food. He dug experimentally with a fork.

"It'd need some work, for sure," he said. "But it's too early to start making firm plans."

"Right," Sara said, backing off. "Of course."

"So," Tom said dutifully. "How was your day?"

"Fine," Sara managed. "The usual."

"Good," he said. "The usual is good."

They regarded each other across the empty countertop. Outside, a dog barked. A sprinkler hissed, dropped into machine-gun bursts, then hissed again.

"Well," Tom said after a moment. "There's a couple things I should close up before bed."

"Should I wait up?"

"Don't bother. I won't be long."

Sara watched him move across the room toward the study. In

166

that moment she decided she would not tell him about the fax from Chicago or the letter she'd written to the Gapps. She would let him make his plans and she would make hers. Two lives, parallel lines, not touching.

14

Kjell watching me, smiling.

Happy birthday.

Me blinking, yawning. The boathouse, drab and cluttered. Frost on the wood, yellow leaves blowing.

Kjell fixing eggs on a camp stove. Cutting butter, stirring with his knife.

Where's the skiff?

He got the motor running this morning and went collecting. Oshie's picking berries for your cake.

It's not my birthday.

Kjell smiles.

We eat, four eggs apiece, sausages, coffee. Then he looks at me.

I need your help with something.

A thump of recognition. This is it. This is the day.

Over at the lagoon entrance. We'll need buckets. A tarp. Rope, too.

Moving automatically, as if we've done it many times before. Gathering the gear, walking down the beach. To a flat spot between two large rocks. Above us, the root screen, the dark hole of the apartment behind.

Here, Kjell says.

Sitting on our haunches, waiting. The day turning beautiful;

windless, fat Hawaiian clouds. Digging a hole with the heel of my boot, watching it slowly fill with water.

When do you think he'll come?

Midtide. An hour. Maybe more.

The water lapping to our feet, scooting back.

How's lucky seven? I ask.

Kjell flexing his leg. Not bad. Doesn't hurt much anymore.

Silence. Each of us in our thoughts.

Ever notice how barnacles pop when they sense a shadow?

Kjell's hand moving like a conjurer. A light crackling.

It's the sound of them closing their trapdoors tighter. They close them loosely when the tide is out, but if they sense a predator, they shut them tighter.

Predators should stay in the shadows.

Kjell smiling. You learn fast, Chicago.

Me, nervous now, rooting around. Finding a few bones, a midden of curved ribs, skulls. A small tidepool with sculpins, mussels, red hermit crabs, and anemones like palm trees. Plucking a mussel from a neighboring rock, laying it open with my knife, and dropping it in.

First the sculpins, snatching and rotating their bodies like miniature crocodiles, tearing the flesh away. Then hermit crabs underneath; one of them climbing out of its shell to get a small piece. Then the anemones leaning forward, searching for floating particles, breathing the smoke.

Dropping another mussel, and another. The tide lapping at my boots. Kjell tilting his head, listening.

He's coming, Kjell says.

I stand and face him, obedient.

I'm going to go back there, okay?

I follow his finger to the apartment, the dense screen of roots.

You wave him in here, pretend you want to show him something.

Okay.

Pulling a canvas package from his pack. Unwrapping the pistol. Heavy and black. Carved wooden handle.

This used to be his father's, Kjell said. Used it in the war.

Dark metal. The trigger, curved and delicate.

This is the way things have to be, Samuel.

Watching him spring up the rocks toward the apartment, barnacles sizzling in his wake. Me walking closer to the water-line, to a large, flat-sided boulder. Leaning against it like a chair. Waiting.

Closing my eyes and concentrating on the sound of the tide, water rising through rock. Filling in blank places. Pressing everything out but itself.

Then. Opening my eyes to see the *Leira* roar into view. Climbing to my feet, waving.

Spero standing in the boat at full bore. Upright, leg propped on gas can, knees bent as he cuts the turn, working the tiller gently, tilting the outdrive, coasting into shore on its wake. Looking like Kjell.

Ahoy, lad.

His voice cheery, loud. The skiff grinding ashore. Spero stepping to the bow, eyes quick.

What's the matter? Cat got your tongue?

My mouth moving, but no words. Him leaning out, looking at my bucket. Pushing his hat back on his head.

Did you gather these here?

Nod.

A slow, rueful smile.

This is where we used to dump our garbage. The tide washes most of it out, but the heavier things sink – the shells and the –

Go.

My hand grabbing his arm. The words coming quickly.

Go. Right now. Kjell's going to do something.

Spero not seeming to hear. Me pushing him toward the boat. Frantic now.

But Spero won't. Pushes me aside, eyes roving the beach. His massive head up, daring him. His voice echoing.

Come on, boy. What are you waiting for?

Don't. Don't tempt –

But Spero still standing, shrugging me off. Arms spread. Turning to me, smiling.

You see? He can't –

A sharp crack, Spero jostled sideways. Regaining his balance, patting his hand on his coat pocket, pulling out a finger coated in bright red. A child with a fingerful of batter.

Another, catching Spero on the shoulder, spinning him to the deck. Then another, trailing out in the water.

A seagull darting off. A crab edging beneath kelp. Sculpins scatter. Spero ducking, pressing his body into the bow, pulling back, and pushing forward again. Me turning away, toward the apartment.

Stop.

The fourth shot splintering *Leira*'s rail. Looking up to the roots, seeing Kjell pull the pistol from its resting place and set it in a higher place for a better angle.

Stop. Kjell, stop it.

More bullets, hitting with soft, wet sounds. Spero making a breathy *ah* sound, pausing for a moment, then resuming his curious rocking, as if he could somehow burrow through the hull of the skiff into the safe gravel below. His shoulder ramming, the boat moving, and I see his purpose: Spero is trying to free the boat, to loose it into the rising tide. His voice thick and whispery.

Push me off.

Kjell reloading. The click and spin of the cylinder.

Push me off, Samuel. Don't let him do this.

I close my eyes. I tried to warn him. Too late now. Too late.

Spero rams again. The stern moves. Afloat, but hung up on some unseen rock.

Goddammit, Spero says, standing upright. Bullets coming quickly, tearing his coat, hitting him in the arm, the shoulder, the hip. His big body tipping, falling out of the boat, scrabbling in the wet gravel. Rousing himself to hands and knees, facing me. His hat flopping behind his head, ivory bead against his throat.

More soft, wet sounds, but he doesn't seem to feel them anymore. Crawling on his belly toward the boat, then changing his mind. Moving toward me, extending his hand. An oval stain under his arm. His eyes are open, his mouth full of blood.

Then Kjell's footsteps coming down the beach. Coming fast. His eyes on me.

I couldn't.

His hand on my shoulder, squeezing hard.

You couldn't.

Stop.

You couldn't.

You're hurting me.

Him letting go, pushing me to the ground. Unrolling the tarp. Dragging his father onto it. Me staring at Spero. His ankles crossed in a casual, floppy way.

Kjell rolling him up like a carpet, grabbing the tarp, hauling it toward the boat. Lifting, but it's too heavy. Trying again, no use. Turning to me.

172

Who you going to help now, Chicago?

I take the feet and Kjell grabs the head. Lifting him into the air, swaying between us like a hammock. Kjell lifting the head on the gunwale, and me feeling a hot stream of blood on my leg. Letting go of the tarp, and it unrolls like a window shade, Spero hitting the ground with one arm out and the other folded against himself.

I step back. Expecting Spero to stand up with that disappointed blue gaze – *how careless*. But he doesn't stand up. He stays the way he is, neck bent, arm splayed out, eyes opened into the gravel.

Kjell working alone now. Me shaking, useless, trying to clean my pants. Kjell rolling him again, hoisting him into the boat. Wrapping the tarp with the rope. Seven times, over and over. Finishing with constrictor knots, half hitches. A package, nothing more. Watching Kjell gather some large rocks in the buckets. Then both of us into the skiff, pushing off.

Sitting in the bow, careful not to let the tarp touch me. If the tarp doesn't touch me, then it's not real. Kjell pulling the starter cord and me staring ahead, finding relief in the movement.

Kjell pointing us into the lagoon, toward the cabin. Me surprised, thinking he'd go to the ocean. But I say nothing. Focusing on the sound of wind, the shapes and colors. Here is a seagull. Here is an otter, eating an urchin. Here is our wake, a V on green water. Here is the blue sky. Here is the smooth coolness of rock.

Now Kjell stopping the boat, lifting rocks into the buckets, tying the bucket handles to the tarp line. Then looking at me.

Inching the body over the rail. Head, then shoulders, then

173

legs. A slight shove, the tarp bellying out like a sail, a red curtain of bubbles. Falling until the color of the tarp blends with the color of the water, and then disappearing. Winking out, just like that.

Kjell and I in the boat, alone. Tying it in the alders, hidden. Walking the beach back to the boathouse, moving quietly. Washing our hands, changing our clothes. When it's done we're standing on the boardwalk. Watching the birds dive for herring.

So. What am I to do with you?

I say nothing. His voice gentle.

Everything set up. Everything perfect. And you fuck it up.

Kjell, I –

After what I've done for you, Samuel. What I've done for you.

It wasn't right.

You have no right to say that. You have no idea.

Him moving toward me, grabbing my arm and twisting it hard. Then stopping. Hearing something, footsteps. Turning to see Oshie walking down the boardwalk, berry pails in hand, waving. Releasing my arm to wave at her. Her voice clear in the cool air.

Hi there.

Closer now. Her cheeks flushed, eyes bright. A twig dangling on her shirt.

So where's Dad?

Kjell shrugging, pointing to me.

Samuel saw him last.

Both of them looking at me. Their eyes, so similar.

He went collecting, I say finally. To Egg Rock.

Oshie's face puzzled, demanding more.

He said he'd be back in a day or so. Not to worry.

Oshie frowns exaggeratedly. But he'll miss your party.

I don't mind. It'll be more fun without him.

Kjell's voice soft in my ear.

Happy birthday, Samuel.

15

When Sara walked in, Josephine picked up the telephone and aimed it like a gun.

"Did you do it?"

"Yes."

"Did you leave a message?"

"Two yesterday, one this morning."

"It's dinnertime," Josephine said. "Leave another."

"Maybe they're already on a plane. Maybe they'll walk through that door any second."

Josephine watched sternly as Sara dialed the Gapps' Chicago number. They'd gone through this ritual for three days now. But each time Sara called, she got the machine. The post office told her that the letter had been signed for by Yvonne Gapp. Sara let it ring, then heard a click and a now-familiar deep voice – William, she guessed – pronounce the recorded greeting. *Hello, you've reached the Gapp home* . . .

"Maybe they're on vacation," Sara said. "Maybe somebody else signed her name."

"Doesn't make sense," Josephine said. "Somebody's got to be around."

"My name is Sara Black," she told the anwering machine. "I have news about your son Samuel."

She felt a momentary urge to blurt out everything. She wanted to tell them that terrible things had happened, but their son had at least tried to do the right thing in the end. Hadn't he? She tried to imagine how she'd tell the story. She'd have to clean it up, simplify everything, wait for Samuel to tell her more. But for now, that's what she'd say – that Samuel had tried to do the right thing. That would be enough.

"Please call me at your earliest convenience."

"Good," Josephine said. "Now that you did the trick, you get a treat."

Sara looked on, noticing for the first time the stopwatch around Josephine's neck.

"But first things come first," Josephine said, pulling up a chair for Sara. "It wouldn't be a show without refreshments."

Josephine produced two airline bottles of whiskey from her purse and poured them into paper cups. Then she stood by the tall man's bed and pulled back the scrim. Her face was theatrical, full of tricks.

"Your attention, please," she said, and pushed a button. The bed emitted a hum, and the tall man tilted into view. Josephine had cut his hair and shaved him and dressed him in dark brown pants and a nice new blue shirt with a collar on it. He had new sneakers – Josephine's high-tops, Sara couldn't help but notice. He looked almost handsome, in a sloppy, artistic sort of way that put Sara in mind of a young English professor at an eastern college. She held her hand to her mouth, and Josephine kept pushing the button, a smile on her face. She'd inserted the stopper in his trach and buckled the restraints on his arms and legs, so she could tilt him until he was nearly vertical.

"Hello, Sara."

Sara stared at the tall man, her vision suddenly blurred by tears.

"Hello, Samuel," she managed.

Josephine paid no attention, unbuckled the restraints on his arms and legs. The tall man's feet slid to the floor, and he balanced there for a moment as Sara held her breath. Josephine extended her hands in the manner of a gentleman asking a lady to dance. He blinked, stared.

"Stand up," Josephine shouted, and jerked him to his feet.

The tall man wobbled for a moment. Sara flinched, picturing his wasted leg muscles, his soft feet. Then, in response to Josephine's firm pull, he took a single shuffling step. He recovered his balance quickly, Sara noticed.

"Good boy, Sam," Josephine said. "Again."

Supported by the massive bulwarks of Josephine's forearms, the tall man took another step. His breath rasped. His foot moved in slow motion, sliding along the linoleum. Sara watched, terrified that he would fall, her fright ebbing as she counted his steps: five, six, seven . . .

"Your turn," Josephine commanded.

Sara began to protest, but too late. In one quick move, Josephine transferred the tall man's hands to Sara's forearms; she felt his tenacious grip, the surprising weight of his body. She looked at his face, which was above hers for the first time. The tall man paused for a moment, then he moved his right leg forward. She lightly drew back her left, feeling the rods and pins stir inside her knee, and slowly they began to move together across the black-and-white checks, forearms clasped. Sara felt light-headed and had to concentrate to keep her balance. She felt the tall man's body moving with hers, step by step.

Josephine checked her stopwatch. "We've been making it to

the desk and back inside three minutes," she said. "He's a little faster every day."

Slowly, Sara led him around the room and lowered him gently to his bed. The tall man sat there sweating, gasping, his eyes radiating their shared pleasure.

Josephine sat down and handed Sara a cup of whiskey. They toasted, and Josephine threw hers back.

"When did this start?"

"Two weeks, maybe," Josephine said, wiping her mouth. "You do go home sometimes, you know. Sammy here doesn't like to sleep much, so I figured I'd tire him out."

"What about the infection?"

"It's in his brain, not his legs. It put us back for a while, but he's stronger than you'd think. A fast learner."

Sara wiped her eyes. "Josephine, you are amaz – "

"Tips only, please," Josephine said.

Josephine undressed Samuel. She was rougher than Sara would have been, unbuttoning and brusquely pulling the clothes away from him, letting the sleeves go inside out. The illusion vanished; the tall man was suddenly and reassuringly naked, himself again.

Sara helped pull on his gown, tying it gently in the back. She moved to wet a washcloth, and that was when the telephone rang.

"What's that?" Sara said, as if she'd never heard the sound in her life.

Josephine answered. A curious look came over her face.

"Hold your horse," she said, mildly irritated. "She's right here."

Sara picked up the phone, and her stomach jumped as she recognized the oiled baritone of William Gapp.

"Is this Sara Black, then?"

His voice was deep and modulated and possessed a lilting midwestern assurance. *Walter Cronkite,* she thought.

"I would like to let you know that my wife and I don't appreciate your sense of humor, if that's what you call it."

"What do you – "

"What I mean is that if this is your idea of a sick joke, then you can kindly leave our family out of it. We've been through enough without this kind of cruelty."

"Mr. Gapp, I'm sorry, but I don't understand what you – "

"Samuel is dead. He drowned nearly two years ago, on an island off Alaska."

"No," Sara said. Her voice was level, and hearing it, she felt a small burst of pride. She was unflappable, a worthy match for Mr. Gapp. "No, that's not true. As it turned out, he didn't drown. He was found, off Cape Flattery. It can all be explained."

"I don't know who you are or what you're trying to do," Mr. Gapp said. "But when I say my son is dead, that is precisely what I mean." His voice cracked slightly. Sara could hear a thin voice in the background – Yvonne, no doubt – urging him on: "Tell her. Tell her," the voice chirped.

"That's not possible," Sara said. Her hand went to her knee, pressing the pins. "He can't speak much yet, but he has told us his name and an account of what happened to him. I am looking at him now."

"Miss Black, I find it strange that you are telling me what is possible and what is impossible."

"Tell her, tell her," the tiny voice urged.

Mr. Gapp took a deep breath. "When Samuel's body was found there had been some . . . ahhh . . . decomposure. Naturally we were hopeful that it wasn't our son, and so we pursued every possible avenue. We checked dental records, X-

180

rays, hair samples, everything. Everything matched one hundred percent."

Sara felt her insides make a bewildering lurch. "Perhaps there was some mistake, a mix-up. Perhaps there was another boy, someone the same size, with the same color hair."

Mr. Gapp's voice went low and resumed its irrefutable Cronkitian rhythm. "One hundred percent, Ms. Black. Dental records are not mistakes. X-rays are not mistakes. DNA samples are not mistakes."

"How can you be – "

"My son died two years ago. If you don't believe me, I invite you to check with the Records Department of Northwestern Hospital."

"It can't – "

Now Yvonne grabbed the phone and shouted, "You've caused enough suffering as it is!"

"I'm sorry," Sara said in a barely audible voice, then realized that they had hung up. She set the receiver carefully back on the hook. She looked away from the tall man, toward the window, into the void of air. A white shape flew past, and she couldn't see it, couldn't concentrate her vision.

"Here," Josephine said.

Sara took the paper cup and drank the whiskey without noticing the taste.

She turned toward the tall man, and she saw his body as if for the first time: the large pale eyes, the lean muscles, the strong square hands. The sinews of his forearms rose beneath his skin, the taut skin of his face shone like a mask.

She looked into his eyes and felt a prickling sensation around the top of her head. She moved behind the tall man in one long transfixed motion and placed her head next to his, close enough to feel the heat of his skin. She extended her hand and grasped the fringed edge of the thin white blanket. She slowly pulled it down to reveal his legs, so that she could see the long pink scar not from an observer's angle, but rather as the tall man himself would see it. A perfect and graceful seven.

Sara stood up and pushed herself away from the bed, staggering a little. She picked up her coat and moved toward the door, not hearing Josephine's shouted question, not feeling the tile beneath her feet. She pushed open the red door and began walking quickly down the fluorescent-lit hallways, dodging stretchers, feeling only the air on her face. Several figures said hello, but she could neither see them nor answer.

She got into the elevator and headed down, eyes closed. Heard the tinkling music. Felt shadows breathing. She waited until everyone else got off, until the elevator reached the lowest level of the parking garage. She stepped off onto a small balcony favored by smokers. There was a small bench, an ashtray, and a pay phone. A hideaway, a place of concrete and cinders. Shafts of granular light.

She stood with her palms against the wall, pressing her forehead into the corner. Inhaling the sharpness of tobacco and concrete. Feeling the top layer of waxy blue paint. She pressed harder, needing the pain, feeling the pinpricks of the rocks that lay beneath.

She dropped to the floor and put her head in her hands. The tears were a relief, falling hot and fast on the concrete. But beneath them lay the shame for her own blindness. The pain she had caused because she hadn't seen the truth that was there all along. Reaching for her. A fast learner indeed.

Hello Sara.

Sara beat the floor with her fists. She hated the tall man, hated his body, hated his brain that had tricked them both. She held herself and shook with silent fury and despair. How did she not know? How could this have happened?

Sara wiped her eyes, tried to gather her thoughts. *Think*, she told herself. But thoughts wouldn't come. All she could see were those saintly eyes, all she could hear was that voice.

His eyes on me all the time.

Sara heard a shuddery moan, which she belatedly recognized as the elevator. Moving toward her. She scrambled to her feet, preparing herself for the sight of Josephine or Nurse Larch or, improbably, the tall man. But when the doors clattered open, the elevator was empty.

16

On a still, cloudless August morning when she was seven and a half years old, Sara ran away from home. She'd prepared the night before, carefully loading a canvas knapsack with a sweater, a hat, a pair of shorts, a pair of underwear, tennis shoes, a peanut-butter sandwich, an almost full package of Oreos, and her father's leather wallet with six wrinkled $20 bills. It seemed like a lot of luggage to Sara at the time, but then she'd long witnessed her mother packing for journeys and knew that a good traveler should never be caught without what Vera grandly called "the minimal accoutrements." So that morning, her mother asleep and her father working the fields, she hefted the bulging package on her skinny shoulders, leaned forward mulishly, and began to walk toward town.

She was running away because of a bike. Sara had been looking at it in the Sears window in town for a month now. It was a chrome-plated dream: upswept handlebars with pink tassels, whitewall tires, a wicker basket, and a paint job exactly the same blue as her mother's Lincoln Continental. On their weekly shopping trips, Sara stood fixed in front of the window, memorizing its shape, feeling rough electricity moving within her spine. The bike was meant for her. After all, her birthday was coming up. Besides, she could ride two-wheeled – was practically expert at it. But when she asked if maybe, just maybe, they could take a closer look, her mother had smiled and purred no; her father had stoically agreed. It was a big-kids' bike, they said. Maybe when she was ten. That wouldn't be so long, would it?

In a crystalline burst of defiance, Sara had decided to prove them wrong. That night, under cover of darkness, she had extracted her father's wallet from the satiny inner pocket of his leather jacket. She unfolded the wallet and inhaled its carnal aroma, felt the mysterious authority of the grown-up world. She closed her eyes and traced her fingertip along the braille of its stitching, feeling her plan take shape. She would walk the five miles to town, purchase the bike, and ride it somewhere far away. She would take a big trip, like Mommy did. Too little? She would show them.

The day grew hot, and after what seemed like hours of walking Sara grew weary and felt compelled to lighten her load. First came the sweater, folded neatly on a flat rock. Then the shorts, hung by their waistband on the branches of a scrubby tree. A pile of Oreos, stacked next to a culvert. She kept trudging through the wavering heat and the locust-spun air, leaving a breadcrumb trail of belongings. Thirsty and miserable, she walked on until she could not bear the hot weight of the knapsack and heaved it, wallet and all, into the bushes.

When she heard her father's old car rumble alongside, Sara would not look at it. She kept walking, feeling its hot mechanical breath next to her, focusing on the tightrope of her determination. She lasted a few minutes, then tripped on a pebble and collapsed in tears, struck down by the immensity of her folly. She lay on the gravel, weeping for her weariness, for her foolishness, for the tongue-lashing her mother had in store, for the punishment that would follow. This was worse than disaster, worse than anything she'd ever known.

Her father lifted Sara gently in the car, wiped her eyes, snugged the seat belt around her. He had to know about the wallet – he was wearing the jacket he kept it in – but to Sara's surprise he did not scold her. In fact, he didn't say anything at all, except for "Hello there, girl."

He turned the car around and they drove slowly home, stopping to pick up the supplies she had abandoned on the road. Her father seemed to view the undertaking as a sport, taking faint but perceptible pleasure in the spotting and retrieval of each item. It was only later that Sara under- stood the gift her father was giving her. He withheld all judgment, as if he were a kindly police officer. Later, at home, he would gradually transform back into her father, but for the duration of this ride, he behaved like a courteous stranger.

The night she told Tom about the tall man, Sara saw the same expression in Tom's face. She saw it when he came to pick her up in the hospital garage, when he helped her into the car, when he handed her a tissue, when he helped her take a seat at their kitchen table. It was the same Officer Friendly treatment, a cool, dispassionate gaze.

Sara told Tom everything. The story spooled out of her with uncontrollable, almost violent force, and he sat with his palms on the table, listening. He learned forward sympathetically when she explained why she kept the tall man's ability to speak a secret from the hospital. He focused intently as she told the story of Kjell and the island. He closed his eyes when she told of telling stories about Luke. But through it all he kept his face cemented in the calm mask, listening and waiting. *Hello there, girl.*

As Tom grew calmer, Sara became more disquieted. She spoke on, overexplaining everything, her words arriving on dizzying waves of guilt and fear. She apologized for not telling him sooner, choking on the inadequacy of the word, and he looked away. Sara wanted to reach for him but didn't dare. Tom seemed to have pulled back into a remote middle distance. His eyes blinked, cameralike. Then he leaned forward.

"So who does this patient think he is right now?"

"I don't know."

"What does your gut tell you?"

"I don't know," she said finally. "It's like there's no person left, just the story."

"Have the Gapps put it together yet?"

"Put what together?"

"That your patient probably killed their son."

"But we don't know that," Sara started. "Samuel – "

"His name is Kjell," Tom said softly. "He's been Kjell all along, hidden in there. It's almost admirable, in a Darwinian sort of way – he had a problem, and he solved it by adapting. But the fact is, he probably had something to do with the Gapp boy's death. And the parents will want to see him. Talk to him, at the very least."

Tom kept talking, outlining a plan. First, Sara should not go to see the tall man anymore – it was unnecessary and potentially dangerous. Second, she should try to get the police report from Chicago, look into neurologists, inform Josephine. His reassuring voice warmed up, began to hum and resound. The cogs were spinning.

Sara nodded. It was a relief to feel Tom's mind working on the problem, sensing its precise dimensions, drilling inexorably toward some conclusion. He picked up the phone receiver and placed it on the table between them.

"Do you want to tell the hospital now? Or do you want to call the Gapps back, tell them the whole story?"

187

Tom saw her hesitate. He tapped the table with his finger-nails, spoke with excruciating slowness.

"What do you want to do, Sara?"

Sara looked down at her hands, still feeling the pressure of the tall man's grip. She flexed them.

"I can't do that."

"You've taken him a great distance," Tom said, the faintest edge rising into his voice. "But now it's time to let go."

Sara closed her eyes. She pictured the tall man's face as he walked across the floor. Saw his eyes.

A stretch of unassailably blue weather blew in the following week, and it seemed to Sara as if time had stopped. She called in sick, telling Larch that she'd reinjured her knee. She embarked on long driving trips, soothed by the scroll of cloudless sky. She inflated tiny errands into half-day expeditions; she sat for hours on street benches, watching for patterns in the whirl of dry leaves. She took long walks after dark, saw glowing tableaux framed by her neighbors' windows: older couples doing dishes, kids bathed in TV's deep-sea light, Mrs. Wooding standing at the hall mirror in her turquoise velour sweatsuit, touching a careful palm to her hair. It all looked alien, impossible.

Sara and Tom shared meals, kissed hello and good-bye. Tom maintained his distant demeanor, but Sara could feel the steady pressure of his will. He said little, but his message was clear: Contact the Gapps and tell them what she could about their son. Tell the hospital and let the experts take over. He said it a thousand times, a thousand ways. *Let go*, his irresistible voice whispered, and in those moments Sara felt herself beginning to sway.

Yet she could not submit the tall man to the psych ward,

to that white-coated battalion of Toms, digging, prodding, dissolving whatever core still existed. *Why do you trust him?* Tom pressed. *Is it his voice? His eyes? His face? Tell me what you have faith in,* he said, and in desperation Sara would cling to the narrow thread of medical argument: *He is delusional; his circuits are scrambled.* Even so, Sara could not bring herself to face the tall man. She stayed home for four days, preferring to receive updates from Josephine, who continued to roll forward under the belief that nothing had fundamentally changed. Josephine telephoned each morning, and Tom watched Sara's face as she took in the news. His fever had returned, she said; his blood pressure was rising. The doctors were tinkering with his medication. When was Sara coming back?

"This can't go on forever," Tom said as he prepared to go to work on the fifth morning. "You have to test him. At least call him Kjell and see how he responds."

Sara kept buttering her toast, her hand machinelike.

"You have to try something," Tom said, and Sara heard his voice crack. She sensed his struggle to keep self-control, the strain in his dark eyes.

"I know," she said. "But I want it to be the right thing."

"He's fooling you," Tom said darkly. "Just like he fooled Samuel."

Sara slapped the knife on the counter. "He has a bullet in his brain. *In his brain,* Tom. Do you honestly think he thinks he can get away with this? If he was so clever, he'd have thought of that, wouldn't he?"

"That's for the doctors to — "

"No, it's for us to say." Sara noticed she was shouting now. "Because if we don't, then he'll go to the doctors and we'll have missed our chance."

"What chance?"

"To do something good." Sara struggled to find words. "To bring someone back into the world who was outside of it."

Tom stepped back. Squinted at Sara.

"You haven't been there," she said. "You don't know how it feels to reach down into the dark and feel someone reaching back toward you. To feel a person come to life, no matter what that life is. He did awful things — I know. But there's another part of him, and that's what I'm reaching for."

Tom stood, his coat half on. He poked his big hand through the sleeve, fixed it with a clinical gaze.

"This won't make things better, Sara. It won't cure anything."

"I need to do this, Tom."

"I can't do this with you, hon. I can't get there."

"I'm not asking you to."

They stood in front of the door, the sunlight beyond. Tom took his briefcase from her hand, turned, and walked away.

For the first few weeks after Luke died, Sara occupied herself by playing logic games: He could have survived this crash only to die of leukemia or cancer, or he could have been hit by a drunk driver. She and Tom kept busy, each possessed by frenetic energy. Sara worked on the funeral and on recovering from her injuries; Tom worked on the house, dealt with insurance companies, made lists, wrote thank-you notes. When she came home from her final surgery, the two stood on the threshold of the house for a long time, listening and watching, feeling the changes that silence brings. Then they simply stepped in, a hollow *thunk* of her cast on the entry tile. *See?* she'd said. *It isn't that hard.*

Sara spent the greater part of one sunny afternoon deciding what to call the event. "Crash" seemed wrong. "Rollover" was vaguely litigious. "Wreck" seemed close – *My son died in a car wreck* – but the words made it sound as if Luke were older, a teen struck down on prom night. Sara finally settled on "accident." She even looked it up in the dictionary and was satisfied to find that it came from the Latin root *cadere*, which means "to fall." Luke fell, that's what happened. We both fell. She looked in a mirror, squaring her shoulders and peering at the hollow-eyed woman within. Our accident, the accident, this accident my son had. *My son died in a car accident*, the woman in the mirror said. *He was four.* She tried it again, and by the end of the third day she was almost able to do it without crying. They were words, she told herself. Just words, nothing more.

At first, friends marveled at their resilience. The hospital psychiatrist, however, was less impressed. He swamped them with a rising tide of pamphlets, books, tapes, and videos. Sara, with Tom's backing, turned it all down. They were fine, couldn't they see that? Oh, there were times that seemed more difficult – how could there not be? But they would keep moving. They would move past it, together. The psychiatrist sucked on his pen and warned them that this stage would pass, that they would have difficult days ahead, that they needed to slow down. *Talk to me*, he said. *Tell me what you're feeling.* Finally, more to pacify him than anything else, they agreed to attend a group meeting at a local junior high school. But at the last minute Tom was called in by a client, so he dropped her off. Sara limped into a room whose walls were decorated with a merrily colored mural of circus performers – trapeze artists, lion tamers, tightrope walkers. *Perfect*, she thought darkly. *Let the show begin!*

There were six parents – or ex-parents, as someone jokily put it – and a group leader. Everyone smiled, pronounced their names with unusual clarity, as if she spoke a foreign language. Then, in a practiced, almost pleasant fashion they proceeded to relate the stories of their children's deaths. Tumors. Guns. Bike accident. Some of the parents cried; most were stoic and even mildly funny. They were hoary veterans of the circuit, smoothly relating pool drownings and bathtub electrocutions as if they were parables, all the same parable, the moral residing not in the fact of the death, but in the parent's powerlessness, in the crummy, unerring happenstances of fate that united them. Unloaded guns that fired real bullets. Stop signs overgrown by hedges. A stray microbe, an arbitrary twist of DNA. The lethal, unthinking mass of the physical world turning, for a moment, against them. *If only I'd been there*, went the unspoken refrain. *Everything would be different.*

Then it was Sara's turn. She experienced a brief impulse to tell them that her son died of AIDS or leukemia, something tidier. But she didn't. She told the truth. When she was done with her story, the room was completely silent. A stiff-haired woman in a pink Minnie Mouse sweater – her son had died of pancreatic cancer – turned to her. She wore a button with a picture of her son, plucky, bald, wearing a too-big baseball cap.

"So you were there, in the car?" Sara noticed that she didn't have the courage to say "driving the car."

"The roof caved in," Sara said automatically. "I couldn't reach him."

"Ohh." Heads bobbed in infinite understanding. "Of course you couldn't," someone said.

"He knew how to unbuckle himself," she said. "I taught him."

Sara looked up and felt other eyes on her. In their own children's deaths, they were all onlookers, helpless witnesses, but Sara was different. Sara hadn't merely seen it, she had been there; she had played a role. She had had a chance to save him, and she had blown it. *He knew how to unbuckle himself?* She sensed the horror and thrill beneath their smiles. They knew it was her fault, they smelled it on her. Minnie Mouse reached out a puffy hand and touched Sara's damaged knee.

"It must be so hard for you."

"Really, it's a piece of cake," Sara said, and was instantly sorry.

The group murmured.

"I was joking," Sara said.

"Yes," the group leader spoke. He was a tiny, rotund man given to dramatic pronouncement. He reminded Sara of a human cannonball. "Humor can be an effective tool."

The group nodded earnestly. Sara looked at him, openly puzzled.

"What I mean," the cannonball said, spreading his arms to cultivate an appearance of general agreement, "is that we need tools to forgive ourselves before we can move forward with our lives. We need forgiveness. Unconditional love. That's the only truth."

"Forgiveness," Minnie Mouse shouted, slapping a meaty hand over her button. "That's what got me through Jeremy's death. I know it's hard, Sara, but you've got to realize that whatever happened, it wasn't your fault."

"Jesus forgives you," someone whispered.

"We forgive you."

Sara looked around and felt an uncomfortable lurch. She didn't like the way these people looked at her, their hungry smiles, their eagerness to absolve her. They were like everyone else, rushing to forgive her, crowding around her, smothering her in their soft embraces, crushing out all memory of what had come before.

"I don't want to be forgiven," she said quietly, and the group turned to look at her in surprise.

"But you're in so much pain," Minnie said. "I can feel it."

"What if that pain is good?"

"No pain is good," the leader whispered uncomfortably. "You may feel as if you deserve it, but pain for its own sake does no good."

"I'm not saying that I desire it. I'm just saying it is real, okay? I'm just saying that if I lose the pain, I'm afraid . . ." She struggled for words. "That I'll forget. That I'll lose him again. And I can't do that."

The rotund man smiled relievedly, spying a comfort zone in the distance. "Yet wouldn't it be better to get past the pain, so that other things may touch you again? So that you may reconnect with your husband, move on together?"

Move on. Forgive and move on, reconcile and move on, bury and sing and commemorate and move on. Something in those words, in the certainty of the round man's utterance, made Sara crack. She turned away from the round man and addressed the group.

"Can you still remember?"

They looked at her, but Sara hardly noticed. The words spilled out. "Can you still remember the way they held their fork, or the way they ran down the stairs, or the way they blew out their birthday candles? Can you close your eyes and see that exactly as it happened? Can you feel it?"

"I remember everything," Minnie said confidently. "Every single thing."

"Of course you do," the round man said. "How could we ever forget?"

A long silence ensued. People shifted in their chairs.

"My son used to run," said a skinny man finally. "He had this funny way of running, kind of like a bird – back and forth, real quicklike, as if he was looking for something. For years I would close my eyes and it would be there. But then one morning last year I woke up and I couldn't find it. It was gone."

"I forget things, too," said another voice.

"Yes," Sara said. "That's what I'm talking about."

Sara was speaking too loudly now. But she could not stop. She sensed a path in front of her, a road that she could take alone.

"I want the pain because I want the memories," she said. "I don't want you or anybody else taking it away."

When the session was over, Tom had picked her up outside the school. His kiss was tangy with Scotch and cigars. He regarded her across the front seat.

"So how'd it go in there?"

"Fine," Sara said quickly. "How was your night?"

"It was a doozy," he said. His big fingers rapped the steering wheel, working out some hidden tune. "You would not believe the way some of these Japanese guys can drink. I'm trying to figure out how big an order they want, and all they can do is keep toasting me, and the cow, and the soil that made the grass, and the grass that made the cow. Then they start with the singing, and I'm trying to talk numbers with them, and they keep singing the numbers back to me, like it's part of the song. I swear to God, I was lucky to get out of there with my shirt."

"Did they sign?"

"I think so," he said, patting his pocket. "Either that or we now own swampland near Osaka."

Sara smiled. She liked seeing him like this, so much a part of the world. So full of smoke and talk, the lingering thrill of the game. Thirteen months after the accident, and he was reentering the world, letting it wash over him.

Tom sensed it, too.

"It was funny," he said. "From the time we got to the restaurant until I got back in the truck, I didn't think about him. Almost three hours."

He checked her, continued.

"I felt sort of guilty at first. As if I'd abandoned him somehow. But then I realized – this is how he would want it. He'd want us to let go – like you used to always tell me, you know, as a parent. To let him go, let him go. Well, I let him go for three hours, and it felt pretty good."

"I'm glad," Sara said.

They drove on, speeding up as they turned onto the four-lane road that led to their neighborhood. The streetlights slipped past.

"So," Tom said. "What did the group talk about?"

Sara hesitated. "Not much. Everyone told stories about their kids."

"Stories, huh?"

"Yes."

Tom braked for a stoplight, glanced over. "Well . . ."

"Well what?"

"Well, what stories did you tell?"

Sara said nothing, gazed studiously into the lights.

Tom looked over, curious. She saw his reflection in the window, curved and glowing, a friendly inhabitant of another

196

planet. She felt a warm pulse of love for him, and as she opened her mouth to tell him what had happened, she felt something clench. It was a small thing, the spasm of a mother's protective instinct – *Don't tell*. Yet it contained everything.

How could she tell him? He was already climbing out, reentering the world. How could she pull him back down?

Their truck boomed through the darkened suburban landscape, past minimalls and across bridges, moving toward their empty house. In the gloom, the spruce looked jungly and prehistoric. They drove along a ditch and she could see a thread of water in its center. For an unbearable second, Sara was tempted to grab the steering wheel and wrench it to the side. Her heart beat fast as she pictured what the truck would look like descending the embankment, its tires etching deep lines in the wet earth, its headlight beams splintering as they hit the water. She pictured the look on Tom's face.

"They never got to me," she said after a moment. "We ran out of time."

17

Sara didn't see the Gapps at first. They were standing next to the scrim, watching her from the shadows. When they stepped out, resplendent in their overcoats, their palms raised peaceably, Sara stared in disbelief. Then she heard the approaching whisper of sandals, and she knew.

"Oh, good," Nurse Larch said when she opened the door. "I see you've already met."

Sara closed her eyes. That morning, Larch had called her in with a special request to work a noon ER shift, claiming that she was out of nurses. Feeling guilty and eager to get out of the house, Sara had agreed, and Larch had dispatched her to this surgery prep room. To check on a patient, she'd said. Now Sara looked more closely behind the scrim, saw the familiar outline of the tall man. Her heart plummeted.

Yvonne stepped forward, releasing a cinnamony burst of perfume. "So good to meet you," she said, fixing Sara with her avid brown gaze. "We want to apologize for the confusion on the telephone – I'm sure you understand." William nodded stiffly, his hair like brushed steel.

Sara said nothing. Nurse Larch circled around and stood between the Gapps and Sara. She spread her arms in her best beseeching style, her soft blue eyes radiating waves of empathy and understanding.

"As you can see, we have a bit of a mystery," Nurse Larch said, nodding toward the bed. "Mr. and Mrs. Gapp are interested in finding out what happened to their son Samuel. They seem to think that this gentleman might be able to help them do that. Do you think so?"

"That's tough to say," Sara said steadily.

"I'm sure there's an answer here that makes sense, but it appears that perhaps you haven't been, shall we say, forthcoming." Nurse Larch smiled sympathetically. "I'm sure you have your reasons, and I'm also sure that those reasons are valid, but at the same time, you need to know that you've put the hospital in a, well, kind of a sticky spot."

"We're prepared to do whatever it takes," William announced, his Cronkite voice echoing off the tiles.

Nurse Larch beamed him a pacifying smile. "I think we need to start off by acknowledging that we're all interested in the same thing," she said. "We have a common problem, and I think if we operate from that place, we can work together to find a common solution. Can't we, Sara?"

"This is wrong," Sara said, finding her voice. "You can't barge in here and take him."

"Right and wrong are tricky words, don't you think, Sara?" Nurse Larch said. "I know you want the best for him. And so do we."

Sara pulled back, unsure. She wished Josephine were here. Or Tom. She wished she could pull back the scrim and see his face. He was sleeping, she could tell, breathing steadily. She felt Nurse Larch's stony hand on the small of her back.

"It's not just their child, either," Nurse Larch said. "There's the matter of the other victim's family."

"What?"

"Didn't you know?"

"No."

Nurse Larch shifted her innocent gaze to Mr. Gapp. "You didn't tell her?"

"Didn't tell me *what*?"

Mr. Gapp cleared his throat. "When Samuel was found, there was another body with his. A Jane Doe, no more than fifteen or sixteen years old, the pathologist estimated. They were wrapped up; the lines were tangled around both of them and tied to some kind of heavy piece of steel, a dredge of some sort."

Sara felt the floor shift beneath her. She placed her palm on the wall, inhaled deeply.

"Tangled around them like a kind of a cage. As if it were done with intent." He stepped back, let the words sink in.

Sara shook her head obstinately. "He would not have done that," she said. "He would not have hurt Oshie. Or your son."

Yvonne leaned in. "He told you that? Has he said as much?"

"No. But I know," Sara continued. "He had no reason – " She stopped, conscious of how impossibly vague she sounded. How could she communicate it to them? How could she say that such an ending made no sense, that it was not where the tall man's story was destined to go? But to the Gapps, such words were an insult. Their son was dead, replaced by a stranger.

"This person – " William began, and stopped. He re-arranged his shoulders in a vaguely military manner. An unexpected ripple of sympathy passed through Sara. She saw the sadness and anger wavering behind his gray eyes.

"This person is involved in my son's death," he said. "I want to know what happened. And I'm prepared to do what it takes to find out."

"The Gapps have been kind enough to offer the services of several prominent neurologists to help find an answer," Nurse Larch interjected smoothly. "Their consensus is that the chances of a good outcome would be greatly increased by the presence of someone the patient trusts. 'Facilitator' is too clinical a word. We're looking for a guide, a friend. A voice in the darkness."

"We want you to work with the neurologists," William continued. "Keep him talking. Recover the rest of his memories."

"Why?"

"To get the facts," William said. "To find out."

There was a silence. Sara's eyes went to the scrim.

"You want to prove he did it," she said softly. "You want to pin it on him."

William did not blink. "There's good reason to believe this person murdered my son," he said.

"This man is injured and delusional. He is harmless," Sara said. "How does putting him in prison help you?"

"I have a difficult time seeing how you can tell me what matters," William said. "How can we get to the truth if we don't know the facts? How can we get any justice?"

Justice. Sara saw it now, in the scrupulous, satisfied way his mouth tasted the word. This was not about their son, not at all. It was about finding reasons, about evening scores. Making up for some deeper guilt they bore, a guilt for which the tall man would now pay.

"He is weak," Sara said. "This could kill him."

"Our doctors are among the best," William said decisively.

"And whoever said anything about prison?" Yvonne said, dredging up a laugh.

"We're prepared to offer compensation," William said. "Double your salary, for the duration of the project."

"Listen to them, Sara," Larch said. "What they say makes sense."

Their mouths kept moving, until Sara could only dimly hear the sounds, until she had the distinct sense that the room was filling up with words. Their words, their desires, pouring on top of one another, swirling and rising like icy water around her chest. She tried to breathe. She glanced sideways toward the door, the sweet lighted air of the hallway beyond.

Yvonne touched her arm. "Nurse Larch told us you've suffered your own loss not so long ago," she said. "I trust that you understand. I'm sure your son meant a lot to you. But this isn't your boy. You don't have to protect him, not anymore."

"Help them, Sara," Larch whispered, her voice low and sweet as if she were singing a lullaby.

Sara did not move. "I won't," she whispered. "He's innocent."

Larch exchanged a glance with the Gapps and moved toward Sara. She smiled, gripped Sara's elbows.

"Are you sure?"

Sara nodded.

"Then I want to thank you for everything you've done here. None of this could be done without you, and that's why this is going to be so difficult."

"What?"

Nurse Larch hugged her, and that's when Sara knew she had been fired.

*   *   *

202

Josephine must have called, because Tom came without saying a word. He took her shoulders gently and they got into the car and drove out of the garage, circling upward within its gray depths. As they emerged onto the street and accelerated onto the blacktop, Sara felt something within her unclench, a feeling of sadness and relief.

It's over, she thought. *He's gone. It's all come to nothing.* Sara pressed her forehead to the glass.

"You fought for him," Tom said softly. "Remember that." Sara looked out at the road.

He was right. She hadn't given in. Sara looked out at the blur of lights, holding on to that thought as they moved together through the darkness. She had fought.

18

Mrs. Wooding was almost finished with the pansies and advancing steadily on the dahlias. She was wearing her usual attire: an avocado green velour gardening frock, blue jeans, and a battered sombrero-like hat. Kneeling, she ranged widely from side to side, snipping offending sprigs with a swordsman's flair. Sara adjusted the venetian blinds and leaned back in her chair. After the dahlias would come the pansies, then the daffodils, then the Johnny-jump-ups. Then Mrs. Wooding would switch to the other side and the whole procedure would begin anew.

Sara had been watching for six days now. She had memorized the aristocratic way Mrs. Wooding adjusted her straw hat, the fussy pluckings of staticky velour, the painterly head tilts. She'd memorized them because they were part of her own routine, located as they were just after her shower and before the telephone call that she never answered.

They put lover boy upstairs, in a big room. Nicer than we've got, like a hotel almost. Big bed, three monitors, full-time EKG, EEG, the works.

When Mrs. Wooding completed the row, she turned and waved to Sara, and Sara waved back. This was a new addition to the routine, proof of the awareness that had developed between the two women over the last week. It had started slowly – a fraternal nod when she left the house, a salutatory wave of the clippers. It was not a relationship, or even a friendship – it was simply an awareness – *you are there, I am here* – that passed through the double pane. Mrs. Wooding limped slightly on her left side, Sara noticed. Perhaps a hip replaced.

When Mrs. Wooding trundled inside, Sara took it as a signal to begin her day. She did the dishes, then the laundry, then picked a room to clean from top to bottom. She had never liked housework of any kind, but now she used it as a kind of haiku, losing herself in the verbs. Wiping, rinsing, lifting, dusting, scrubbing. After the third day she'd told Josephine to stop calling – she didn't want to hear any more. The tall man was gone now, beyond her power to help. She had done her best, she said, and now it was up to fate and doctors. But her friend didn't seem to hear, broadcasting her booming rasp over the answering machine with the crackly urgency of a covert wartime broadcast. Radio Free Josephine.

Twenty-seven electrodes now, can you believe it? Mostly on the skull, but all over, too. Sometimes he wears a hood that's all electrodes – I'm not sure what that does, but it makes him rashy.

Everybody heard about what you did. Some of the Psych staff refused to work with the Chicago doctors, and Larch almost had a rebellion on her hands. She talked her way out of it, but they're still short staffed up there.

Afternoons, Sara tried to escape the house. She drove, tracing byzantine routes into the city. She watched the Technicolor flow of Pike Street tourists; she watched the huddles of the lunchtime cabals. She found herself drawn to traffic jams, malls, crowded beaches; only in a crowd could she feel properly alone. She lost herself in traffic, rolling up and down I-5 gridlock. She flicked through the radio stations one by one, letting the voices flow into the car in the hope that they would wash away other voices.

Oh, he's talking some, but they're not having much luck. The doctors do something called confrontational therapy, where they try to convince him that he's Kjell – showing evidence, calling him by name. But he doesn't hear them. Mostly, he just sleeps.

Tom usually arrived home around five-thirty. The terrain shifted with his arrival; she felt his discerning gaze, the tension between them. Each evening he walked in the door with that careful smile and Sara prepared herself for the words that would lead to their split-up. He had done as much as drawn up the plans, hadn't he? She knew exactly how he'd start, the five slow, reasoned words with which he broached every crossroad: *I've been doing some thinking.*

Sara tried to fill the silence with talk. She talked in a bright, effortful voice, telling him about Mrs. Wooding and her flower beds, and the Olivers' new riding lawn mower with a cup holder (ole Derek had wisely given up hope of becoming a handyman). Once, halfway through a mildly amusing anecdote of an angry mailman and two brazen squirrels, Sara caught Tom looking at her strangely. Her stomach clenched.

"I already told you that one, didn't I," she said.

Tom took her hand.

"Dammit," Sara said. "It's like I can't think straight."

"It's okay," he said, a terrible look of pity in his eyes.

Sara rearranged her peas. Tom twirled his fork. He spoke the words they'd both been avoiding for six days.

"So. How's he doing?"

"Not so well."

"I'm sorry to hear that." His voice was formal. "Did they

206

find out if he . . . you know, was the one who hurt the Gapp boy?"

Sara shook her head. "He hasn't said anything about that. The infection is worse. And the doctors aren't getting anywhere."

"Are the parents still around?"

"They took a room on the square," Sara said. "They're not giving up."

Tom nodded circumspectly. "I wouldn't expect them to."

"Apparently they're with him most of the day. Helping the doctors."

Tom's brow creased. "How do you know all this? I thought he was under tight security."

"Josephine has her ways. I think she's dating someone from Psych."

Tom smiled. "Man or woman?"

"I don't think she notices anymore."

Tom laughed, and Sara felt it like an unexpected burst of sunshine. Here was her husband, laughing in that soundless, vaguely spastic way she remembered, tilting his head back, the tectonic plates of his shoulders shifting against each other as if his big body were on the verge of collapse. Sara watched him and felt borne up by a wave of fondness. She felt an urge to go to him, to fix her mouth over the O of his lips, but that was impossible, unthinkable. So she poked at her casserole, letting the secret warmth wash through her.

When she looked up, Tom was gazing at the wall behind her.

"I've been doing some thinking," he said. He set his elbows on the table and twined his fingers.

So this was it. Sara gripped her fork, braced for the inevitable.

"I want to paint the kitchen," he said. "Didn't you bring home a couple gallons of paint a long time ago? Green?"

Sara breathed. "Forest glade, I think."

The kitchen walls were pale blue. They'd never liked it, had planned on changing it, had always put it off. Glacier blue, they called it. But why now? Tom stood, placed his hands on the island, and looked around as if he were surveying the back forty.

"You know," he said, checking his watch, "we could start right now."

"Are you sure?"

Tom's knuckles rat-a-tatted on the countertop. "It won't take long. The setup is the hardest part. And if we're going to do it, we have to start sometime, don't we?"

Sara was slightly put off by the brusqueness of his manner, the clank and rattle with which he organized their work party. Yet beneath she sensed something softer, a furtive, rabbitty awareness that reminded her of their first awkward dates. She remembered that rainy night of the prom, the hulking way he stood on her front porch after that dance, his eyes wet berries beneath that thicket of hair.

After all, we just started to get to know each other.

Tom found the paint in the garage and hauled in a bucket with dropcloths and brushes. After a while Sara joined in. They didn't paint a test patch or see how the color matched the windows or engage in the debates they'd held when the house was new. They worked silently, stripping tape into a line, marking off the ceiling. Covering their stove and refrigerator with sheets, their actions forming a tacit agreement. They would eat takeout for a few days. They would put off talking. They would see what happened.

*   *   *

When Luke was a toddler, it had been Sara's habit to replay each day with Tom before they went to bed. The official idea was to fill him in on what she and Luke had done; the unofficial idea was to allow Sara a chance to reflect. Was she playing with Luke too much? Too little? Should he have more chores, or was it enough already? What about that new girl whose family moved in down the street – was that friendship worth cultivating? Was she being too lenient? Too harsh?

"Come on," Tom would say, cajoling. "Quit analyzing so much."

"Why?"

"When we were growing up, our parents had no idea what we were doing half the time."

"And what exactly were you doing?"

"Playing in the woods, probably. Shooting each other with BBs. Torturing frogs – you know, wholesome kid stuff."

"That world doesn't exist anymore. It's all organized. It all comes in a box or on a screen."

"That doesn't make it bad, necessarily. Or dangerous. I mean, there's more dangerous stuff in the woods than in a video game."

"Animals are at least honest about wanting to eat you. But these things . . ." Sara struggled to find words. "These things eat you up and you don't even know."

"They won't eat Luke. He lives in a different world than we did. He needs to learn how to be part of it."

"I don't see how playing Pokémon makes him a part of it."

"It's not that. It's just being with other kids, that's all. Doing the things they do. Not everything has to be so pure, you know?"

Sara hesitated. She didn't mean to be a dictator. After all, there were already many things that she purposefully overlooked, like the small truckload of toys Tom bought at Christmas, and the marshmallow-laden breakfast cereal that kept mysteriously appearing in the cupboard. Moderation – that was the key. A few indulgences were fine, but only a few, the better to keep Luke's boat firmly on its track, clear from the whirlpools. Because, Sara reminded herself, her approach was working. Luke was growing into a strong, self-sufficient boy. At four, he was capable of occupying himself for hours building Legos or plinking out sounds on a toy piano. He was starting to read. He was bright and confident and utterly himself. If this was purity, she told Tom, then so be it.

Tom assented on most of these matters, but sometimes Sara got an unsettling feeling that something was happening just out of her ken. Particularly on Fridays, when Tom would leave work early and spend the afternoon with Luke. Whenever Sara asked where they'd gone, Luke and Tom would always exchange a wink before answering, "To the park." Luke wasn't yet a good winker, he used his hands. But it was a wink nevertheless, and it indicated a secret. *A good secret*, Sara told herself, *some father-son intimacies that they should have*. The kind, she couldn't help but notice, that she wanted to have with Luke.

One day Sara trailed Tom and Luke. She planned to watch them from her car, her husband and her son playing, the two men in her life. It felt strange, tailing her own family, but she liked it. She followed them to the park and watched them play on the slide for a few minutes. Then Tom waved Luke over and whispered a few words in his ear. Wide-eyed, Luke listened and laughed, a silly, high laugh that Sara didn't recognize, and she felt a pang of jealousy. Then they walked together back to the car, got in, and drove off in the opposite direction of the house.

Sara followed them a few miles until they turned into the mall parking lot and the gigantic, cheddar yellow door of

Chuck E. Cheese's Family Entertainment Center. Sara watched the door swing open, loosing a concentrated burst of sound and light – the howls of sugar-fueled children, the frantic bells and slashing lasers of video gamers, the narcotizing multithroated drone of entertainment. She watched her son stride confidently inside, and she felt dizzy and furious. This? This was their secret? Tom knew how she felt about these sorts of places, and this place in particular. They'd even joked about it, come up with a name for it – the Cheesers, shorthand for the sorts of parents who came here every week.

She waited, then slipped inside. Her eyes adjusted slowly to the light, and through the lasery gloom she saw what seemed like a thousand children hurtling like atomic particles through the semidarkness. Sara felt as if she had entered the very brains of the children this place was designed to create. She moved gingerly through the strobe lights, practicing the words she'd speak. She'd keep it light, she decided, but not so light that Tom wouldn't get the message. *Well*, she'd say. *Imagine meeting you here!*

She found them hunched over a pinball machine. Tom was holding Luke on his lap and they were operating the flippers together, their faces reflected in the glass. She took a step toward them, intending to stand there until they noticed her.

"Nice one, Dad," Luke said. "Way to go."

Something in his voice made her stop.

"Hit it again, boy," he said. "Come on."

Sara took a step back into the shadows and watched. She watched for half an hour, watched them play pinball and whack-a-mole and bowling and Pac-Man. She watched Luke spend ten unsuccessful minutes trying to use a metal claw to pick up a stuffed mouse. He kept dropping it, but he would not

211

give up, and Tom kept surreptitiously pumping tokens into the machine until, with a yelp of triumph, he finally lifted the mouse clear of the jumble.

As she was putting Luke to bed that night, Sara asked how the park was.

"Fun," he said loudly.

"What did you do there?"

He looked at her. He was a terrible liar.

"Lots of stuff. The slide, mostly."

"Slides are fun."

"Uh-huh."

A long pause.

"Luke," she said, "do you think you and I should do more . . . fun stuff?"

"Okay," he said carefully. "Like what?"

"Like playing games. Going out for pizza. Maybe watching a video. That kind of stuff."

Luke nearly smiled. "With you?"

"Yeah." Sara managed not to sound defensive. "With me."

"I dunno," he said slowly.

Sara winced inwardly, maintained her composure.

"Why couldn't we?" she continued. "I've been thinking, I can be a pretty strict mom sometimes, can't I?"

Luke thought this over. Sara watched him, in exquisite pain.

"What I mean is," she said, "I think that sometimes I say no to a lot of stuff, and maybe it's okay to sometimes say yes."

His brow furrowed. The semantics were too complex for a four-year-old. Sara was trying to find a way to phrase it when she suddenly felt his hand on her arm, patting it.

"It's okay," he said. "As long as you do your best."

That's what he said.

Was that forgiveness? Sara wasn't sure back then, and now

she was no more certain. What else could a four-year-old offer, except to echo some phrase that he'd heard a thousand times? Seven words he'd heard so often that they'd become a part of him, words that he now sent back to her. *As long as you do your best.*

Sara lay awake, looking at the moonscape of the bedroom ceiling. She closed her eyes and tried to visualize the tall man's face. She concentrated on his eyes, but they would not come; their edges wavered and fell apart. It had started. He was beginning to disappear, to blur into all the other faces. Tom snored with hydraulic vigor; Sara rolled over and submerged her head beneath the covers, counted slowly to one hundred. Finally she walked downstairs to the kitchen and poured herself a glass of milk. She drank it slowly, concentrating on the way it eased the hollowness in her stomach.

Three days and scarcely any news on the tall man. Josephine kept tabs as well as she could, but the Chicago doctors were working behind closed doors. "Say the word and I'll get you in there," Josephine had offered, but even she had seemed half-hearted about it. What could be done now? What could Sara do that she hadn't already tried?

She was about to return upstairs when she saw a pile of clothes Tom had left by the door, the tailings from another of his reorganizing projects. Idly curious, she dug in. It wasn't much. Hats, a few pairs of boots from their ranch days, a dusty pair of once favorite sunglasses. She touched each, trying to capture any faint emanations of memory that might remain.

At the bottom of the pile, she found her mother's red suitcase. She shook it loose and pulled it into the dim yellow light and took a close look. It had been in their closet since her mother's funeral. Its dried-out leather skin bore a thousand miles of hatch lines; its hinges were sugary with rust, its hooped wooden handle as thin as an old wedding ring.

Sara stood up. She slid her fingers into the handle. Many times as a child, she imagined what it would have felt like to be her mother, to be a desirable woman alone on the open road, headed to some far-off city full of tuxedoed men and jazz clubs. The queen of the West Coast. Sara took a step, and as she did she felt something shift. She stopped, surprised. The only time she'd opened the suitcase, after her mother's funeral, it had been empty.

The lock gave way on the third hammer blow. Sara grasped the metal edges with her fingernails and pried, and the rusted hinges grudgingly relented. She felt along the silky interior, and her fingers found a lump at the bottom. She slid her hand under the elastic loop and pulled out a large manila envelope, folded over on itself and tied with red string. She hesitated, weighing the envelope in her hand, prolonging the thrill.

She undid the knot and opened the envelope, and a stack of road maps slid out into her hand. Wrinkled and tattered, held together by a blue rubber band. Sara looked on, disappointed. She'd expected something suitably dramatic – a perfumey clutch of love letters, perhaps, or a black book crammed with suitors' names and cryptic jottings. But this? A stack of ninety-five-cent, accordion-fold gas station maps? She'd never imagined that her mother, of all people, would need any help to get where she was going, never pictured her hunched over the wheel, pulled over at some nameless rest stop in Oregon or California, puzzling over a web of blue and red lines. Never pictured the many nights she must have spent alone in roadside motels, trying to figure out a route. Yet here they were, carefully folded and held together with yellowing poultices of tape, marked with hieroglyphs of coffee stain and cigarette burns, irrefutable. Here they were, proof that she'd found her way.

The idea did not have a beginning. It was simply something that was not there and then it was, like a wave in a perfectly calm sea, fast and whole and right. Sara closed the suitcase, picked it up and let herself out the front door, and walked outside on the lawn in her bare feet. An observer would have thought her insane, a smiling woman in a thin white robe standing ghostlike on the suburban lawn, haloed by sprinklers, the distantly veering headlights lighting her robe with a fire-fly's glow. She stood there for a moment, extending her arms into the darkness. Then she left the suitcase on the curb for the garbageman.

Sara dialed Josephine, didn't wait for a hello.

"Can you get me up there?"

"What?"

"Up there. To see him, tonight."

She heard a rustle of sheets, Josephine shushing someone. Sara tapped the notebook impatiently.

"Give me half an hour."

Sara went upstairs and dressed. She walked to the door and turned back to get her keys and noticed Tom sleeping. His head was tipped and his mouth was open, as if he were laughing. His hair was pressed to one side; his hand lay tenderly next to his cheek, palm up. She watched him breathe a few seconds, seeing his big chest moving in and out, in and out.

Sara cupped his hand and squeezed gently. He woke up slowly, squinting, pulling her hand instinctively to his warm cheek.

"I'm going to see him," she whispered. "I wanted you to know."

Tom nodded slowly. He got up and followed her to the open

215

door. Stood there in his boxers, his bare feet. Their breath turning to mist.

He smiled – a tight smile, but a smile nonetheless.

"Good luck," he said.

19

The tall man was sitting up, eyes closed. His hands and feet were pinned to the bed with blue Velcro cuffs and infiltrated with three IV lines. His head was newly shaved and studded with a dozen tiny blue electrodes whose red and black wires formed a cruel simulacrum of hair. His trach had been replaced and fitted with a permanent stopper. A large monitor chimed with each pulse and respiration. Sara adjusted the cuffs and retaped one of the IVs, which was pinching his skin. He opened his eyes.

"They said," he said laboriously. "They said you . . ."

"No," Sara said. "I'm here."

His enunciation was better; they'd evidently done speech therapy in the two weeks since she'd seen him. But he seemed weaker. His voice was barely a whisper. His temperature was 102, his skin beaded with sweat. Sara dabbed his forehead with a cool towel.

"They – " His tongue hunted blindly for leverage. "They t-tell – "

A pearl of saliva escaped his lip.

"They tell me things."

"I know," she soothed, trying to slow her jackhammering heart. She glanced through the window toward the cool blue oasis of the nurses' station, where Josephine was flirting with the night nurse. Sara had posed as a new trainee touring the floor, an unnecessary guise considering Josephine's tanklike irresistibility. Above the window, inside the room, Sara saw a camera mounted in its blocky greenish case, its red eye blinking steadily. It was wired for sound, Josephine had pointed out, so that the ever thorough Gapps would not miss any evidence that arrived while they were asleep.

Sara loosened the cuffs, massaged blood into his arms.

"I can't," he said. His nostrils flared, his hand went to a fist. "I try, I c-can't remember."

He took her arm; he still had some strength. Her tendons shifted under his grip, his fingers finding the groove below her bone. She felt his desperation.

"Samuel, it's okay."

His fingers squeezed harder. His head twitched from side to side in misery and confusion.

"It's okay."

"It wasn't me," he rasped. "N-not me."

The tall man began to cry silently. He tried to speak.

"Shhh," Sara said, taking his face in her hands, touching their foreheads. "Close your eyes now. There's another story I want you to hear."

He closed his eyes, seemed to relax. The monitors played their musical tones. Outside, Sara could see the night nurse writing her phone number down for Josephine. The light from the hallway streamed in through the opened door, a parallelogram of white across the dark tile. Sara pulled the yellow notebook from her bag. It looked ancient, its wire binding bent, its cover creased and tattered. She found the page she wanted, smoothed it.

"He's watching me," she read. "That's how it begins."

She felt him tense, continued. "An island, a cabin in the trees. Me, curled on the floor, asleep. Then waking up."

The tall man's face tipped toward the ceiling. Sara could see a turbulence beneath his eyelids.

"On one side, Kjell. Long hair. Muscular arms. Sharp face, pale eyes like a cat's. Then me, soft in city clothes. He's the hero, the wild island boy. I'm the exile, the misfit. We look at each other, agree . . ."

"Hey," she said.

"Hey," the tall man echoed faintly.

Sara read as she had first heard it, in that familiar, hesitating voice that hunted for each sound. Josephine looked on through the window, curious. The camera's red eye blinked. The words rose from the page and moved through Sara's mouth.

Sara read for ninety minutes, working her way slowly through the notebook. When she had read the final entry, she looked up. The tall man's eyes were open. The monitors rang like church bells.

"T-tangled," he said, the word slipping through chapped lips. "I'm tangled."

"What?"

"A line on my l-leg. But I don't see it."

"Where are you?" Sara asked gently.

"The boats. It's dark. Oshie's with me."

"You're on the dock," Sara said, enunciating slowly. "You and Oshie on the dock. Is Kjell there?"

He shook his head.

"Just us. Wanting to tell her about Spero. About what Kjell did."

"Do you tell her?"

The tall man didn't seem to hear her. He raised his head, all alertness now.

"What is it?" Sara asked.

"Footsteps. C-c-coming at us."

His head swung from side to side. "Can't see us here – hide, quick, over here."

He froze for a moment, then arched his back, gasped, clenched into a fetal hunch. His mouth opened and closed soundlessly. He threw his body toward the wall, the sheets twisting around him.

"Samuel," Sara said, becoming alarmed. "Can you hear me? What's happening?"

"T-too heavy," he said, choking. "T-tight."

Resisting an urge to comfort him, she put her hands on the mattress and leaned into his ear.

"Tell me what's happening," she said urgently. "Tell me, Samuel."

His hands went to his face; his abdominal muscles writhed.

"S-someone. Coming to m-me." He sucked in a breath and then let it go. "Trying to h-help. T-tangled now. Spinning. Too fast."

He hunched over, closed his eyes. His body convulsed.

Sara put a hand on his arm, checked the monitors.

"Samuel," she said slowly. "Did Kjell push you and Oshie in? Was he trying to hurt you?"

He didn't seem to hear. Sara gripped harder.

"Samuel, this is important. Tell me – did Kjell push you? Or was it an accident?"

Samuel stopped moving for a moment. His pulse slowed. Then he spoke, his voice muffled by the sheets.

"F-fallen," he said. "So clum-sy."

Sara felt a helium bubble of relief move through her abdomen.

"You fell."

"Y-yes."

"That's good." She took his head in her arms. "That's very, very good."

He seemed to quiet. Then he tipped his face to hers, his eyes alive with a secret.

"Kjell th-thinks we're still down there. But we're c-clever, Oshie and I."

He peered at the window, pleased, foxlike.

"Him looking, trying to pull up. But we're not th-there anymore."

"Can you see him?" Sara asked.

"We're watching him," he said "W-watching *him* now."

"What does he do?"

"Ohhh . . ." The tall man's face furrowed in a sympathy that was both genuine and somehow jeering. "Nothing for him now. Nothing. All his plans and now . . ."

He smiled and wept at the same time, the tears pooling in the hollows beneath his eyes.

"Nothing," he said. "Gone."

Tears came to Sara's eyes. "It's safe to come out now, Samuel," she said. "Kjell is gone. He left in the skiff."

"Gone," he repeated. "Gone."

Summer arrived cold, windless, and rainy. The weatherman attributed it to a milewide lens of icy water that blew over from the Aleutian chain, but Jeanne Wooding held to her physicist ex-husband's weather theory. Her disregard for her ex (Sara had yet to learn his name; he was referred to solely as "the Jackass") seemed in inverse proportion to her regard for his hypotheses, which involved the building up and releasing of atmospheric pressures, like so many balloons at a party.

"A warm wind will release the pressure, push the rain away," she would intone. "It's the needle in the balloon."

Whatever its cause, the balloon was set so firmly around Seattle that by the third week of May the rains seemed almost cheerful. Gutters overflowed and transformed the streets into river deltas; the lawns of MountainLake Hills were decorated with a snowfall of tiny white mushrooms that defied every attempt to get rid of them.

Since the inclement weather slowed business, Tom spent most afternoons around the house. Repainting was becoming their shared habit, moving from the kitchen to the entry and then to the first-floor bath, Tom and Sara falling into a companionable rhythm of taping and draping, rolling and daubing. They didn't talk about the tall man, but Sara had the impression that Josephine kept Tom apprised of the events that followed her visit: how the Gapps had gone ballistic when they learned about Sara's visit; how their howling changed to chastened silence when their doctors issued a formal diagnosis of "dissociative identity disorder"; how the Gapps had struck a deal with the hospital to evaluate the tall man in three months if he showed "significant signs of change or improvement." How the tall man had been returned to the TBI ward. How Josephine, in a series of Machiavellian maneuvers, positioned herself to fill out those selfsame evaluations.

"I don't care if he's doing back flips, reciting Shakespeare," Josephine told Sara. "Those dickholes won't get their hands on him again."

Josephine still called occasionally with updates. The tall man seemed to spend most of his days suspended in a fog, calling out for Oshie, revisiting his story again and again. Most of the time, Josephine surmised, he was walking around the island, peering into tidepools.

222

Sara's days were getting busier. She had landed a new job as an ER nurse down in St. Cabrini Hospital. The Rini, as the hospital was called, was located in the international district, a gritty neighborhood that had become home to Asian and Pacific Island immigrants. The ER supervisor was a tiny, energetic Grenadian named Julius who ran the unit as if it were a British naval vessel, insisting that all handrails be wiped down "thrice daily" with disinfectant, that nurses wear lightly starched white uniforms, and that beds be made with verifiable hospital corners. The work was constant and exhausting – a smorgasbord of inner-city problems.

"Diabetes, heart problems, abscesses, vitamin deficiencies – you must be prepared for anything," Julius told her on her first day. "You are the first contact many of these people have had with the Western medical system. Often they don't trust doctors or technology, but they will trust a nurse."

"I don't trust doctors either," Sara said.

Julius laughed. "So it appears we will get along just fine."

So they did. The Rini nurses were a mismatched crew: a Cleopatra-eyed Nigerian who listened to Tony Bennett on headphones, a hulking and whispery Tongan man who was rumored to be a fallen priest, a toothily radiant Filipina who reminded Sara of an Asiatic Brenda Oliver. "The UNN," Julius called it. "United Nations of Nursing." The nurses treated one another with a refreshing formality that found its model in Julius's voice: a brisk, fluty tone brimming with if you pleases and thank you very muches. Working at the Rini, Sara thought, was a little like serving high tea in the middle of a busy city street.

If Tom was less than thrilled about the Rini's location, he didn't let on. Instead, he paid business calls on a nearby noodle shop, attempting to persuade them to add grass-fed organic prime rib to their offerings of chow mein and happy lucky chicken. Sara suspected he'd chosen the shop just so he could pop in on her every so often, but she didn't say anything, either. Because, she realized, she looked forward to his visits, to the steady clomp of his brown shoes as he walked down the hallway toward her.

Sara was doing dishes when Josephine called and told her the tall man had died. An aneurysm. The brain tissue, weakened by the infection, had given way all at once like a leaky dam. They'd hustled him to ICU, but within fifteen minutes he had stopped breathing.

Sara listened, held up her soapy hands. She flexed her hand into a fist and watched the bubbles burst. They sent flecks into the air; little explosions.

"Did he feel anything?"

"Freight train," Josephine said.

Sara looked out the window and saw empty sky. A color of blue so pure that she thought she had never seen anything like it.

"They were getting ready to send the body out for cremation, and I told them to hang on to it," Josephine continued. "Do you want to see him one last time?"

Sara kept looking at the sky. There was one small cloud up high, thin and gauzy. Not a cloud as much as a notion of a cloud; a hollowed-out idea to be filled in. She felt it moving inside her; she felt struck by waves of sadness and pure relief. He was gone. It was over. There was no more she could do.

She became aware of Josephine's voice within the earpiece.

"So what should I tell them?" her friend asked. "Are you coming in?"

"No," Sara said, clearing her throat. "Let him go."

Two days later Sara attended a service in the hospital's chapel presided over by a Russian Orthodox priest Josephine had enlisted. The service was brief: Russian priests, Josephine later explained, had a lot of practice at burying people. The tall man's ashes were placed in a blue ceramic box and drenched in clouds of incense. The priest said several blessings, lifting the box into the air to gesture toward each compass direction, then covering it with a white cloth over which he made the sign of the cross seven times. His beard was black and rippling; his voice sounded like the ocean.

Afterward the two women drove forty-five minutes north to the cemetery to meet Mr. Giddings, the officious, penguinlike state employee contracted by the hospital to oversee interments. After taking possession of the box, he led them to an unmarked stone building filled with drawers; it reminded Sara of a post office. Mr Giddings unlocked drawer No. 4668. He set the box on a corner table, opened it, and lifted out a black plastic bag as big as a softball.

"Hold on," Josephine said. "He doesn't stay in the box?"

"We reuse these," Mr. Giddings said apologetically. "State regs."

Josephine reared. "I thought he got the box. A man should be put in a proper container, not just in some sandwich bag."

"Sorry," Mr. Giddings said. "Those are the rules. And I must point out, it is high-quality plastic. Vacuum-packed."

Sara expected Josephine to continue battling. But she was surprised to see her friend aim a slow smile at the bureaucrat.

"Ah, yes," she said, sounding impressed. She traced her red fingernails over the bag, then fixed Mr. Giddings with a leonine gaze infused with enough raw sexuality to cause him to stutter and blush. "It's very hard."

"It's standard procedure," he said, his arms flapping ineffectually at his sides.

"Yes, I suppose it has to be," Josephine purred, threading her hair behind her ear. "And the bag does look like it does a good job."

"Twelve-millimeter," Giddings managed.

"Ooooh." Josephine leaned up against the shelves, effectively pinning the now sweating bureaucrat in the corner.

Sara registered the rest of Josephine's maneuvers with faint irritation: the chatting, the arm touching, the rifling through the purse for a pen and paper. By the time it was over, Giddings (who, arm flapping aside, displayed a degree of composure sufficient to cause Sara to wonder if this wasn't the first time he'd found a potential date in this gloomy locale) was clicking the drawer closed and leading Josephine by the arm toward the door.

Sara was relieved to be alone. She looked at the drawer, a brass plate that held a blurred reflection of her face. She tried to picture the tall man's face, to say some kind of a prayer, but every word that came to mind felt stilted, forced. She kept trying, closing her eyes, folding her hands, until she heard Josephine leaning on the car horn. She waited until the third honk.

"Well," she said finally. "Good-bye, Samuel."

The two women drove in silence back to the hospital. Sara wasn't angry with Josephine for flirting and hurrying her – one could no sooner be angry at the tide for rising. But she was irritated with herself. Why couldn't she find it in herself to concentrate? To have one pure moment when the world did not intrude?

"So," Sara said as the truck pulled up to the hospital's back entrance, "did you make a date with him?"

"Perhaps," Josephine said, a catlike look on her face. She reached in her purse and pulled out the black plastic bag of cremains. She held it by its corners, then she planted it on the seat between them. The bag listed slightly toward Sara, and she flinched.

"Wait," Sara said. "What am I supposed – "

"What else would he have wanted? Who else is there?"

"I'll just return it to the cemetery," Sara said, her voice rising to a schoolmarmish pitch. "That's all I can do."

"As you wish," Josephine said evenly, leaning over to plant a kiss on Sara's cheek. "But it is your choice to make."

Then the door was slamming and Josephine was striding away and Sara was alone with the bag in the idling truck. She gripped the steering wheel, fiddled with the radio. The bag sat plumply on the seat. Inscrutable.

Sara drove through the city, concentrating on the sky, the shape of the buildings. Feeling hemmed in, she pointed the truck toward the highway, the fastest route to the cemetery. On the cloverleaf the bag tipped over and Sara nervously righted it, grasping its edge between her thumb and forefinger, tamping it back into the seat. She briefly pictured it spilling in the car; considered buckling it in a seat belt.

She turned the radio up loud and drove north up the shore, catching the westbound road to the cemetery. She passed through the smattering of strip malls and neighborhoods that marked the city's edges. She punched up a classical station and let herself be carried along by the music. The light came in thick, tubular shafts through the clouds; she could see the shadow play of distant storms. She passed a red farmhouse, then three black dogs running along a fence, their bodies like silk against the evergreens. She found herself along the Sound, seeing the waves roll to the smoothly accelerating rhythms of Handel's violins.

She felt it a few seconds before she arrived. Something in the rhythm of the turns, the shape of the road. The knowledge arrived quietly, like a cold but familiar handshake. *This is the curve. This is where it happened.*

There was no turnout, so she had to drive a hundred feet past until she found a place safe to pull over. She clicked on the hazards and sat for a moment, feeling herself breathe. There was no traffic in either direction. She looked across the seat at the bag, its taut, rounded shape like a monstrous lozenge.

She opened the door.

She walked slowly along the roadside, trying not to feel the weight of the bag in her hand. The wind seemed to pick up as she approached the curve, and she leaned forward, noticing that it was warm. The needle in the balloon.

The state had replaced the guardrail with a new one made of tubular steel. Sara ran a hand along it, feeling the broad bolt heads that protruded buttonlike from its surface. Her fingers located faint abradings where an unlucky bumper had skidded. She plucked an end and pulled, unzipping a slender thread of black plastic. She held it and watched the wind pull it into shapes too fast for her eye to follow.

The bank was steeper and shorter than she'd pictured, fifteen feet at the most. Her bad leg squawking in protest, Sara gripped the bag and stepped onto the rocky bank. The road noise vanished, replaced by the rush and gurgle of waves. She picked her way down to the water in the manner of a drunken woman descending a staircase. Near the water's edge, the bank was upholstered with bright green moss. Funny, she'd remembered it as black rock, as if she'd climbed out of a quarry. But now she saw how soft it was, how coated in life.

She scanned the shore, hoping to find a placid tidepool. But there was only a narrow edging of rock and seaweed, the bottom planing off deeply. She checked the wind – a seaward breeze. Now she looked at the bag and for the first time felt its compacted weight, the tensed blockiness. She squeezed it, but it was like squeezing a brick. She pulled at the top seam, but the bag would not give. She tore at the side, resisting the impulse to use her teeth.

"Twelve-millimeter," she said under her breath.

Her house key cut into it on the second try, and Sara heard an inhalatory hiss. She flinched, expecting a smoky plume to rise from the opening, but none did. She squeezed, and her fingers sank easily into the bag. For a moment she was transfixed by the oddly pleasurable transformation – how could something so hard turn soft in an instant? – but her pleasure turned to mild alarm when she saw a lobe of solid ash extruding through the opening. She tipped the bag and let the lobe drop into the water; it floated briefly (like cocoa powder, Sara could not help but think), then broke apart, some of it sinking and some of it blown into the air.

Sara widened the opening and reached in, feeling the grit and, within it, the harder chunks like pebbles. She pulled out her hand and looked. The ash was whiter than she had expected – closer to snowflakes than cinders. She felt the weight of it in her palm and let some slide down her fingertips into the water. There was something vaguely culinary about the act, as if she were spreading some precious spice. She closed her eyes and took another handful, feeling a faint tickle on her face as the wind swirled. The ash scattered, some sinking, some glinting in the fading light, some cohering to form miniature islands that rose and fell on the incoming waves.

Sara scattered the ashes, thinking of everything and nothing. Of the Minnie Mouse woman. Nurse Larch. William Gapp's sad pilot eyes. Jeanne Wooding's tulips. Brenda Oliver's hair. The soapy smell of Luke's skin. They all flowed through her mind, fusing and tumbling in a way that made them all seem equal to one another, and as they did she sensed the flow of life, the whole unmanageable torrent of it, and something within her gave way. She couldn't put a word on it — forgiveness, perhaps? — but all she knew was that she felt lighter than before. She didn't feel happy; there was too much work left to be done for that. But she felt light and strong, as if she could leap back to the road in a single bound, as if she could run all the way home in long strides. Yet she didn't want to do those things or anything else. She wanted only to be here, now, standing on the rocky shore beneath a pale bright sky, releasing handful after handful of ash into the freshening wind.

The big man in the white shirt and tie must have been calling for a minute or two, because when Sara finally heard him, he was stepping over the guardrail. He was middle-aged, in a suit and tie, a worried look tensing his broad face. A businessman, on his way home. A friendly stranger, checking if he could help.

"Thank you," Sara shouted, raising her voice so it could be heard over the waves. "I'm okay."

Sara drove quickly home, enjoying the lightness of acceleration as she moved down the highway. She left the shore and cut inland, into the funneling flow of evening traffic. As she passed the exit to the hospital, she felt a stab of regret. Through it all, she'd never properly thanked Josephine for everything she'd done. But how to make it up to her?

Roses, she decided, turning into a mall at the entrance to MountainLake Hills. A dozen – no, two dozen. She would have them sent to the nurses' station, signed "Your Secret Admirer."

Sara smiled – it would create a stir; Josephine would love it. Sara strode into the shop, selected the blooms from the case, and handed her credit card to the clerk.

"Don't you want this on your account, Mrs. Black?" she asked.

Sara's brow creased. "I don't believe I have an account here."

"Oh, that's right," the clerk said, and began to blush.

Tom was in the living room, watching a Mariners game on television. Sara walked to the couch and stood in front of him, sunflowers in hand.

"It's you," she said.

A flicker of protest crossed Tom's face, then he gave it up. He smiled and looked down bashfully. Sara took him in her arms, put a hand beneath his chin. She felt something within her soften.

"Why didn't you tell me, all this time? Why did you let me think it was Brenda?"

Tom looked at her, his eyes squinty and shining beneath that dark tangle of hair. Sara put her hand in it, above his ear. She felt small soft underhairs, the heat radiating from his scalp. She stood there, her hand in his hair. She felt frozen; this was unfamiliar ground. But she couldn't bring herself to remove her hand; she liked the heat, she liked the liquid feel of it around her fingers. It was up to Tom to make the move.

"It's a good ball game," he said, taking her hand and pulling her down next to him. "Bottom of the ninth, tie score."

He kept hold of her hand, put his arm around her. It felt heavy and unfamiliar. She tucked her head into his shoulder. They readjusted, then readjusted again.

"Who's going to win?"

"I guess we'll have to see."

That night, in the half-light of their bedroom, they made love for the first time in nearly five months. They undressed quickly, greedily. It seemed too good to be true: this light, this soft bed, the solid warmth of his body separated from her by thin fabric, a measly zipper. *Now Mommy's naked.* It was almost funny, but they could not laugh; laughing would break the spell. He was tender, awkward; his body was exactly as she remembered, but somehow improved. She ran her hands over him, feeling the muscles of his back, his legs. Touching his arms, the edges of his knees, the flat of his hips.

"Hey," he said softly. "Remember me?"

In answer, Sara tugged the covers aside and lay back, creating space, showing herself to him. Tom watched her intently, his face frozen in concentration, his hands open at his sides. She reached for him, and they moved into each other, Sara's mind registering only the smooth curving contact of skin on skin, feeling the miraculous familiarity of his body with each stroke. His taste in her mouth, his breath in her ear. Each of them moving to a place where there were no words, where they could be together without any pain or the faintest memory of pain.

20

The forest was thick, thicker than it looked on the map. Shadowy and luxuriant, it grew close over the thin gravel road they traveled, its leaves swabbing the truck, licking away any residue of the city. Birch and cottonwood grew along the road edge, but beyond, the forest consisted of old-growth spruce whose trunks were so completely enveloped in moss that they seemed less like trees and more like a congregation of sleekly furred beasts. Pale light filtered down from the distant canopy, a green and painterly glow that seemed designed to reveal half-hidden secrets – a silvery caterpillar extending itself along a branch, a glistening purple berry peeking warily beneath a leafy eyelid. Every so often the forest relented, opening into blazing meadows that forced them to squint.

"Are you sure this is the road?" Sara asked.

"Has to be," Tom said. "I think."

They'd been driving on roads like this for two hours, searching for the cabin that had become, in yesterday's stroke of a county auctioneer's hammer, their legal property. Finding the cabin, however, was proving to be more complicated. Unmarked and poorly maintained, the road circled endlessly through the forested foothills as if tracing the whorls of a giant fingerprint. They splashed through small rocky creeks and followed sinuous ridges. Their hearts rose several times as they approached a picturesque log cabin, only to fall as they found out it wasn't the one.

"There are only a half dozen cabins in this area," Tom said, regripping the steering wheel. "We've got to bump into it sooner or later."

"Definitely." Sara tried to sound confident. When the phone had rung with the long-awaited news about the cabin, Tom had seized on the idea. They would go out there together for the day—unwrap the surprise package, as he put it. Besides, getting out of the house would be good for them both. So they'd packed the truck and headed out, working their way through the channeled hive of the suburbs, looping around Puget Sound, then heading north and west, crossing that borderland between civilization and the undersea hush of the deep woods. They'd chatted, slightly giddy with velocity. As the morning wore on, however, Sara felt her nervousness growing. They were headed toward their cabin in the woods, that mythical destination they'd talked about for years. Sara tried not to think about what it meant. She concentrated on the motion, the sense of expanding distance.

Finally, just before noon, they rounded a hairpin corner and came upon a thicket of blackberry bushes. The road seemed to end, but Tom saw something beyond. He eased the old truck forward, and the spiky branches parted like a curtain.

Sara watched Tom's face go slack.

The structure stood at the far edge of a small meadow, as if cowering from the sunlight. At first glance it was not a cabin so much as a parody of a cabin: a roof swaybacked enough to lend a vaguely pagodalike appearance to the bedraggled mass of weathered logs. The front porch appeared to be half devoured by an army of moss and mushrooms, the stovepipe crushed like a discarded cigarette. Its east wall appeared to be supported mostly by a moraine of trash and old tires and what appeared to be a bedspring. Yet the outlines were unmistakable. This was the cabin – their cabin. Sara recognized the shape from Tom's drawings.

Neither of them spoke.

Tom swallowed. "I guess that photo must have been taken a couple years ago."

A nervous hilarity rose up in Sara, but she could not permit herself to laugh. Laughter would be cruel; it would ruin everything. They'd talked about this for so many years, their dream cabin. And now . . . this.

They circled the property with slow reverence, as if visiting a hallowed battlefield. They saw the ribwork of naked rafters exposed by a falling tree. The mattresses stacked like a failed breakwater along the creek that marked the property's boundary. The fifty-gallon oil barrels piled like children's toys in the cottonwoods. The toilet perched like a throne on a tree stump, a cottonwood sapling sprouting from its bowl. The red Chevy Nova carcass standing over what must have once been a rudimentary garden. Bean plants grew inside, stalks curling against the windshield.

Warily, they climbed the porch and opened the door, releasing an eye-watering gust of mold and moss. They peered in, saw a modest kitchen gilded in cobwebs and dust, the confetti of mice droppings. A yellow foam mattress stood in the corner, its corners nibbled and redistributed around the room in small, neat piles. A small pyramid of clothes – overalls and a red plaid shirt, by the looks of them – lay in the center of the room, as if their previous occupant had spontaneously combusted.

They walked outside. Tom glanced at her, but Sara looked away. *Your call*, she thought silently.

*　　　*　　　*

The mattresses came first, waterlogged and slippery, leaving snail-like tracks on the long grass. Then the tires, extracted from the pile and stacked near the road. Then the oil barrels, rusted to lace but still surprisingly heavy, heaved out of the cottonwoods and pushed toward the road like runaway steamrollers. Tom used one as a burn barrel, siphoning gas from the truck and setting a pile of cardboard alight with a *whoosh*. Sara moved near the flame, felt its dry heat.

They worked on opposite ends of the property, Tom near the house and Sara in the surrounding brush, harvesting the trash that had blown into the alders. She plucked magazines, pizza boxes, a pair of women's underwear, candy bar wrappers, and innumerable blue plastic grocery bags. She noticed that the trash seemed to have organized itself over the years, drifting into piles of like-seeming materials: the plastic milk and soda jugs lay mostly in the lower bushes, while the tarps and plastics flew higher. Her fingers grew adept at extracting those grocery bags, which were twisted into complicated knots. She threw paper in the burn barrel; the rest was piled in the back of the truck.

By lunchtime, Sara had finished the west side and moved to the east, plucking and tugging out each piece, shoving it into a garbage bag, and plucking more. She began to enjoy the process, her eyes roving to repeatedly compare the newly cleaned bush with the trash-festooned ones that lay ahead. The alder leaves were waxy and supple beneath her hands. It was almost peaceful, working there among the birdsong and the insect whirr. She tugged an old tarp from the grasp of weeds, saw wet earth beneath. A patch of tiny white seedlings, fine as baby's hair.

She watched Tom across the yard. He was hunched like a miner on the pile of rubble at the east wall with a rake, patiently scraping his way down to ground level. Sara could see the cords in his forearms rise and rearrange themselves with each stroke, and she was reminded of the first time she saw him after her father died, out there in the fields. She always loved watching him from a distance; she could see him more clearly. He cleared away a space, then lay on his belly and disappeared beneath the house. A few minutes later his head reemerged.

"Creosote pilings," he called. "All but two in decent shape."

They worked all afternoon. Three times they made deliveries to the Port Lucy landfill. Returning to the cabin after the third trip, Sara noticed with a start that the sun was nearly down. It was only then, standing in the blackberries in the low light of evening, that she could see how much they had left to accomplish. The cabin stood starkly against the darkened trees, the completeness of its ruin more evident now than before.

As the shadows grew, they packed up for a last run to the landfill before returning to Seattle. Tom backed the truck across the yard to the creek's edge, where a last cache of oil barrels lay in the swampy earth around the cottonwoods. They loaded five barrels, then Tom threw it in gear. The old truck shuddered forward a few inches, then sank down and refused to move.

Tom grimaced, downshifted, and tried again. Nothing.

For the next hour they worked at extracting the wheels, but they remained lodged axle deep in the leafy bog, marooned in black soil so soft and moist that it seemed more chocolate pudding than dirt. Tom considered walking the six miles to Port Lucy, then decided against it.

"It's kind of funny, if you think about it," Sara said.

"I'd rather not," Tom said, looking warily at the cabin.

For a half hour they sat in the truck with the radio on to a top 40 station, taking shelter in the music, putting off the inevitable as long as possible. Then as darkness fell they packed what meager supplies they could find – a blue tarp, a windbreaker, a lighter, a half-eaten pack of Rolos – and climbed out into a surprisingly cold wind. The grass whipped their legs; the spruce seemed to rustle and bounce in anticipation.

The cabin seemed bigger in the darkness, its roof curving toward them like the flank of a mountain. Sara leaned against Tom's shoulder as they worked their way across the crumbling porch, shuffling like skiers along the joists. As they opened the door they heard an urgent scratching, claws on wood. Sara pictured a mother raccoon watching her with its red eyes, its brace of needled teeth.

Tom flicked the lighter, and they heard a rustling. Then nothing.

"Home sweet home," he said, and Sara was surprised to hear a slight quaver in his voice.

They stood like statues in the doorway. Sara waited for Tom to go first, but he seemed frozen. She glanced at her husband and in the faint light saw that his shoulders were hunched, his elbows held close like a child's. It would be different with Luke, she realized. If Luke were here, Tom would not be hesitant. He would have claimed this place with bold strides. He would have been someone else. She looked closer and sensed the depth of his fears, and she was moved to tenderness.

Sara picked up a board and began to wave it ahead of her like an avenging sword; Tom followed, ducking slightly. In this way they moved to the center of the room, near the wood stove, where the mold smell seemed least strong. Shards of moonlight came through roof chinks; dust motes rose and spun like planets.

Tom, moving as gingerly as he could, found some old newspapers and lit them in the stove. By its faint light they could make out the rest of the room: the skeleton of a couch, a broken rocking chair, a small city of broken teacups and plates around the sink. Tom wrenched a few dry boards up from the porch and tucked them in the fire. Sara found two candle stubs and set them in teacups. They spread the tarp on the floor, then put a crate in the center with the candles. They sat down, felt the reassuring crinkle of clean nylon.

Tom smoothed a space between them and made a show of laying out the Rolos on their foil wrapper.

"We have some filet mignon tonight, very nicely done, with peppercorns, leeks, and American squash." He reached across and slipped one in her mouth. Sara felt the brush of his thumb against her lip.

"Medium rare," she said. "Perfect."

They ate the candy and watched the fire. They leaned against each other for comfort and then for security, concentrating on the flames and trying to ignore the rustling sounds all around them.

From behind, Sara put her arms around him. She drew the windbreaker closer and put her head on his shoulder. She could feel each breath.

"You sleepy?" he asked.

"Not really." Her voice was quick and light.

"I was just remembering that time when we got kicked out of Lamaze class."

"That was your fault."

"No, that was definitely your fault."

"You were making me laugh. We were supposed to be

239

concentrating on each breath and you kept breathing too heavily. You sounded like a pervert."

"It's not my fault if I have big lungs," he said. "Besides, at least I remembered the part about the ice chips during labor."

"Which part was that?" Sara asked teasingly. "The part where you keep shoving them in my mouth until I choke?"

"Gagging helped," Tom observed. "You went from three to six centimeters."

"If you would have strangled me, I might have gotten to ten."

"That's probably true," Tom allowed.

Sara leaned in and pulled her hands tighter around his body. The fire popped and wavered; the walls glowed.

"So who do you think lived here?" Sara asked.

She felt Tom tip back his head. She could see him, closing his eyes, giving it proper thought.

"An old man," he said. "An old man with lots of pets."

"And no wife."

"And no broom."

Tom leaned forward to put another board on the fire.

"Buford," Sara said suddenly.

"Yes, his name was Buford," Tom said, picking it up smoothly. "Buford Mayflower. An old cowboy from Montana."

"Ex–rodeo rider," Sara said, closing her eyes. "Knees shot. All gimped up, but training for a comeback. With his pets."

"Cats" Tom continued. "That's why he came here. Teaching tricks to his cats. That's why he needed all the mattresses and oil barrels, for the different stunts. He had twenty-seven cats. Toms, Siamese, tabbies. All kinds."

"Ahh," Sara said. She felt a tickle of pleasure, as if hearing the rhythm of a long-forgotten song.

"His big plan was to get back on the rodeo as a sideshow

act," Tom said, his voice deepening. "And he almost did it, too. He trained the cats to jump through hoops and do flips and fetch. Taught them to balance balls on their noses."

"But then they rebelled," Sara said. "One day the cats stopped cooperating."

"Oh yes," Tom said. "Buford tried everything – different kinds of feed, different rules. But the cats went wild. Wrecked the house, chewed up all the clothes. It wasn't in their nature."

"Buford was a stubborn old bastard," Sara said. "He didn't give up easily."

"It must have turned into a war," Tom agreed. "They trashed the house and tried to see who was going to blink first. The house got worse and worse. The roof started to go, the porch fell in. Everything started to rot. They left the dishes where they stood, the clothes in the closet. Waiting to see who would give in."

"So what happened in the end?"

"That's the mystery," Tom said softly. "Maybe Buford got fed up and left. Maybe the cats ran off to new homes. Either way, all that's left is this cabin."

Sara peered at the fire. "Buford's cabin," she said.

They sat a long time in the darkness, watching the fire. The wind picked up, rattling the windows, slapping the loose tar paper. Pinpricks of rain fell, slowly at first, and then in sheets, and Sara imagined a gust ripping the roof off, a great Noachian flood. But that didn't happen. The roof held, and the drops arrived, patting on the wooden floor like a coded message, each washing away a speck of dirt.

After a long while, Tom spoke. His voice was thin and strange.

"Tell me a story."

He nestled his body into hers.

Tomorrow they would wake up in sunlight. Tomorrow they would act brisk and slightly awkward; they would concentrate on the job of getting to Port Lucy and getting the car pulled out. But now they were here, together in the firelight, and Tom was asking her to give in. Submitting to fear and asking that she do the same. Sara felt her body shake with nervousness. She closed her eyes and took a breath.

ACKNOWLEDGMENTS

Thanks to Todd Balf, Kate Boie, Chip Brown, Mark Bryant, Tom Bursch, Lisa Chase, Jonathan Coyle, Maury and Agnes Coyle, Hal Espen, Rob Fisher, Laura Hohnhold, Tom Kizzia, Steven G. Miller, Mike Paterniti, and Marshall Sella for their friendship and advice. Thanks to Lara Carrigan for her unerring editorial instincts and her wisdom. Thanks to David Black, Lucy Stille, Joy Tutela, Jason Sacher, Gary Morris, Sona Vogel, and Leigh Ann Eliseo for their talent and support. Thanks to Tammy Enders and Kathy Peluso of Grace Hospital for their research assistance. Most of all, thanks to my wife, Jen, who awakens all that's good in this book and in our home.

A NOTE ON THE AUTHOR

Daniel Coyle is a contributing editor at *Outside* magazine and the author of the nonfiction book *Hardball: A Season in the Projects*, which was named best sports book of the year by the *Sporting News* and made into a movie by Paramount Pictures. A former resident of Chicago, Coyle lives with his wife and four children in Homer, Alaska.

A NOTE ON THE TYPE

The text of this book is set in Bodoni Book.
Giambattista Bodoni designed his typefaces at the end
of the eighteenth century. The Bodoni types were the
culmination of nearly three hundred years of evolution in
roman type design. Bodoni is recognized by its high
contrast between thick and thin strokes, pure vertical
stress, and hairline serifs.